D0199132

PENGUIN MODERN CLASSICS

IN THE CAGE AND OTHER STORIES

Henry James was born in 1843 in Washington Place, New York, of Scottish and Irish ancestry. His father was a prominent theologian and philosopher and his elder brother, William, was also famous as a philosopher. He attended schools in New York and later in London, Paris, and Geneva, entering the Law School at Harvard in 1862. In 1865 he began to contribute reviews and short stories to American journals. In 1875, after two prior visits to Europe, he settled for a year in Paris, where he met Flaubert, Turgenev, and other literary figures. However, the next year he moved to London, where he became such an inveterate diner-out that in the winter of 1878–9 he confessed to accepting 107 invitations. In 1898 he left London and went to live at Lamb House, Rye, Sussex. Henry James became naturalized in 1915, was awarded the O.M., and died early in 1916.

In addition to many short stories, plays, books of criticism, autobiography, and travel he wrote some twenty novels, the first published being *Roderick Hudson* (1875). They include *The Europeans*, *Washington Square*, *The Portrait of a Lady*, *The Bostonians*, *The Princess Casamassima*, *The Spoils of Poynton*, *The Awkward Age*, *The Wings of the Dove*, *The Ambassadors*, and *The Golden Bowl*.

HENRY JAMES

In The Cage and Other Stories

SELECTED BY S. GORLEY PUTT

PENGUIN BOOKS

Penguin Books Ltd, Harmondsworth, Middlesex, England
Penguin Books, 625 Madison Avenue, New York, New York 10022, U.S.A.
Penguin Books Australia Ltd, Ringwood, Victoria, Australia
Penguin Books Canada Ltd, 2801 John Street, Markham, Ontario, Canada L3R 1B4
Penguin Books (N.Z.) Ltd, 182–190 Wairau Road, Auckland 10, New Zealand

'In The Cage' first published by Duckworth 1898
'The Siege of London' first published in *Cornhill Magazine* 1883
'Crapy Cornelia' first published in *Harper's Magazine* 1909
This collection published in Penguin Books 1974
Reprinted 1983

In the United States of America 'Creepy Cornelia' copyright 1909 by Harper & Brothers; copyright renewed 1936 by Harper & Brothers. Collected in *The Finer Grain*, copyright 1910 by Chas. Scribner's Sons; copyright renewed 1938 by Henry James. Reprinted in the United States of America by permission of Charles Scribner's Sons

This selection copyright © Penguin Books Ltd, 1972

Made and printed in Great Britain by
Hazell Watson & Viney Ltd, Aylesbury, Bucks
Set in Linotype Times

Except in the United States of America,
this book is sold subject to the condition
that it shall not, by way of trade or otherwise,
be lent, re-sold, hired out, or otherwise circulated
without the publisher's prior consent in any form of
binding or cover other than that in which it is
published and without a similar condition
including this condition being imposed
on the subsequent purchaser

CONTENTS

IN THE CAGE

1

It had occurred to her early that in her position – that of a young person spending, in framed and wired confinement, the life of a guinea-pig or a magpie – she should know a great many persons without their recognizing the acquaintance. That made it an emotion the more lively – though singularly rare and always, even then, with opportunity still very much smothered – to see any one come in whom she knew, as she called it, outside, and who could add something to the poor identity of her function. Her function was to sit there with two young men – the other telegraphist and the counter-clerk; to mind the 'sounder', which was always going, to dole out stamps and postal-orders, weigh letters, answer stupid questions, give difficult change and, more than anything else, count words as numberless as the sands of the sea, the words of the telegrams thrust, from morning to night, through the gap left in the high lattice, across the encumbered shelf that her forearm ached with rubbing. This transparent screen fenced out or fenced in, according to the side of the narrow counter on which the human lot was cast, the duskiest corner of a shop pervaded not a little, in winter, by the poison of perpetual gas, and at all times by the presence of hams, cheese, dried fish, soap, varnish, paraffin, and other solids and fluids that she came to know perfectly by their smells without consenting to know them by their names.

The barrier that divided the little post-and-telegraph-office from the grocery was a frail structure of wood and wire; but the social, the professional separation was a gulf that fortune, by a stroke quite remarkable, had spared her the necessity of contributing at all publicly to bridge. When Mr Cocker's young men stepped over from behind the other counter to change a five-pound note – and Mr Cocker's situation, with the cream of the 'Court Guide' and the dearest furnished apartments,

Simpkin's, Ladle's, Thrupp's, just round the corner, was so select that his place was quite pervaded by the crisp rustle of these emblems – she pushed out the sovereigns as if the applicant were no more to her than one of the momentary appearances in the great procession; and this perhaps all the more from the very fact of the connection – only recognized outside indeed – to which she had lent herself with ridiculous inconsequence. She recognized the others the less because she had at last so unreservedly, so irredeemably, recognized Mr Mudge. But she was a little ashamed, none the less, of having to admit to herself that Mr Mudge's removal to a higher sphere – to a more commanding position, that is, though to a much lower neighbourhood – would have been described still better as a luxury than as the simplification that she contented herself with calling it. He had, at any rate, ceased to be all day long in her eyes, and this left something a little fresh for them to rest on of a Sunday. During the three months that he had remained at Cocker's after her consent to their engagement, she had often asked herself what it was that marriage would be able to add to a familiarity so final. Opposite there, behind the counter of which his superior stature, his whiter apron, his more clustering curls and more present, too present, h's had been for a couple of years the principal ornament, he had moved to and fro before her as on the small sanded floor of their contracted future. She was conscious now of the improvement of not having to take her present and her future at once. They were about as much as she could manage when taken separate.

She had, none the less, to give her mind steadily to what Mr Mudge had again written her about, the idea of her applying for a transfer to an office quite similar – she couldn't yet hope for a place in a bigger – under the very roof where he was foreman, so that, dangled before her every minute of the day, he should see her, as he called it, 'hourly,' and in a part, the far N.W. district, where, with her mother, she would save, on their two rooms alone, nearly three shillings. It would be far from dazzling to exchange Mayfair for Chalk Farm, and it was something of a predicament that he so kept at her; still, it was nothing to the old predicaments, those of the early times of their great misery, her own, her mother's, and her elder sister's – the last of whom had succumbed to all but absolute want when, as conscious, incredulous ladies, suddenly bereaved, betrayed, overwhelmed, they had slipped faster and faster down the steep slope at the bottom of which she alone had rebounded. Her mother had never rebounded any more at the bottom than on the way; had only rumbled and grumbled down and down, making, in respect of caps and conversation, no effort whatever, and too often, alas! smelling of whisky.

2

IT was always rather quiet at Cocker's while the contingent from Ladle's and Thrupp's and all the other great places were at luncheon, or, as the young men used vulgarly to say, while the animals were feeding. She had forty minutes in advance of this to go home for her own dinner; and when she came back, and one of the young men took his turn, there was often half an hour during which she could pull out a bit of work or a book – a book from the place where she borrowed novels, very greasy, in fine print and all about fine folks, at a ha'penny a day. This sacred pause was one of the numerous ways in which the establishment kept its finger on the pulse of fashion and fell into the rhythm of the larger life. It had something to do, one day, with the particular vividness marking the advent of a lady whose meals were apparently irregular, yet whom she was destined, she afterwards found, not to forget. The girl was *blasée*; nothing could belong more, as she perfectly knew, to the intense publicity of her profession; but she had a whimsical mind and wonderful nerves; she was subject, in short, to sudden flickers of antipathy and sympathy, red gleams in the grey, fitful awakings and followings, odd caprices of curiosity. She had a friend who had invented a new career for women – that of being in and out of people's houses to look after the flowers. Mrs Jordan had a manner of her own of sounding this allusion; 'the flowers,' on her lips, were, in happy homes, as usual as the coals or the daily papers. She took charge of them, at any rate, in all the rooms, at so much a month, and people were quickly finding out what it was to make over this delicate duty to the widow of a clergyman. The widow, on her side, dilating on the initiations thus opened up to her, had been splendid to her young friend over the way she was made free of the greatest houses – the way, especially when she did the dinner-tables, set out so often for twenty, she felt that a single step more would socially, would absolutely, introduce her. On its being asked of her, then, if she circulated only in a sort of tropical solitude, with the upper servants for picturesque natives, and on her having to assent to this glance at her limitations, she had found a reply to the girl's invidious question. 'You've no imagination, my dear!' – that was because the social door might at any moment open so wide.

Our young lady had not taken up the charge, had dealt with it good-humouredly, just because she knew so well what to think of it. It was at once one of her most cherished complaints and most secret supports that people didn't understand her, and it was accordingly a matter of indifference to her that Mrs Jordan shouldn't; even though Mrs Jordan, handed down from their early twilight of gentility and also the victim of reverses, was the only member of her circle in whom she recognized an equal. She was perfectly aware that her imaginative life was the life in which she spent most of her time; and she would have been ready, had it been at all worth while, to contend that, since her outward occupation didn't kill it, it must be strong indeed. Combinations of flowers and greenstuff, forsooth! What *she* could handle freely, she said to herself, was combinations of men and women. The only weakness in her faculty came from the positive abundance of her contact with the human herd; this was so constant, had the effect of becoming so cheap, that there were long stretches in which inspiration, divination and interest, quite dropped. The great thing was the flashes, the quick revivals, absolute accidents all, and neither to be counted on nor to be resisted. Some one had only sometimes to put in a penny for a stamp, and the whole thing was upon her. She was so absurdly constructed that these were literally the moments that made up – made up for the long stiffness of sitting there in the stocks, made up for the cunning hostility of Mr Buckton and the importunate sympathy of the counter-clerk, made up for the daily, deadly, flourishy letter from Mr Mudge, made up even for the most haunting of her worries, the rage at moments of not knowing how her mother did 'get it'.

She had surrendered herself moreover, of late, to a certain expansion of her consciousness; something that seemed perhaps vulgarly accounted for by the fact that, as the blast of the season roared louder and the waves of fashion tossed their spray further over the counter, there were more impressions to be gathered and really – for it came to that – more life to be led. Definite, at any rate, it was that by the time May was well started the kind of company she kept at Cocker's had begun to strike her as a reason – a reason she might almost put forward for a policy of procrastination. It sounded silly, of course, as yet, to plead such a motive, especially as the fascination of the place was, after all, a sort of torment. But she liked her torment; it was a torment she should miss at Chalk Farm. She was ingenious and uncandid, therefore, about leaving the breadth of London a little longer between herself and that austerity. If she had not quite the courage, in short, to say to Mr Mudge that her actual chance for a play of mind was worth, any week, the three shillings he desired to help her to save, she yet saw something happen in the course of the month that, in her heart of hearts at least, answered the subtle question. This was connected precisely with the appearance of the memorable lady.

3

SHE pushed in three bescribbled forms which the girl's hand was quick to appropriate, Mr Buckton having so frequent a perverse instinct for catching first any eye that promised the sort of entertainment with which she had her peculiar affinity. The amusements of captives are full of a desperate contrivance, and one of our young friend's ha'pennyworths had been the charming tale of *Picciola*. It was of course the law of the place that they were never to take no notice, as Mr Buckton said, whom they served; but this also never prevented, certainly on the same gentleman's own part, what he was fond of describing as the underhand game. Both her companions, for that matter, made no secret of the number of favourites they had among the ladies; sweet familiarities in spite of which she had repeatedly caught each of them in stupidities and mistakes, confusions of identity and lapses of observation that never failed to remind her how the cleverness of men ended where the cleverness of women began. 'Marguerite, Regent Street. Try on at six. All Spanish lace. Pearls. The full length.' That was the first; it had no signature. 'Lady Agnes Orme, Hyde Park Place. Impossible to-night, dining Haddon. Opera tomorrow, promised Fritz, but could do play Wednesday. Will try Haddon for Savoy, and anything in the world you like, if you can get Gussy. Sunday, Montenero. Sit Mason Monday, Tuesday. Margueriete awful. Cissy.' That was the second. The third, the girl noted when she took it, was on a foreign form: 'Everard, Hôtel Brighton, Paris. Only understand and believe. 22nd to 26th, and certainly 8th and 9th. Perhaps others. Come. Mary.'

Mary was very handsome, the handsomest woman, she felt in a moment, she had even seen – or perhaps it was only Cissy. Perhaps it was both, for she had seen stranger things than that – ladies wiring to different persons under different names. She had seen all sorts of things and pieced together all sorts of mysteries. There had once been one – not long before – who, without winking, sent off five over five different signatures. Perhaps these represented five different friends who had asked her – all women, just as perhaps now Mary and Cissy, or one or other of them, were wiring by deputy. Sometimes she put in too much – too much of her own sense; sometimes she put in too little; and in either case this often came round to her afterwards, for she had an extraordinary way of keeping clues. When she noticed, she noticed; that was what it came to. There were days and days, there were weeks sometimes, of vacancy. This arose often from Mr Buckton's devilish and successful subterfuges for keeping her at the sounder whenever it looked as if anything might amuse; the sounder, which it was equally his business to mind, being the innermost cell of captivity, a cage within the cage, fenced off from the rest by a frame of ground glass. The counter-clerk would have played into her hands; but the counter-clerk was really reduced to idiocy by the effect of his passion for her. She flattered herself moreover, nobly, that with the unpleasant conspicuity of this passion she would never have consented to be obliged to him. The most she would ever do would be always to shove off on him whenever she could the registration of letters, a job she happened particularly to loathe. After the long stupors, at all events, there almost always suddenly would come a sharp taste of something; it was in her mouth before she knew it; it was in her mouth now.

To Cissy, to Mary, whichever it was, she found her curiosity going out with a rush, a mute effusion that floated back to her, like a returning tide, the living colour and splendour of the beautiful head, the light of eyes that seemed to reflect such utterly other things than the mean things actually before them; and, above all, the high, curt consideration of a manner that, even at bad moments, was a magnificent habit and of the very essence of the innumerable things – her beauty, her birth, her father and mother, her cousins, and all her ancestors – that its possessor couldn't have got rid of if she had wished. How did our obscure little public servant know that, for the lady of the telegrams, this was a bad moment? How did she guess all sorts of impossible things, such as, almost on the very spot, the presence of drama, at a critical stage, and the nature of the tie with the gentleman at the Hôtel Brighton? More than ever before it floated to her through the bars of the cage that this at last was the high reality, the bristling truth that she had hitherto only patched up and eked out – one of the creatures, in fine, in whom all the conditions for happiness actually met, and who, in the air they made, bloomed with an unwitting insolence. What came home to the girl was the way the insolence was tempered by something that was equally a part of the distinguished life, the custom of a flowerlike bend to the less fortunate – a dropped fragrance, a mere quick breath, but which in fact pervaded and lingered. The apparition was very young, but certainly married, and our fatigued friend had a sufficient store of mythological comparison to recognize the port of Juno. Marguerite might be 'awful', but she knew how to dress a goddess.

Pearls and Spanish lace – she herself, with assurance, could see them, and the 'full length' too, and also red velvet bows, which, disposed on the lace in a particular manner (she could have placed them with the turn of a hand) were of course to adorn the front of a black brocade that would be like a dress in a picture. However, neither Marguerite, nor Lady Agnes, nor Haddon, nor Fritz, nor Gussy was what the wearer of this garment had really come in for. She had come in for Everard – and that was doubtless not *his* true name either. If our young lady had never taken such jumps before, it was simply that she had never before been so affected. She went all the way. Mary and Cissy had been round together, in their single superb person, to see him – he must live round the corner; they had found that, in consequence of something they had come, precisely, to make up for or to have another scene about, he had gone off – gone off just on purpose to make them feel it; on which they had come together to Cocker's as to the nearest place; where they had put in the three forms partly in order not to put in the one alone. The two others, in a manner, covered it, muffled it, passed it off. Oh yes, she went all the way, and this was a specimen of how she often went. She would know the hand again any time. It was as handsome and as everything else as the woman herself. The woman herself had, on learning his flight, pushed past Everard's servant and into his room; she had written her missive at his table and with his pen. All this, every inch of it, came in the waft that she blew through and left behind her, the influence that, as I have said, lingered. And among the things the girl was sure of, happily, was that she should see her again.

4

SHE saw her, in fact, and only ten days later; but this time she was not alone, and that was exactly a part of the luck of it. Being clever enough to know through what possibilities it could range, our young lady had ever since had in her mind a dozen conflicting theories about Everard's type; as to which, the instant they came into the place, she felt the point settled with a thump that seemed somehow addressed straight to her heart. That organ literally beat faster at the approach of the gentleman who was this time with Cissy, and who, as seen from within the cage, became on the spot the happiest of the happy circumstances with which her mind had invested the friend of Fritz and Gussy. He was a very happy circumstance indeed as, with his cigarette in his lips and his broken familiar talk caught by his companion, he put down the half-dozen telegrams which it would take them together some minutes to despatch. And here it occurred, oddly enough, that if, shortly before, the girl's interest in his companion had sharpened her sense for the messages then transmitted, her immediate vision of himself had the effect, while she counted his seventy words, of preventing intelligibility. *His* words were mere numbers, they told her nothing whatever; and after he had gone she was in possession of no name, of no address, of no meaning, of nothing but a vague, sweet sound and an immense impression. He had been there but five minutes, he had smoked in her face, and, busy with his telegrams, with the tapping pencil and the conscious danger, the odious betrayal that would come from a mistake, she had had no wandering glances nor roundabout arts to spare. Yet she had taken him in; she knew everything; she had made up her mind.

He had come back from Paris; everything was re-arranged; the pair were again shoulder to shoulder in their high encounter with life, their large and complicated game. The fine, soundless pulse of this game was in the air for our young woman while they remained in the shop. While they remained? They remained all day; their presence continued and abode with her, was in everything she did till nightfall, in the thousands of other words she counted, she transmitted, in all the stamps she detached and the letters she weighed and the change she gave, equally unconscious and unerring in each of these particulars, and not, as the run on the little office thickened with the afternoon hours, looking up at a single ugly face in the long sequence, nor really hearing the stupid questions that she patiently and perfectly answered. All patience was possible now, and all questions stupid after his – all faces ugly. She had been sure she should see the lady again; and even now she should perhaps, she should probably, see her often. But for him it was totally different; she should never, never see him. She wanted it too much. There was a kind of wanting that helped – she had arrived, with her rich experience, at that generalization; and there was another kind that was fatal. It was this time the fatal kind; it would prevent.

Well, she saw him the very next day, and on this second occasion it was quite different; the sense of every syllable he despatched was fiercely distinct; she indeed felt her progressive pencil, dabbing as if with a quick caress the marks of his own, put life into every stroke. He was there a long time – had not brought his forms filled out, but worked them off in a nook on the counter; and there were other people as well – a changing, pushing cluster, with every one to mind at once and endless right change to make and information to produce. But she kept hold of him throughout; she continued, for herself, in a relation with him as close as that in which, behind the hated ground glass, Mr Buckton luckily continued with the sounder. This morning everything changed, but with a kind of dreariness too; she had to swallow the rebuff to her theory about fatal desires, which she did without confusion and indeed with absolute levity; yet if it was now flagrant that he did live close at hand – at Park Chambers – and belonged supremely to the class that wired everything, even their expensive feelings (so that, as he never wrote, his correspondence cost him weekly pounds and pounds, and he might be in and out five times a day), there was, all the same, involved in the prospect, and by reason of its positive excess of light, a perverse melancholy, almost a misery. This was rapidly to give it a place in an order of feelings on which I shall presently touch.

Meanwhile, for a month, he was very constant. Cissy, Mary, never re-appeared with him; he was always either alone or accompanied only by some gentleman who was lost in the blaze of his glory. There was another sense, however – and indeed there was more than one – in which she mostly found herself counting in the splendid creature with whom she had originally connected him. He addressed this correspondent neither as Mary nor as Cissy; but the girl was sure of whom it was, in Eaton Square, that he was perpetually wiring to – and so irreproachably! – as Lady Bradeen. Lady Bradeen was Cissy, Lady Bradeen was Mary, Lady Bradeen was the friend of Fritz and of Gussy, the customer of Marguerite, and the close ally, in short (as was ideally right, only the girl had not yet found a descriptive term that was), of the most magnificent of men. Nothing could equal the frequency and variety of his communications to her ladyship but their extraordinary, their abysmal propriety. It was just the talk – so profuse sometimes that she wondered what was left for their real meetings – of the happiest people in the world. Their real meetings must have been constant, for half of it was appointments and allusions, all swimming in a sea of other allusions still, tangled in a complexity of questions that gave a wondrous image of their life. If Lady Bradeen was Juno it was all certainly Olympian. If the girl, missing the answers, her ladyship's own outpourings, sometimes wished that Cocker's had only been one of the bigger offices where telegrams arrived as well as departed, there were yet ways in which, on the whole, she pressed the romance closer by reason of the very quantity of imagination that it demanded. The days and hours of this new friend, as she came to account him, were at all events unrolled, and however much more she might have known she would still have wished to go beyond. In fact she did go beyond; she went quite far enough.

But she could none the less, even after a month, scarce have told if the gentlemen who came in with him recurred or changed; and this in spite of the fact that they too were always posting and wiring, smoking in her face and signing or not signing. The gentlemen who came in with him were nothing, at any rate, when he was there. They turned up alone at other times – then only perhaps with a dim richness of reference. He himself, absent as well as present, was all. He was very tall, very fair, and had, in spite of his thick pre-occupations, a good-humour that was exquisite, particularly as it so often had the effect of keeping him on. He could have reached over anybody, and anybody – no matter who – would have let him; but he was so extraordinarily kind that he quite pathetically waited, never waggling things at her out of his turn or saying 'Here!' with horrid sharpness. He waited for pottering old ladies, for gaping slaveys, for the perpetual Buttonses from Thrupp's; and the thing in all this that she would have liked most unspeakably to put to the test was the possibility of her having for him a personal identity that might in a particular way appeal. There were moments when he actually struck her as on her side, arranging to help, to support, to spare her.

But such was the singular spirit of our young friend, that she could remind herself with a sort of rage that when people had awfully good manners – people of that class, – you couldn't tell. These manners were for everybody, and it might be drearily unavailing for any poor particular body to be overworked and unusual. What he did take for granted was all sorts of facility; and his high pleasantness, his relighting of cigarettes while he waited, his unconscious bestowal of opportunities, of boons, of blessings, were all a part of his magnificent security, the instinct that told him there was nothing such an existence as his could ever lose by. He was, somehow, at once very bright and very grave, very young and immensely complete; and whatever he was at any moment, it was always as much as all the rest the mere bloom of his beatitude. He was sometimes Everard, as he had been at the Hôtel Brighton, and he was sometimes Captain Everard. He was sometimes Philip with his surname and sometimes Philip without it. In some directions he was merely Phil, in others he was merely Captain. There were relations in which he was none of these things, but a quite different person – 'the Count'. There were several friends for whom he was William. There were several for whom, in allusion perhaps to his complexion, he was 'the Pink 'Un'. Once, once only by good luck, he had, coinciding comically, quite miraculously, with another person also near to her, been 'Mudge'. Yes, whatever he was, it was a part of his happiness – whatever he was and probably whatever he wasn't. And his happiness was a part – it became so little by little – of something that, almost from the first of her being at Cocker's, had been deeply with the girl.

5

THIS was neither more nor less than the queer extension of her experience, the double life that, in the cage, she grew at last to lead. As the weeks went on there she lived more and more into the world of whiffs and glimpses, and found her divinations work faster and stretch further. It was a prodigious view as the pressure heightened, a panorama fed with facts and figures, flushed with a torrent of colour and accompanied with wondrous world-music. What it mainly came to at this period was a picture of how London could amuse itself; and that, with the running commentary of a witness so exclusively a witness, turned for the most part to a hardening of the heart. The nose of this observer was brushed by the bouquet, yet she could never really pluck even a daisy. What could still remain fresh in her daily grind was the immense disparity, the difference and contrast, from class to class, of every instant and every motion. There were times when all the wires in the country seemed to start from the little hole-and-corner where she plied for a livelihood, and where, in the shuffle of feet, the flutter of 'forms', the strayings of stamps and the ring of change over the counter, the people she had fallen into the habit of remembering and fitting together with others, and of having her theories and interpretations of, kept up before her their long procession and rotation. What twisted the knife in her vitals was the way the profligate rich scattered about them, in extravagant chatter over their extravagant pleasures and sins, an amount of money that would have held the stricken household of her frightened childhood, her poor pinched mother and tormented father and lost brother and starved sister, together for a lifetime. During her first weeks she had often gasped at the sums people were willing to pay for the stuff they transmitted – the 'much love's, the 'awful' regrets, the compliments and wonderments and vain, vague gestures that cost the price of a new pair of boots. She had had a way then of glancing at the people's faces, but she had early learned that if you became a telegraphist you soon ceased to be astonished. Her eye for types amounted nevertheless to genius, and there were those she liked and those she hated, her feeling for the latter of which grew to a positive possession, an instinct of observation and detection. There were the brazen women, as she called them, of the higher and the lower fashion, whose squanderings and graspings, whose struggles and secrets and love-affairs and lies, she tracked and stored up against them, till she had at moments, in private, a triumphant, vicious feeling of mastery and power, a sense of having their silly, guilty secrets in her pocket, her small retentive brain, and thereby knowing so much more about them than they suspected or would care to think. There were those she would have liked to betray, to trip up, to bring down with words altered and fatal; and all through a personal hostility provoked by the lightest signs, by their accident of tone and manner, by the particular kind of relation she always happened instantly to feel.

There were impulses of various kinds, alternately soft and severe, to which she was constitutionally accessible and which were determined by the smallest accidents. She was rigid, in general, on the article of making the public itself affix its stamps, and found a special enjoyment in dealing, to that end, with some of the ladies who were too grand to touch them. She had thus a play of refinement and subtlety greater, she flattered herself, than any of which she could be made the subject; and though most people were too stupid to be conscious of this, it brought her endless little consolations and revenges. She recognized quite as much those of her sex whom she would have liked to help, to warn, to rescue, to see more of; and that alternative as well operated exactly through the hazard of personal sympathy, her vision for silver threads and moonbeams and her gift for keeping the clues and finding her way in the tangle. The moonbeams and silver threads presented at moments all the vision of what poor *she* might have made of happiness. Blurred and blank as the whole thing often inevitably, or mercifully, became, she could still, through crevices and crannies, be stupefied, especially by what, in spite of all seasoning, touched the sorest place in her consciousness, the revelation of the golden shower flying about without a gleam of gold for herself. It remained prodigious to the end, the money her fine friends were able to spend to get still more, or even to complain to fine friends of their own that they were in want. The pleasures they proposed were equalled only by those they declined, and they made their appointments often so expensively that she was left wondering at the nature of the delights to which the mere approaches were so paved with shillings. She quivered on occasion into the perception of this and that one whom she would, at all events, have just simply liked to *be*. Her conceit, her baffled vanity were possibly monstrous; she certainly often threw herself into a defiant conviction that she would have done the whole thing much better. But her greatest comfort, on the whole, was her comparative vision of the men; by whom I mean the unmistakable gentlemen, for she had no interest in the spurious or the shabby, and no mercy at all for the poor. She could have found a sixpence, outside, for an appearance of want; but her fancy, in some directions so alert, had never a throb of response for any sign of the sordid. The men she did follow, moreover, she followed mainly in one relation, the relation as to which the cage convinced her, she believed, more than anything else could have done, that it was quite the most diffused.

She found her ladies, in short, almost always in communication with her gentlemen, and her gentlemen with her ladies, and she read into the immensity of their intercourse stories and meanings without end. Incontestably she grew to think that the men cut the best figure; and in this particular, as in many others, she arrived at a philosophy of her own, all made up of her private notations and cynicisms. It was a striking part of the business, for example, that it was much more the women, on the whole, who were after the men than the men who were after the women: it was literally visible that the general attitude of the one sex was that of the object pursued and defensive, apologetic and attenuating, while the light of her own nature helped her more or less to conclude as to the attitude of the other. Perhaps she herself a little even fell into the custom of pursuit in occasionally deviating only for gentlemen from her high rigour about the stamps. She had early in the day made up her mind, in fine, that they had the best manners; and if there were none of them she noticed when Captain Everard was there, there were plenty she could place and trace and name at other times, plenty who, with their way of being 'nice' to her, and of handling, as if their pockets were private tills, loose, mixed masses of silver and gold, were such pleasant appearances that she could envy them without dislike. *They* never had to give change – they only had to get it. They ranged through every suggestion, every shade of fortune, which evidently included indeed lots of bad luck as well as of good, declining even toward Mr Mudge and his bland, firm thrift, and ascending, in wild signals and rocket-flights, almost to within hail of her highest standard. So, from month to month, she went on with them all, through a thousand ups and downs and a thousand pangs and indifferences. What virtually happened was that in the shuffling herd that passed before her by far the greater part only passed – a proportion but just appreciably stayed. Most of the elements swam straight away, lost themselves in the bottomless common, and by so doing really kept the page clear. On the clearness, therefore, what she did retain stood sharply out; she nipped and caught it, turned it over and interwove it.

6

SHE met Mrs Jordan whenever she could, and learned from her more and more how the great people, under her gentle shake, and after going through everything with the mere shops, were waking up to the gain of putting into the hands of a person of real refinement the question that the shop-people spoke of so vulgarly as that of the floral decorations. The regular dealers in these decorations were all very well; but there was a peculiar magic in the play of taste of a lady who had only to remember, through whatever intervening dusk, all her own little tables, little bowls and little jars and little other arrangements, and the wonderful thing she had made of the garden of the vicarage. This small domain, which her young friend had never seen, bloomed in Mrs Jordan's discourse like a new Eden, and she converted the past into a bank of violets by the tone in which she said, 'Of course you always knew my one passion!' She obviously met now, at any rate, a big contemporary need, measured what it was rapidly becoming for people to feel they could trust her without a tremor. It brought them a peace that – during the quarter of an hour before dinner in especial – was worth more to them than mere payment could express. Mere payment, none the less, was tolerably prompt; she engaged by the month, taking over the whole thing; and there was an evening on which, in respect to our heroine, she at last returned to the charge. 'It's growing and growing, and I see that I must really divide the work. One wants an associate – of one's own kind, don't you know? You know the look they want it all to have? – of having come, not from a florist, but from one of themselves. Well, I'm sure *you* could give it – because you *are* one. Then we *should* win. Therefore just come in with me.'

'And leave the P.O.?'

'Let the P.O. simply bring you your letters. It would bring you lots, you'd see: orders, after a bit, by the dozen.' It was on this, in due course, that the great advantage again came up:

'One seems to live again with one's own people.' It had taken some little time (after their having parted company in the tempest of their troubles and then, in the glimmering dawn, finally sighted each other again) for each to admit that the other was, in her private circle, her only equal; but the admission came, when it did come, with an honest groan; and since equality *was* named, each found much personal profit in exaggerating the other's original grandeur. Mrs Jordan was ten years the older, but her young friend was struck with the smaller difference this now made: it had counted otherwise at the time when, much more as a friend of her mother's, the bereaved lady, without a penny of provision, and with stopgaps, like their own, all gone, had, across the sordid landing on which the opposite doors of the pair of scared miseries opened and to which they were bewilderedly bolted, borrowed coals and umbrellas that were repaid in potatoes and postage-stamps. It had been a questionable help, at that time, to ladies submerged, floundering, panting, swimming for their lives, that they *were* ladies; but such an advantage could come up again in proportion as others vanished, and it had grown very great by the time it was the only ghost of one they possessed. They had literally watched it take to itself a portion of the substance of each that had departed; and it became prodigious now, when they could talk of it together, when they could look back at it across a desert of accepted derogation, and when, above all, they could draw from each other a credulity about it that they could draw from no one else. Nothing was really so marked as that they felt the need to cultivate this legend much more after having found their feet and stayed their stomachs in the ultimate obscure than they had done in the upper air of mere frequent shocks. The thing they could now oftenest say to each other was that they knew what they meant; and the sentiment with which, all round, they knew it was known had been a kind of promise to stick well together again.

Mrs Jordan was at present fairly dazzling on the subject of the way that, in the practice of her beautiful art, she more than peeped in – she penetrated. There was not a house of the great kind – and it was, of course, only a question of those, real homes of luxury – in which she was not, at the rate such people now had things, all over the place. The girl felt before the picture the cold breath of disinheritance as much as she had ever felt it in the cage; she knew, moreover, how much she betrayed this, for the experience of poverty had begun, in her life, too early, and her ignorance of the requirements of homes of luxury had grown, with other active knowledge, a depth of simplification. She had accordingly at first often found that in these colloquies she could only pretend she understood. Educated as she had rapidly been by her chances at Cocker's, there were still strange gaps in her learning – she could never, like Mrs Jordan, have found her way about one of the 'homes'. Little by little, however, she had caught on, above all in the light of what Mrs Jordan's redemption had materially made of that lady, giving her, though the years and the struggles had naturally not straightened a feature, an almost super-eminent air. There were women in and out of Cocker's who were quite nice and who yet didn't look well; whereas Mrs Jordan looked well and yet, with her extraordinarily protrusive teeth, was by no means quite nice. It would seem, mystifyingly, that it might really come from all the greatness she could live with. It was fine to hear her talk so often of dinners of twenty and of her doing, as she said, exactly as she liked with them. She spoke as if, for that matter, she invited the company. 'They simply *give* me the table – all the rest, all the other effects, come afterwards.'

7

'THEN you *do* see them?' the girl again asked.

Mrs Jordan hesitated, and indeed the point had been ambiguous before. 'Do you mean the guests?'

Her young friend, cautious about an undue exposure of innocence, was not quite sure. 'Well – the people who live there.'

'Lady Ventnor? Mrs Bubb? Lord Rye? Dear, yes. Why, they *like* one.'

'But does one personally *know* them?' our young lady went on, since that was the way to speak. 'I mean socially, don't you know? – as you know *me*.'

'They're not so nice as you!' Mrs Jordan charmingly cried. 'But I *shall* see more and more of them.'

Ah, this was the old story. 'But how soon?'

'Why, almost any day. Of course,' Mrs Jordan honestly added, 'they're nearly always out.'

'Then why do they want flowers all over?'

'Oh, that doesn't make any difference.' Mrs Jordan was not philosophic; she was only evidently determined it shouldn't make any. 'They're awfully interested in my ideas, and it's inevitable they should meet me over them.'

Her interlocutress was sturdy enough. 'What do you call your ideas?'

Mrs Jordan's reply was fine. 'If you were to see me some day with a thousand tulips, you'd soon discover.'

'A thousand?' – the girl gaped at such a revelation of the scale of it; she felt, for the instant, fairly planted out. 'Well, but if in fact they never do meet you?' she none the less pessimistically insisted.

'Never? They *often* do – and evidently quite on purpose. We have grand long talks.'

There was something in our young lady that could still stay her from asking for a personal description of these apparitions; that showed too starved a state. But while she considered, she took in afresh the whole of the clergyman's widow. Mrs Jordan couldn't help her teeth, and her sleeves were a distinct rise in the world. A thousand tulips at a shilling clearly took one further than a thousand words at a penny; and the betrothed of Mr Mudge, in whom the sense of the race for life was always acute, found herself wondering, with a twinge of her easy jealousy, if it mightn't after all then, for *her* also, be better – better than where she was – to follow some such scent. Where she was was where Mr Buckton's elbow could freely enter her right side and the counter-clerk's breathing – he had something the matter with his nose – pervade her left ear. It was something to fill an office under Government, and she knew but too well there were places commoner still than Cocker's; but it never required much of a chance to bring back to her the picture of servitude and promiscuity that she must present to the eye of comparative freedom. She was so boxed up with her young men, and anything like a margin so absent, that it needed more art than she should ever possess to pretend in the least to compass, with any one in the nature of an acquaintance – say with Mrs Jordan herself, flying in, as it might happen, to wire sympathetically to Mrs Bubb – an approach to a relation of elegant privacy. She remembered the day when Mrs Jordan *had*, in fact, by the greatest chance, come in with fifty-three words for Lord Rye and a five-pound note to change. This had been the dramatic manner of their reunion – their mutual recognition was so great an event. The girl could at first only see her from the waist up, besides making but little of her long telegram to his lordship. It was a strange whirligig that had converted the clergyman's widow into such a specimen of the class that went beyond the sixpence.

Nothing of the occasion, all the more, had ever become dim; least of all the way that, as her recovered friend looked up from counting, Mrs Jordan had just blown, in explanation, through her teeth and through the bars of the cage. 'I *do* flowers, you know.' Our young woman had always, with her little finger crooked out, a pretty movement for counting; and she had not forgotten the small secret advantage, a sharpness of triumph it might even have been called, that fell upon her at this moment and avenged her for the incoherence of the message, an unintelligible enumeration of numbers, colours, days, hours. The correspondence of people she didn't know was one thing; but the correspondence of people she did had an aspect of its own for her, even when she couldn't understand it. The speech in which Mrs Jordan had defined a position and announced a profession was like a tinkle of bluebells; but, for herself, her one idea about flowers was that people had them at funerals, and her present sole gleam of light was that lords probably had them most. When she watched, a minute later, through the cage, the swing of her visitor's departing petticoats, she saw the sight from the waist down; and when the counter-clerk after a mere male glance, remarked, with an intention unmistakably low, 'Handsome woman!' she had for him the finest of her chills: 'She's the widow of a bishop.' She always felt, with the counter-clerk, that it was impossible sufficiently to put it on; for what she wished to express to him was the maximum of her contempt, and that element in her nature was confusedly stored. 'A bishop' *was* putting it on, but the counter-clerk's approaches were vile. The night, after this, when, in the fulness of time, Mrs Jordan mentioned the grand long talks, the girl at last brought out: 'Should *I* see them? – I mean if I *were* to give up everything for you.'

Mrs Jordan at this became most arch. 'I'd send you to all the bachelors!'

Our young lady could be reminded by such a remark that she usually struck her friend as pretty. 'Do *they* have their flowers?'

'Oceans. And they're the most particular.' Oh, it was a wonderful world. 'You should see Lord Rye's.'

'His flowers?'

'Yes, and his letters. He writes me pages on pages – with the most adorable little drawings and plans. You should see his diagrams!'

8

THE girl had in course of time every opportunity to inspect these documents, and they a little disappointed her; but in the meanwhile there had been more talk, and it had led to her saying, as if her friend's guarantee of a life of elegance were not quite definite: 'Well, I see every one at *my* place.'

'Every one?'

'Lots of swells. They flock. They live, you know, all round, and the place is filled with all the smart people, all the fast people, those whose names are in the papers – mamma has still the *Morning Post* – and who come up for the season.'

Mrs Jordan took this in with complete intelligence. 'Yes, and I dare say it's some of your people that *I* do.'

Her companion assented, but discriminated. 'I doubt if you "do" them as much as I! Their affairs, their appointments and arrangements, their little games and secrets and vices – those things all pass before me.'

This was a picture that could impose on a clergyman's widow a certain strain; it was in intention, moreover, something of a retort to the thousand tulips. 'Their vices? Have they got vices?'

Our young critic even more remarkably stared; then with a touch of contempt in her amusement: 'Haven't you found *that* out?' The homes of luxury, then, hadn't so much to give. '*I* find out everything,' she continued.

Mrs Jordan, at bottom a very meek person, was visibly struck. 'I see. You do "have" them.'

'Oh, I don't care! Much good does it do me!'

Mrs Jordan, after an instant, recovered her superiority. 'No – it doesn't lead to much.' Her own initiations so clearly did. Still – after all; and she was not jealous: 'There must be a charm.'

'In seeing them?' At this the girl suddenly let herself go. 'I hate them; there's that charm!'

Mrs Jordan gaped again. 'The *real* "smarts"?'

'Is that what you call Mrs Bubb? Yes – it comes to me; I've had Mrs Bubb. I don't think she has been in herself, but there are things her maid has brought. Well, my dear!' – and the young person from Cocker's, recalling these things and summing them up, seemed suddenly to have much to say. But she didn't say it; she checked it; she only brought out: 'Her maid, who's horrid – *she* must have her!' Then she went on with indifference: 'They're *too* real! They're selfish brutes.'

Mrs Jordan, turning it over, adopted at last the plan of treating it with a smile. She wished to be liberal. 'Well, of course, they do lay it out.'

'They bore me to death,' her companion pursued with slightly more temperance.

But this was going too far. 'Ah, that's because you've no sympathy!'

The girl gave an ironic laugh, only retorting that she wouldn't have any either if she had to count all day all the words in the dictionary; a contention Mrs Jordan quite granted, the more that she shuddered at the notion of ever failing of the very gift to which she owed the vogue – the rage she might call it – that had caught her up. Without sympathy – or without imagination, for it came back again to that – how should she get, for big dinners, down the middle and toward the far corners at all? It wasn't the combinations, which were easily managed: the strain was over the ineffable simplicities, those that the bachelors above all, and Lord Rye perhaps most of any, threw off – just blew off, like cigarette-puffs – such sketches of. The betrothed of Mr Mudge at all events accepted the explanation, which had the effect, as almost any turn of their talk was now apt to have, of bringing her round to the terrific question of that gentleman. She was tormented with the desire to get out of Mrs Jordan, on this subject, what she was sure was at the back of Mrs Jordan's head; and to get it out of her, queerly enough, if only to vent a certain irritation at it. She knew that what her friend would already have risked if she had not been timid and tortuous was: 'Give him up – yes, give him up: you'll see that with your sure chances you'll be able to do much better.'

Our young woman had a sense that if that view could only be put before her with a particular sniff for poor Mr Mudge she should hate it as much as she morally ought. She was conscious of not, as yet, hating it quite so much as that. But she saw that Mrs Jordan was conscious of something too, and that there was a sort of assurance she was waiting little by little to gather. The day came when the girl caught a glimpse of what was still wanting to make her friend feel strong; which was nothing less than the prospect of being able to announce the climax of sundry private dreams. The associate of the aristocracy had personal calculations – she pored over them in her lonely lodgings. If she did the flowers for the bachelors, in short, didn't she expect that to have consequences very different from the outlook, at Cocker's, that she had described as leading to nothing? There seemed in very truth something auspicious in the mixture of bachelors and flowers, though, when looked hard in the eye, Mrs Jordan was not quite prepared to say she had expected a positive proposal from Lord Rye to pop out of it. Our young woman arrived at last, none the less, at a definite vision of what was in her mind. This was a vivid foreknowledge that the betrothed of Mr Mudge would, unless conciliated in advance by a successful rescue, almost hate her on the day she should break a particular piece of news. How could that unfortunate otherwise endure to hear of what, under the protection of Lady Ventnor, was after all so possible?

9

MEANWHILE, since irritation sometimes relieved her, the betrothed of Mr Mudge drew straight from that admirer an amount of it that was proportioned to her fidelity. She always walked with him on Sundays, usually in the Regent's Park, and quite often, once or twice a month, he took her, in the Strand or thereabouts, to see a piece that was having a run. The productions he always preferred were the really good ones – Shakespeare, Thompson, or some funny American thing; which, as it also happened that she hated vulgar plays, gave him ground for what was almost the fondest of his approaches, the theory that their tastes were, blissfully, just the same. He was for ever reminding her of that, rejoicing over it, and being affectionate and wise about it. There were times when she wondered how in the world she could bear him, how she could bear any man so smugly unconscious of the immensity of her difference. It was just for this difference that, if she was to be liked at all, she wanted to be liked, and if that was not the source of Mr Mudge's admiration, she asked herself, what on earth *could* be? She was not different only at one point, she was different all round; unless perhaps indeed in being practically human, which her mind just barely recognized that he also was. She would have made tremendous concessions in other quarters: there was no limit, for instance, to those she would have made to Captain Everard; but what I have named was the most she was prepared to do for Mr Mudge. It was because *he* was different that, in the oddest way, she liked as well as deplored him; which was after all a proof that the disparity, should they frankly recognize it, wouldn't necessarily be fatal. She felt that, oleaginous – too oleaginous – as he was, he was somehow comparatively primitive: she had once, during the portion of his time at Cocker's that had overlapped her own, seen him collar a drunken soldier, a big, violent man, who, having come in with a mate to get a postal-order cashed, had made a grab at the money before his friend could reach it and had so produced, among the hams and cheeses and the lodgers from Thrupp's, reprisals instantly ensuing, a scene of scandal and consternation. Mr Buckton and the counter-clerk had crouched within the cage, but Mr Mudge had, with a very quiet but very quick step round the counter, triumphantly interposed in the scrimmage, parted the combatants, and shaken the delinquent in his skin. She had been proud of him at that moment, and had felt that if their affair had not already been settled the neatness of his execution would have left her without resistance.

Their affair had been settled by other things: by the evident sincerity of his passion and by the sense that his high white apron resembled a front of many floors. It had gone a great way with her that he would build up a business to his chin, which he carried quite in the air. This could only be a question of time; he would have all Piccadilly in the pen behind his ear. That was a merit in itself for a girl who had known what she had known. There were hours at which she even found him good-looking, though, frankly, there could be no crown for her effort to imagine, on the part of the tailor or the barber, some such treatment of his appearance as would make him resemble even remotely a gentleman. His very beauty was the beauty of a grocer, and the finest future would offer it none too much room to expand. She had engaged herself, in short, to the perfection of a type, and perfection of anything was much for a person who, out of early troubles, had just escaped with her life. But it contributed hugely at present to carry on the two parallel lines of her contacts in the cage and her contacts out of it. After keeping quiet for some time about this opposition, she suddenly – one Sunday afternoon on a penny chair in the Regent's Park – broke, for him, capriciously, bewilderingly, into an intimation of what it came to. He naturally pressed more and more on the subject of her again placing herself where he could see her hourly, and for her to recognize that she had as yet given him no sane reason for delays she had no need to hear him say that he couldn't make out what she was up to. As if, with her absurd bad reasons, she knew it herself! Sometimes she thought it would be amusing to let him have them full in the face, for she felt she should die of him unless she once in a while stupefied him; and sometimes she thought it would be disgusting and perhaps even fatal. She liked him, however, to think her silly, for that gave her the margin which, at the best, she would always require; and the only difficulty about this was that he hadn't enough imagination to oblige her. It produced, none the less, something of the desired effect – to leave him simply wondering why, over the matter of their reunion, she didn't yield to his arguments. Then at last, simply as if by accident and out of mere boredom on a day that was rather flat, she preposterously produced her own. 'Well, wait a bit. Where I am I still see things.' And she talked to him even worse, if possible, than she had talked to Mrs Jordan.

Little by little, to her own stupefaction, she caught that he was trying to take it as she meant it, and that he was neither astonished nor angry. Oh, the British tradesman – this gave her an idea of his resources! Mr Mudge would be angry only with a person who, like the drunken soldier in the shop, should have an unfavourable effect upon business. He seemed positively to enter, for the time and without the faintest flash of irony or ripple of laughter, into the whimsical grounds of her enjoyment of Cocker's custom, and instantly to be casting up whatever it might, as Mrs Jordan had said, lead to. What he had in mind was not, of course, what Mrs Jordan had had: it was obviously not a source of speculation with him that his sweetheart might pick up a husband. She could see perfectly that this was not,

She had to think a moment; then she found something. 'From the "spring meetings". They bet tremendously.'

'Well, they bet enough at Chalk Farm, if that's all.'

'It *isn't* all. It isn't a millionth part!' she replied with some sharpness. 'It's immense fun' – she would tantalize him. Then, as she had heard Mrs Jordan say, and as the ladies at Cocker's even sometimes wired, 'It's quite too dreadful!' She could fully feel how it was Mr Mudge's propriety, which was extreme – he had a horror of coarseness and attended a Wesleyan chapel – that prevented his asking for details. But she gave him some of the more innocuous in spite of himself, especially putting before him how, at Simpkin's and Ladle's, they all made the money fly. That was indeed what he liked to hear: the connection was not direct, but one was somehow more in the right place where the money was flying than where it was simply and meagrely nesting. It enlivened the air, he had to acknowledge, much less at Chalk Farm than in the district in which his beloved so oddly enjoyed her footing. She gave him, she could see, a restless sense that these might be familiarities not to be sacrificed; germs, possibilities, faint foreshowings – heaven knew what – of the initiation it would prove profitable to have arrived at when, in the fulness of time, he should have his own shop in some such paradise. What really touched him – that was discernible – was that she could feed him with so much mere vividness of reminder, keep before him, as by the play of a fan, the very wind of the swift bank-notes and the charm of the existence of a class that Providence had raised up to be the blessing of grocers. He liked to think that the class was there, that it was always there, and that she contributed in her slight but appreciable degree to keep it up to the mark. He couldn't have formulated his theory of the matter, but the exuberance of the aristocracy was the advantage of trade, and everything was knit together in a richness of pattern that it was good to follow with one's finger-tips. It was a comfort to him to be thus assured that there were no symptoms of a drop. What did the sounder, as she called it, nimbly worked, do but keep the ball going?

What it came to, therefore, for Mr Mudge, was that all enjoyments were, in short, interrelated, and that the more people had the more they wanted to have. The more flirtations, as he might roughly express it, the more cheese and pickles. He had even in his own small way been dimly struck with the concatenation between the tender passion and cheap champagne. What he would have liked to say had he been able to work out his thought to the end was: 'I see, I see. Lash them up then, lead them on, keep them going: some of it can't help, some time, coming *our* way.' Yet he was troubled by the suspicion of subtleties on his companion's part that spoiled the straight view. He couldn't understand people's hating what they liked or liking what they hated; above all it hurt him somewhere – for he had his private delicacies – to see anything *but* money made out of his betters. To be curious at the expense of the gentry was vaguely wrong; the only thing that was distinctly right was to be prosperous. Wasn't it just because they were up there aloft that they were lucrative? He concluded, at any rate, by saying to his young friend: 'If it's improper for you to remain at Cocker's, then that falls in exactly with the other reasons that I have put before you for your removal.'

'Improper?' – her smile became a long, wide look at him. 'My dear boy, there's no one like you!'

'I dare say,' he laughed; 'but that doesn't help the question.'

'Well,' she returned, 'I can't give up my friends. I'm making even more than Mrs Jordan.'

Mr Mudge considered. 'How much is *she* making?'

'Oh, you dear donkey!' – and, regardless of all the Regent's Park, she patted his cheek. This was the sort of moment at which she was absolutely tempted to tell him that she liked to be near Park Chambers. There was a fascination in the idea of seeing if, on a mention of Captain Everard, he wouldn't do what she thought he might; wouldn't weigh against the obvious objection the still more obvious advantage. The advantage, of course, could only strike him at the best as rather fantastic; but it was always to the good to keep hold when you *had* hold, and such an attitude would also after all involve a high tribute to her fidelity. Of one thing she absolutely never doubted: Mr Mudge believed in her with a belief—! She believed in herself too, for that matter: if there was a thing in the world no one could charge her with, it was being the kind of low barmaid person who rinsed tumblers and bandied slang. But she forbore as yet to speak; she had not spoken even to Mrs Jordan; and the hush that on her lips surrounded the Captain's name maintained itself as a kind of symbol of the success that, up to this time, had attended something or other – she couldn't have said what – that she humoured herself with calling, without words, her relation with him.

11

SHE would have admitted indeed that it consisted of little more than the fact that his absences, however frequent and however long, always ended with his turning up again. It was nobody's business in the world but her own if that fact continued to be enough for her. It was of course not enough just in itself; what it had taken on to make it so was the extraordinary possession of the elements of his life that memory and attention had at last given her. There came a day when this possession, on the girl's part, actually seemed to enjoy, between them, while their eyes met, a tacit recognition that was half a joke and half a deep solemnity. He bade her good morning always now; he often quite raised his hat to her. He passed a remark when there was time or room, and once she went so far as to say to him that she had not seen him for 'ages'. 'Ages' was the word she consciously and carefully, though a trifle tremulously, used; 'ages' was exactly what she meant. To this he replied in terms doubtless less anxiously selected, but perhaps on that account not the less remarkable, 'Oh yes, hasn't it been awfully wet?' That was a specimen of their give and take; it fed her fancy that no form of intercourse so transcendent and distilled had ever been established on earth. Everything, so far as they chose to consider it so, might mean almost anything. The want of margin in the cage, when he peeped through the bars, wholly ceased to be appreciable. It was a drawback only in superficial commerce. With Captain Everard she had simply the margin of the universe. It may be imagined, therefore, how their unuttered reference to all she knew about him could, in this immensity, play at its ease. Every time he handed in a telegram it was an addition to her knowledge: what did his constant smile mean to mark if it didn't mean to mark that? He never came into the place without saying to her in this manner: 'Oh yes, you have me by this time so completely at your mercy that it doesn't in the least matter what I give you now. You've become a comfort, I assure you!'

She had only two torments; the greatest of which was that she couldn't, not even once or twice, touch with him on some individual fact. She would have given anything to have been able to allude to one of his friends by name, to one of his engagements by date, to one of his difficulties by the solution. She would have given almost as much for just the right chance – it would have to be tremendously right – to show him in some sharp, sweet way that she had perfectly penetrated the greatest of these last and now lived with it in a kind of heroism of sympathy. He was in love with a woman to whom, and to any view of whom, a lady-telegraphist, and especially one who passed a life among hams and cheeses, was as the sand on the floor; and what her dreams desired was the possibility of its somehow coming to him that her own interest in him could take a pure and noble account of such an infatuation and even of such an impropriety. As yet, however, she could only rub along with the hope that an accident, sooner or later, might give her a lift toward popping out with something that would surprise and perhaps even, some fine day, assist him. What could people mean, moreover – cheaply sarcastic people – by not feeling all that could be got out of the weather? *She* felt it all, and seemed literally to feel it most when she went quite wrong, speaking of the stuffy days as cold, of the cold ones as stuffy, and betraying how little she knew, in her cage, of whether it was foul or fair. It was, for that matter, always stuffy at Cocker's, and she finally settled down to the safe proposition that the outside element was 'changeable.' Anything seemed true that made him so radiantly assent.

This indeed is a small specimen of her cultivation of insidious ways of making things easy for him – ways to which of course she couldn't be at all sure that he did real justice. Real justice was not of this world: she had had too often to come back to that; yet, strangely, happiness was, and her traps had to be set for it in a manner to keep them unperceived by Mr Buckton and the counter-clerk. The most she could hope for apart from the question, which constantly flickered up and died down, of the divine chance of his consciously liking her, would be that, without analysing it, he should arrive at a vague sense that Cocker's was – well, attractive; easier, smoother, sociably brighter, slightly more picturesque, in short more propitious in general to his little affairs, than any other establishment just thereabouts. She was quite aware that they couldn't be, in so huddled a hole, particularly quick; but she found her account in the slowness – she certainly could bear it if *he* could. The great pang was that, just thereabouts, post-offices were so awfully thick. She was always seeing him, in imagination, in other places and with other girls. But she would defy any other girl to follow him as she followed. And though they weren't, for so many reasons, quick at Cocker's, she could hurry for him when, through an intimation light as air, she gathered that he was pressed.

When hurry was, better still, impossible, it was because of the pleasantest thing of all, the particular element of their contact – she would have called it their friendship – that consisted of an almost humorous treatment of the look of some of his words. They would never perhaps have grown half so intimate if he had not, by the blessing of heaven, formed some of his letters with a queerness –! It was positive that the queerness could scarce have been greater if he had practised it for the very purpose of bringing their heads together over it as far as was possible to heads on different sides of a cage. It had taken her in reality but once or twice to master these tricks, but, at the cost of striking him perhaps as stupid, she could still challenge them when circumstances favoured. The great circumstance that favoured was that she sometimes actually believed he knew she only feigned perplexity. If he knew it, therefore, he tolerated it; if he tolerated it he came back; and if he came back he liked her. This was her seventh heaven; and she didn't ask much of his liking – she only asked of it to reach the point of his not going away because of her own. He had at times to be away for weeks, he had to lead his life; he had to travel – there were places to which he was constantly wiring for 'rooms': all this she granted him, forgave him; in fact, in the long-run, literally blessed and thanked him for. If he had to lead his life, that precisely fostered his leading it so much by telegraph: therefore the benediction was to come in when he could. That was all she asked – that he shouldn't wholly deprive her.

Sometimes she almost felt that he couldn't have done so even had he been minded, on account of the web of revelation that was woven between them. She quite thrilled herself with thinking what, with such a lot of material, a bad girl would do. It would be a scene better than many in her ha'penny novels, this going to him in the dusk of evening at Park Chambers and letting him at last have it. 'I know too much about a certain person now not to put it to you–excuse my being so lurid–that it's quite worth your while to buy me off. Come, therefore; buy me!' There was a point indeed at which such flights had to drop again – the point of an unreadiness to name, when it came to that, the purchasing medium. It wouldn't, certainly, be anything so gross as money, and the matter accordingly remained rather vague, all the more that *she* was not a bad girl. It was not for any such reason as might have aggravated a mere minx that she often hoped he would again bring Cissy. The difficulty of this, however, was constantly present to her, for the kind of communion to which Cocker's so richly ministered rested on the fact that Cissy and he were so often in different places. She knew by this time all the places – Suchbury, Monkhouse, Whiteroy, Finches, – and even how the parties, on these occasions, were composed; but her subtlety found ways to make her knowledge fairly protect and promote their keeping, as she had heard Mrs Jordan say, in touch. So, when he actually sometimes smiled as if he really felt the awkwardness of giving her again one of the same old addresses, all her being went out in the desire – which her face must have expressed – that he should recognize her forbearance to criticize as one of the finest, tenderest sacrifices a woman had ever made for love.

12

SHE was occasionally worried, all the same, by the impression that these sacrifices, great as they were, were nothing to those that his own passion had imposed; if indeed it was not rather the passion of his confederate, which had caught him up and was whirling him round like a great steam-wheel. He was at any rate in the strong grip of a dizzy, splendid fate; the wild wind of his life blew him straight before it. Didn't she catch in his face, at times, even through his smile and his happy habit, the gleam of that pale glare with which a bewildered victim appeals, as he passes, to some pair of pitying eyes? He perhaps didn't even himself know how scared he was; but *she* knew. They were in danger, they were in danger, Captain Everard and Lady Bradeen: it beat every novel in the shop. She thought of Mr Mudge and his safe sentiment; she thought of herself and blushed even more for her tepid response to it. It was a comfort to her at such moments to feel that in another relation – a relation supplying that affinity with her nature that Mr Mudge, deluded creature, would never supply – she should have been no more tepid than her ladyship. Her deepest soundings were on two or three occasions of finding herself almost sure that, if she dared, her ladyship's lover would have gathered relief from 'speaking' to her. She literally fancied once or twice that, projected as he was toward his doom, her own eyes struck him, while the air roared in his ears, as the one pitying pair in the crowd. But how could he speak to her while she sat sandwiched there between the counter-clerk and the sounder?

She had long ago, in her comings and goings, made acquaintance with Park Chambers, and reflected, as she looked up at their luxurious front, that *they*, of course, would supply the ideal setting for the ideal speech. There was not a picture in London that, before the season was over, was more stamped upon her brain. She went round about to pass it, for it was not on the short way; she passed on the opposite side of the street and always looked up, though it had taken her a long time to be sure of the particular set of windows. She had made that out at last by an act of audacity that, at the time, had almost stopped her heart-beats and that, in retrospect, greatly quickened her blushes. One evening, late, she had lingered and watched – watched for some moment when the porter, who was in uniform and often on the steps, had gone in with a visitor. Then she had followed boldly, on the calculation that he would have taken the visitor up and that the hall would be free. The hall *was* free, and the electric light played over the gilded and lettered board that showed the names and numbers of the occupants of the different floors. What she wanted looked straight at her – Captain Everard was on the third. It was as if, in the immense intimacy of this, they were, for the instant and the first time, face to face outside the cage. Alas! they were face to face but a second or two: she was whirled out on the wings of a panic fear that he might just then be entering or issuing. This fear was indeed, in her shameless deflections, never very far from her, and was mixed in the oddest way with depressions and disappointments. It was dreadful, as she trembled by, to run the risk of looking to him as if she basely hung about; and yet it was dreadful to be obliged to pass only at such moments as put an encounter out of the question.

At the horrible hour of her first coming to Cocker's he was always – it was to be hoped – snug in bed; and at the hour of her final departure he was of course – she had such things all on her fingers'-ends – dressing for dinner. We may let it pass that if she could not bring herself to hover till he was dressed, this was simply because such a process for such a person could only be terribly prolonged. When she went in the middle of the day to her own dinner she had too little time to do anything but go straight, though it must be added that for a real certainty she would joyously have omitted the repast. She had made up her mind as to there being on the whole no decent pretext to justify her flitting casually past at three o'clock in the morning. That was the hour at which, if the ha'penny novels were not all wrong, he probably came home for the night. She was therefore reduced to merely picturing that miraculous meeting toward which a hundred impossibilities would have to conspire. But if nothing was more impossible than the fact, nothing was more intense than the vision. What may not, we can only moralize, take place in the quickened, muffled perception of a girl of a certain kind of soul? All our young friend's native distinction, her refinement of personal grain, of heredity, of pride, took refuge in this small throbbing spot; for when she was most conscious of the abjection of her vanity and the pitifulness of her little flutters and manoeuvres, then the consolation and the redemption were most sure to shine before her in some just discernible sign. He did like her!

13

HE never brought Cissy back, but Cissy came one day without him, as fresh as before from the hands of Marguerite, or only, at the season's end, a trifle less fresh. She was, however, distinctly less serene. She had brought nothing with her, and looked about her with some impatience for the forms and the place to write. The latter convenience, at Cocker's, was obscure and barely adequate, and her clear voice had the light note of disgust which her lover's never showed as she responded with a 'There?' of surprise to the gesture made by the counter-clerk in answer to her sharp inquiry. Our young friend was busy with half a dozen people, but she had despatched them in her most business-like manner by the time her ladyship flung through the bars the light of re-appearance. Then the directness with which the girl managed to receive this missive was the result of the concentration that had caused her to make the stamps fly during the few minutes occupied by the production of it. This concentration, in turn, may be described as the effect of the apprehension of imminent relief. It was nineteen days, counted and checked off, since she had seen the object of her homage; and as, had he been in London, she should, with his habits, have been sure to see him often, she was now about to learn what other spot his presence might just then happen to sanctify. For she thought of them, the other spots, as ecstatically conscious of it, expressively happy in it.

But, gracious, how handsome *was* her ladyship, and what an added price it gave him that the air of intimacy he threw out should have flowed originally from such a source! The girl looked straight through the cage at the eyes and lips that must so often have been so near his own – looked at them with a strange passion that, for an instant, had the result of filling out some of the gaps, supplying the missing answers, in his correspondence. Then, as she made out that the features she thus scanned and associated were totally unaware of it, that they glowed only with the colour of quite other and not at all guessable thoughts, this directly added to their splendour, gave the girl the sharpest impression she had yet received of the uplifted, the unattainable plains of heaven, and yet at the same time caused her to thrill with a sense of the high company she did somehow keep. She was with the absent through her ladyship and with her ladyship through the absent. The only pang – but it didn't matter – was the proof in the admirable face, in the sightless pre-occupation of its possessor, that the latter hadn't a notion of her. Her folly had gone to the point of half believing that the other party to the affair must sometimes mention in Eaton Square the extraordinary little person at the place from which he so often wired. Yet the perception of her visitor's blankness actually helped this extraordinary little person, the next instant, to take refuge in a reflection that could be as proud as it liked. 'How little she knows, how little she knows!' the girl cried to herself; for what did that show after all but that Captain Everard's telegraphic confidant was Captain Everard's charming secret? Our young friend's perusal of her ladyship's telegram was literally prolonged by a momentary daze: what swam between her and the words, making her see them as through rippled, shallow, sunshot water, was the great, the perpetual flood of 'How much *I* know – how much *I* know!' This produced a delay in her catching that, on the face, these words didn't give her what she wanted, though she was prompt enough with her remembrance that her grasp was, half the time, just of what was *not* on the face. 'Miss Dolman, Parade Lodge, Parade Terrace, Dover. Let him instantly know right one, Hôtel de France, Ostend. Make it seven nine four nine six one. Wire me alternative Burfield's.'

The girl slowly counted. Then he was at Ostend. This hooked on with so sharp a click that, not to feel she was as quickly letting it all slip from her, she had absolutely to hold it a minute longer and to do something to that end. Thus it was that she did on this occasion what she never did – threw off an 'Answer paid?' that sounded officious, but that she partly made up for by deliberately affixing the stamps and by waiting till she had done so to give change. She had, for so much coolness, the strength that she considered she knew all about Miss Dolman.

'Yes – paid.' She saw all sorts of things in this reply, even to a small, suppressed start of surprise at so correct an assumption; even to an attempt, the next minute, at a fresh air of detachment. 'How much, with the answer?' The calculation was not abstruse, but our intense observer required a moment more to make it, and this gave her ladyship time for a second thought. 'Oh, just wait!' The white, begemmed hand bared to write rose in sudden nervousness to the side of the wonderful face which, with eyes of anxiety for the paper on the counter, she brought closer to the bars of the cage. 'I think I must alter a word!' On this she recovered her telegram and looked over it again; but she had a new, obvious trouble, and studied it without deciding and with much of the effect of making our young woman watch her.

This personage, meanwhile, at the sight of her expression, had decided on the spot. If she had always been sure they were in danger, her ladyship's expression was the best possible sign of it. There was a word wrong, but she had lost the right one, and much, clearly, depended on her finding it again. The girl, therefore, sufficiently estimating the affluence of customers and the distraction of Mr Buckton and the counter-clerk, took the jump and gave it. 'Isn't it Cooper's?'

It was as if she had bodily leaped – cleared the top of the cage and alighted on her interlocutress. 'Cooper's?' – the stare was heightened by a blush. Yes, she had made Juno blush.

This was all the more reason for going on. 'I mean instead of Burfield's.'

Our young friend fairly pitied her; she had made her in an instant so helpless, and yet not a bit haughty nor outraged. She was only mystified and scared. 'Oh, you know –?'

'Yes, I know!' Our young friend smiled, meeting the other's eyes, and, having made Juno blush, proceeded to patronize her. '*I'll* do it' – she put out a competent hand. Her ladyship only submitted, confused and bewildered, all presence of mind quite gone; and the next moment the telegram was in the cage again and its author out of the shop. Then quickly, boldly, under all the eyes that might have witnessed her tampering, the extraordinary little person at Cocker's made the proper change. People were really too giddy, and if they *were,* in a certain case, to be caught, it shouldn't be the fault of her own grand memory. Hadn't it been settled weeks before? – for Miss Dolman it was always to be 'Cooper's'.

14

BUT the summer 'holidays' brought a marked difference; they were holidays for almost everyone but the animals in the cage. The August days were flat and dry, and, with so little to feed it, she was conscious of the ebb of her interest in the secrets of the refined. She was in a position to follow the refined to the extent of knowing – they had made so many of their arrangements with her aid – exactly where they were; yet she felt quite as if the panorama had ceased unrolling and the band stopped playing. A stray member of the latter occasionally turned up, but the communications that passed before her bore now largely on rooms at hotels, prices of furnished houses, hours of trains, dates of sailings and arrangements for being 'met': she found them for the most part prosaic and coarse. The only thing was that they brought into her stuffy corner as straight a whiff of Alpine meadows and Scotch moors as she might hope ever to inhale; there were moreover, in especial, fat, hot, dull ladies who had out with her, to exasperation, the terms for seaside lodgings, which struck her as huge, and the matter of the number of beds required, which was not less portentous: this in reference to places of which the names – Eastbourne, Folkstone, Cromer, Scarborough, Whitby – tormented her with something of the sound of the plash of water that haunts the traveller in the desert. She had not been out of London for a dozen years, and the only thing to give a taste to the present dead weeks was the spice of a chronic resentment. The sparse customers, the people she did see, were the people who were 'just off' – off on the decks of fluttered yachts, off to the uttermost point of rocky headlands where the very breeze was then playing for the want of which she said to herself that she sickened.

There was accordingly a sense in which, at such a period, the great differences of the human condition could press upon her more than ever; a circumstance drawing fresh force, in truth, from the very fact of the chance that at last, for a change, did squarely meet her – the chance to be 'off', for a bit, almost as far as anybody. They took their turns in the cage as they took them both in the shop and at Chalk Farm, and she had known these two months that time was to be allowed in September – no less than eleven days – for her personal, private holiday. Much of her recent intercourse with Mr Mudge had consisted of the hopes and fears, expressed mainly by himself, involved in the question of their getting the same dates – a question that, in proportion as the delight seemed assured, spread into a sea of speculation over the choice of where and how. All through July, on the Sunday evenings and at such other odd times as he could seize, he had flooded their talk with wild waves of calculation. It was practically settled that, with her mother, somewhere 'on the south coast' (a phrase of which she liked the sound) they should put in their allowance together;

but she already felt the prospect quite weary and worn with the way he went round and round on it. It had become his sole topic, the theme alike of his most solemn prudences and most placid jests, to which every opening led for return and revision and in which every little flower of a foretaste was pulled up as soon as planted. He had announced at the earliest day – characterizing the whole business, from that moment, as their 'plans', under which name he handled it as a syndicate handles a Chinese, or other, Loan – he had promptly declared that the question must be thoroughly studied, and he produced, on the whole subject, from day to day, an amount of information that excited her wonder and even, not a little, as she frankly let him know, her disdain. When she thought of the danger in which another pair of lovers rapturously lived, she inquired of him anew why he could leave nothing to chance. Then she got for answer that this profundity was just his pride, and he pitted Ramsgate against Bournemouth and even Boulogne against Jersey – for he had great ideas – with all the mastery of detail that was some day, professionally, to carry him far.

The longer the time since she had seen Captain Everard, the more she was booked, as she called it, to pass Park Chambers; and this was the sole amusement that, in the lingering August days and the long, sad twilights, it was left her to cultivate. She had long since learned to know it for a feeble one, though its feebleness was perhaps scarce the reason for her saying to herself each evening as her time for departure approached: 'No, no – not tonight.' She never failed of that silent remark, any more than she failed of feeling, in some deeper place than she had even yet fully sounded, that one's remarks were as weak as straws, and that, however one might indulge in them at eight o'clock, one's fate infallibly declared itself in absolute indifference to them at about eight-fifteen. Remarks were remarks, and very well for that; but fate was fate, and this young lady's was to pass Park Chambers every night in the working week. Out of the immensity of her knowledge of the life of the world there bloomed on these occasions a specific remembrance that it was regarded in that region, in August and September, as rather pleasant just to be caught for something or other in passing through town. Somebody was always passing and somebody might catch somebody else. It was in full cognisance of this subtle law that she adhered to the most ridiculous circuit she could have made to get home. One warm, dull, featureless Friday, when an accident had made her start from Cocker's a little later than usual, she became aware that something of which the infinite possibilities had for so long peopled her dreams was at last prodigiously upon her, though the perfection in which the conditions happened to present it was almost rich enough to be but the positive creation of a dream. She saw, straight before her, like a vista painted in a picture, the empty street and the lamps that burned pale in the dusk not yet established. It was into the convenience of this quiet twilight that a gentleman on the door-step of the Chambers gazed with a vagueness that our young lady's little figure violently trembled, in the approach, with the measure of its power to dissipate. Everything indeed grew in a flash terrific and distinct; her old uncertainties fell away from her, and, since she was so familiar with fate, she felt as if the very nail that fixed it were driven in by the hard look with which, for a moment, Captain Everard awaited her.

The vestibule was open behind him and the porter as absent as on the day she had peeped in; he had just come out – was in town, in a tweed suit and a pot hat, but between two journeys – duly bored over his evening and at a loss what to do with it. Then it was that she was glad she had never met him in that way before: she reaped with such ecstasy the benefit of his not being able to think she passed often. She jumped in two seconds to the determination that he should even suppose it to be the first time and the queerest chance: this was while she still wondered if he would identify or notice her. His original attention had not, she instinctively knew, been for the young woman at Cocker's; it had only been for any young woman who might advance with an air of not upholding ugliness. Ah, but then, and just as she had reached the door, came his second observation, a long, light reach with which, visibly and quite amusedly, he recalled and placed her. They were on different sides, but the street, narrow and still, had only made more of a stage for the small momentary drama. It was not over, besides, it was far from over, even on his sending across the way, with the pleasantest laugh she had ever heard, a little lift of his hat and an 'Oh, good evening!' It was still less over on their meeting, the next minute, though rather indirectly and awkwardly, in the middle of the road – a situation to which three or four steps of her own had unmistakably contributed, – and then passing not again to the side on which she had arrived, but back toward the portal of Park Chambers.

'I didn't know you at first. Are you taking a walk?'

'Oh, I don't take walks at night! I'm going home after my work.'

'Oh!'

That was practically what they had meanwhile smiled out, and his exclamation, to which, for a minute, he appeared to have nothing to add, left them face to face and in just such an attitude as, for his part, he might have worn had he been wondering if he could properly ask her to come in. During this interval, in fact, she really felt his question to be just '*How* properly –?' It was simply a question of the degree of properness.

15

SHE never knew afterwards quite what she had done to settle it, and at the time she only knew that they presently moved, with vagueness, but with continuity, away from the picture of the lighted vestibule and the quiet stairs and well up the street together. This also must have been in the absence of a definite permission, of anything vulgarly articulate, for that matter, on the part of either; and it was to be, later on, a thing of remembrance and reflection for her that the limit of what, just here, for a longish minute, passed between them was his taking in her thoroughly successful deprecation, though conveyed without pride or sound or touch, of the idea that she might be, out of the cage, the very shopgirl at large that she hugged the theory she was not. Yes, it was strange, she afterwards thought, that so much could have come and gone and yet not troubled the air either with impertinence or with resentment, with any of the horrid notes of that kind of acquaintance. He had taken no liberty, as she would have called it; and, through not having to betray the sense of one, she herself had, still more charmingly, taken none. Yet on the spot, nevertheless, she could speculate as to what it meant that, if his relation with Lady Bradeen continued to be what her mind had built it up to, he should feel free to proceed in any private direction. This was one of the questions he was to leave her to deal with – the question whether people of his sort still asked girls up to their rooms when they were so awfully in love with other women. Could people of his sort do that without what people of *her* sort would call being 'false to their love'? She had already a vision of how the true answer was that people of her sort didn't, in such cases, matter – didn't count as infidelity, counted only as something else: she might have been curious, since it came to that, to see exactly what.

Strolling together slowly in their summer twilight and their empty corner of Mayfair, they found themselves emerge at last opposite to one of the smaller gates of the Park; upon which, without any particular word about it – they were talking so of other things – they crossed the street and went in and sat down on a bench. She had gathered by this time one magnificent hope about him – the hope that he would say nothing vulgar. She knew what she meant by that; she meant something quite apart from any matter of his being 'false'. Their bench was not far within; it was near the Park Lane paling and the patchy lamplight and the rumbling cabs and 'buses. A strange emotion had come to her, and she felt indeed excitement within excitement; above all a conscious joy in testing him with chances he didn't take. She had an intense desire he should know the type she really was without her doing anything so low as tell him, and he had surely begun to know it from the moment he didn't seize the opportunities into which a common man would promptly have blundered. These were on the mere surface, and *their* relation was behind and below them. She had questioned so little on the way what they were doing, that as soon as they were seated she took straight hold of it. Her hours, her confinement, the many conditions of service in the post-office, had – with a glance at his own personal resources and alternatives – formed, up to this stage, the subject of their talk. 'Well, here we are, and it may be right enough, but this isn't the least, you know, where I was going.'

'You were going home?'

'Yes, and I was already rather late. I was going to my supper.'

'You haven't had it?'

'No, indeed!'

'Then you haven't eaten –?'

He looked, of a sudden, so extravagantly concerned that she laughed out. 'All day? Yes, we do feed once. But that was long ago. So I must presently say good-bye.'

'Oh, deary *me*!' he exclaimed, with an intonation so droll and yet a touch so light and a distress so marked – a confession of helplessness for such a case, in short, so unrelieved – that she felt sure, on the spot, she had made the great difference plain. He looked at her with the kindest eyes and still without saying what she had known he wouldn't. She had known he wouldn't say, 'Then sup with *me*!' but the proof of it made her feel as if she had feasted.

'I'm not a bit hungry,' she went on.

'Ah, you *must* be, awfully!' he made answer, but settling himself on the bench as if, after all, that needn't interfere with his spending his evening. 'I've always quite wanted the chance to thank you for the trouble you so often take for me.'

'Yes, I know,' she replied; uttering the words with a sense of the situation far deeper than any pretence of not fitting his allusion. She immediately saw that he was surprised and even a little puzzled at her frank assent; but, for herself, the trouble she had taken could only, in these fleeting minutes – they would probably never come back – be all there like a little hoard of gold in her lap. Certainly he might look at it, handle it, take up the pieces. Yet if he understood anything he must understand all. 'I consider you've already immensely thanked me.' The horror was back upon her of having seemed to hang about for some reward. 'It's awfully odd that you should have been there just the one time – !'

'The one time you've passed my place?'

'Yes; you can fancy I haven't many minutes to waste. There was a place tonight I had to stop at.'

'I see, I see' – he knew already so much about her work. 'It must be an awful grind – for a lady.'

'It is; but I don't think I groan over it any more than my companions – and you've seen *they're* not ladies!' She mildly jested, but with an intention. 'One gets used to things, and there are employments I should have hated much more.' She had the finest conception of the beauty of not, at least, boring him. To whine, to count up her wrongs, was what a barmaid or a shopgirl would do, and it was quite enough to sit there like one of these.

'If you had had another employment,' he remarked after a moment, 'we might never have become acquainted.'

'It's highly probable – and certainly not in the same way.' Then, still with her heap of gold in her lap and something of the pride of it in her manner of holding her head, she continued not to move – she only smiled at him. The evening had thickened now; the scattered lamps were red; the Park, all before them, was full of obscure and ambiguous life; there were other couples on other benches, whom it was impossible not to see, yet at whom it was impossible to look. 'But I've walked so much out of my way with you only just to show you that – that' – with this she paused; it was not, after all, so easy to express – 'that anything you may have thought is perfectly true.'

'Oh, I've thought a tremendous lot!' her companion laughed: 'Do you mind my smoking?'

'Why should I? You always smoke *there*.'

'At your place? Oh yes, but here it's different.'

'No,' she said, as he lighted a cigarette, 'that's just what it isn't. It's quite the same.'

'Well, then, that's because "there" it's so wonderful!'

'Then you're conscious of how wonderful it is?' she returned.

He jerked his handsome head in literal protest at a doubt. 'Why, that's exactly what I mean by my gratitude for all your trouble. It has been just as if you took a particular interest.' She only looked at him in answer to this, in such sudden, immediate embarrassment, as she was quite aware, that, while she remained silent, he showed he was at a loss to interpret her expression. 'You *have* – haven't you? – taken a particular interest?'

'Oh, a particular interest!' she quavered out, feeling the whole thing – her immediate embarrassment – get terribly the better of her, and wishing, with a sudden scare, all the more to keep her emotion down. She maintained her fixed smile a moment and turned her eyes over the peopled darkness, unconfused now, because there was something much more confusing. This, with a fatal great rush, was simply the fact that they were thus together. They were near, near, and all that she had imagined of that had only become more true, more dreadful and overwhelming. She stared straight away in silence till she felt that she looked like an idiot; then, to say something, to say nothing, she attempted a sound which ended in a flood of tears.

16

HER tears helped her really to dissimulate, for she had instantly, in so public a situation, to recover herself. They had come and gone in half a minute, and she immediately explained them. 'It's only because I'm tired. It's that – it's that!' Then she added a trifle incoherently: 'I shall never see you again.'

'Ah, but why not?' The mere tone in which her companion asked this satisfied her once for all as to the amount of imagination for which she could count on him. It was naturally not large: it had exhausted itself in having arrived at what he had already touched upon – the sense of an intention in her poor zeal at Cocker's. But any deficiency of this kind was no fault in him: *he* wasn't obliged to have an inferior cleverness –

to have second-rate resources and virtues. It had been as if he almost really believed she had simply cried for fatigue, and he had accordingly put in some kind, confused plea – 'You ought really to take something: won't you have something or other *somewhere*?' – to which she had made no response but a head-shake of a sharpness that settled it. 'Why shan't we all the more keep meeting?'

'I mean meeting this way – only this way. At my place there – *that* I've nothing to do with, and I hope of course you'll turn up, with your correspondence, when it suits you. Whether I stay or not, I mean; for I shall probably not stay.'

'You're going somewhere else?' – he put it with positive anxiety.

'Yes; ever so far away – to the other end of London. There are all sorts of reasons I can't tell you; and it's practically settled. It's better for me, much; and I've only kept on at Cocker's for you.'

'For me?'

Making out in the dusk that he fairly blushed, she now measured how far he had been from knowing too much. Too much, she called it at present; and that was easy, since it proved so abundantly enough for her that he should simply be where he was. 'As we shall never talk this way but to-night – never, never again! – here it all is; I'll say it; I don't care what you think; it doesn't matter; I only want to help you. Besides, you're kind – you're kind. I've been thinking, then, of leaving for ever so long. But you've come so often – at times, – and you've had so much to do, and it has been so pleasant and interesting, that I've remained, I've kept putting off any change. More than once, when I had nearly decided, you've turned up again and I've thought, "Oh no!" That's the simple fact!' She had by this time got her confusion down so completely that she could laugh. 'This is what I meant when I said to you just now that I "knew". I've known perfectly that you knew I took trouble for you; and that knowledge has been for me, and I seemed to see it was for you, as if there were something – I don't know what to call it! – between us. I mean something unusual and good – something not a bit horrid or vulgar.'

She had by this time, she could see, produced a great effect upon him; but she would have spoken the truth to herself if she had at the same moment declared that she didn't in the least care: all the more that the effect must be one of extreme perplexity. What, in it all, was visibly clear for him, none the less, was that he was tremendously glad he had met her. She held him, and he was astonished at the force of it; he was intent, immensely considerate. His elbow was on the back of the seat, and his head, with the pot-hat pushed quite back, in a boyish way, so that she really saw almost for the first time his forehead and hair, rested on the hand into which he had crumpled his gloves. 'Yes,' he assented, 'it's not a bit horrid or vulgar.'

She just hung fire a moment; then she brought out the whole truth. 'I'd do anything for you. I'd do anything for you.' Never in her life had she known anything so high and fine as this, just letting him have it and bravely and magnificently leaving it. Didn't the place, the associations and circumstances, perfectly make it sound what it was not? and wasn't that exactly the beauty?

So she bravely and magnificently left it; and little by little she felt him take it up, take it down, as if they had been on a satin sofa in a boudoir. She had never seen a boudoir, but there had been lots of boudoirs in the telegrams. What she had said, at all events, sank into him, so that after a minute he simply made a movement that had the result of placing his hand on her own – presently indeed that of her feeling herself firmly enough grasped. There was no pressure she need return, there was none she need decline; she just sat admirably still, satisfied, for the time, with the surprise and bewilderment of the impression she made on him. His agitation was even greater, on the whole, than she had at first allowed for. 'I say, you know, you mustn't think of leaving!' he at last broke out.

'Of leaving Cocker's, you mean?'

'Yes, you must stay on there, whatever happens, and help a fellow.'

She was silent a little, partly because it was so strange and exquisite to feel him watch her as if it really mattered to him and he were almost in suspense. 'Then you *have* quite recognized what I've tried to do?' she asked.

'Why, wasn't that exactly what I dashed over from my door just now to thank you for?'

'Yes; so you said.'

'And don't you believe it?'

She looked down a moment at his hand, which continued to cover her own; whereupon he presently drew it back, rather restlessly folding his arms. Without answering his question she went on: 'Have you ever spoken of me?'

'Spoken of you?'

'Of my being there – of my knowing, and that sort of thing.'

'Oh, never to a human creature!' he eagerly declared.

She had a small drop at this, which was expressed in another pause; after which she returned to what he had just asked her. 'Oh yes, I quite believe you like it – my always being there and our taking things up so familiarly and successfully: if not exactly where we left them,' she laughed, 'almost always, at least, in an interesting place!' He was about to say something in reply to this, but her friendly gaiety was quicker. 'You want a great many things in life, a great many comforts and helps and luxuries – you want everything as pleasant as possible. Therefore, so far as it's in the power of any particular person to contribute to all that –' She had turned her face to him smiling, just thinking.

'Oh, see here!' But he was highly amused. 'Well, what then?' he inquired, as if to humour her.

'Why, the particular person must never fail. We must manage it for you somehow.'

He threw back his head, laughing out; he was really exhilarated. 'Oh yes, somehow!'

'Well, I think we each do – don't we? – in one little way and another and according to our limited lights. I'm pleased, at any rate, for myself, that you are; for I assure you I've done my best.'

'You do better than any one!' He had struck a match for another cigarette, and the flame lighted an instant his responsive, finished face, magnifying into a pleasant grimace the kindness with which he paid her this tribute. 'You're awfully clever, you know; cleverer, cleverer, cleverer—!' He had appeared on the point of making some tremendous statement; then suddenly, puffing his cigarette and shifting almost with violence on his seat, let it altogether fall.

17

In spite of this drop, if not just by reason of it, she felt as if Lady Bradeen, all but named out, had popped straight up; and she practically betrayed her consciousness by waiting a little before she rejoined: 'Cleverer than who?'

'Well, if I wasn't afraid you'd think I swagger, I should say – than anybody! If you leave your place there, where shall you go?' he more gravely demanded.

'Oh, too far for you ever to find me!'

'I'd find you anywhere.'

The tone of this was so still more serious that she had but her one acknowledgement. 'I'd do anything for you – I'd do anything for you,' she repeated. She had already, she felt, said it all; so what did anything more, anything less, matter? That was the very reason indeed why she could, with a lighter note, ease him generously of any awkwardness produced by solemnity, either his own or hers. 'Of course it must be nice for you to be able to think there are people all about who feel in such a way.'

In immediate appreciation of this, however, he only smoked without looking at her. 'But you don't want to give up your present work?' he at last inquired. 'I mean you *will* stay in the post-office?'

'Oh yes; I think I've a genius for that.'

'Rather! No one can touch you.' With this he turned more to her again. 'But you can get, with a move, greater advantages?'

'I can get, in the suburbs, cheaper lodgings. I live with my mother. We need some space; and there's a particular place that has other inducements.'

He just hesitated. 'Where is it?'

'Oh, quite out of *your* way. You'd never have time.'

'But I tell you I'd go anywhere. Don't you believe it?'

'Yes, for once or twice. But you'd soon see it wouldn't do for you.'

He smoked and considered; seemed to stretch himself a little and, with his legs out, surrender himself comfortably. 'Well, well, well – I believe everything you say. I take it from you – anything you like – in the most extraordinary way.' It struck her certainly – and almost without bitterness – that the way in which she was already, as if she had been an old friend, arranging for him and preparing the only magnificence she could muster, was quite the most extraordinary. 'Don't, *don't* go!' he presently went on. 'I shall miss you too horribly!'

'So that you just put it to me as a definite request?' – oh, how she tried to divest this of all sound of the hardness of bargaining! That ought to have been easy enough, for what was she arranging to get? Before he could answer she had continued: 'To be perfectly fair, I should tell you I recognize at Cocker's certain strong attractions. All you people come. I like all the horrors.'

'The horrors?'

'Those you all – you know the set I mean, *your* set – show me with as good a conscience as if I had no more feeling than a letter-box.'

He looked quite excited at the way she put it. 'Oh, they don't know!'

'Don't know I'm not stupid? No, how should they?'

'Yes, how should they?' said the Captain sympathetically. 'But isn't "horrors" rather strong?'

'What you *do* is rather strong!' the girl promptly returned.

'What *I* do?'

'Your extravagance, your selfishness, your immorality, your crimes,' she pursued, without heeding his expression.

'I *say*!' – her companion showed the queerest stare.

'I like them, as I tell you – I revel in them. But we needn't go into that,' she quietly went on; 'for all I get out of it is the harmless pleasure of knowing. I know, I know, I know!' – she breathed it ever so gently.

'Yes; that's what has been between us,' he answered much more simply.

She could enjoy his simplicity in silence, and for a moment she did so. 'If I do stay because you want it – and I'm rather capable of that – there are two or three things I think you ought to remember. One is, you know, that I'm there sometimes for days and weeks together without your ever coming.'

'Oh, I'll come every day!' he exclaimed.

She was on the point, at this, of imitating with her hand his movement of shortly before; but she checked herself, and there was no want of effect in the tranquillizing way in which she said: 'How can you? How can you?' He had, too manifestly, only to look at it there, in the vulgarly animated gloom, to see that he couldn't; and at this point, by the mere action of his silence, everything they had so definitely not named, the whole presence round which they had been circling became a part of their reference, settled solidly between them. It was as if then, for a minute, they sat and saw it all in each other's eyes, saw so much that there was no need of a transition for sounding it at last. 'Your danger, your danger—!' Her voice indeed trembled with it, and she could only, for the moment, again leave it so.

During this moment he leaned back on the bench, meeting her in silence and with a face that grew more strange. It grew so strange that, after a further instant, she got straight up. She stood there as if their talk were now over, and he just sat and watched her. It was as if now – owing to the third person they had brought in – they must be more careful; so that the most he could finally say was: 'That's where it is!'

'That's where it is!' the girl as guardedly replied. He sat still, and she added: 'I won't abandon you. Good-bye.'

'Good-bye?' – he appealed, but without moving.

'I don't quite see my way, but I won't abandon you,' she repeated. 'There. Good-bye.'

It brought him with a jerk to his feet, tossing away his

of freedom. This relative took her pleasure of a week at Bournemouth in a stuffy back-kitchen and endless talks; to that degree even that Mr Mudge himself – habitually inclined indeed to a scrutiny of all mysteries and to seeing, as he sometimes admitted, too much in things – made remarks on it as he sat on the cliff with his betrothed, or on the decks of steamers that conveyed them, close-packed items in terrific totals of enjoyment, to the Isle of Wight and the Dorset coast.

He had a lodging in another house, where he had speedily learned the importance of keeping his eyes open, and he made no secret of his suspecting that sinister mutual connivances might spring, under the roof of his companions, from unnatural sociabilities. At the same time he fully recognized that, as a source of anxiety, not to say of expense, his future mother-in-law would have weighted them more in accompanying their steps than in giving her hostess, in the interest of the tendency they considered that they never mentioned, equivalent pledges as to the tea-caddy and the jam-pot. These were the questions – these indeed the familiar commodities – that he had now to put into the scales; and his betrothed had, in consequence, during her holiday, the odd, and yet pleasant and almost languid, sense of an anticlimax. She had become conscious of an extraordinary collapse, a surrender to stillness and to retrospect. She cared neither to walk nor to sail; it was enough for her to sit on benches and wonder at the sea and taste the air and not be at Cocker's and not see the counter-clerk. She still seemed to wait for something – something in the key of the immense discussions that had mapped out their little week of idleness on the scale of a world-atlas. Something came at last, but without perhaps appearing quite adequately to crown the monument.

Preparation and precaution were, however, the natural flowers of Mr Mudge's mind, and in proportion as these things declined in one quarter they inevitably bloomed elsewhere. He could always, at the worst, have on Tuesday the project of their taking the Swanage boat on Thursday, and on Thursday that of their ordering minced kidneys on Saturday. He had, moreover, a constant gift of inexorable inquiry as to where and what they should have gone and have done if they had not been exactly as they were. He had in short his resources, and his mistress had never been so conscious of them; on the other hand they had never interfered so little with her own. She liked to be as she was – if it could only have lasted. She could accept even without bitterness a rigour of economy so great that the little fee they paid for admission to the pier had to be balanced against other delights. The people at Ladle's and at Thrupp's had *their* ways of amusing themselves, whereas she had to sit and hear Mr Mudge talk of what he might do if he didn't take a bath, or of the bath he might take if he only hadn't taken something else. He was always with her now, of course, always beside her; she saw him more than 'hourly', more than ever yet, more even than he had planned she should do at Chalk Farm. She preferred to sit at the far end, away from the band and the crowd; as to which she had frequent differences with her friend, who reminded her often that they could have only in the thick of it the sense of the money they were getting back. That had little effect on her, for she got back her money by seeing many things, the things of the past year, fall together and connect themselves, undergo the happy relegation that transforms melancholy and misery, passion and effort, into experience and knowledge.

She liked having done with them, as she assured herself she had practically done, and the strange thing was that she neither missed the procession now nor wished to keep her place for it. It had become there, in the sun and the breeze and the sea-smell, a far-away story, a picture of another life. If Mr Mudge himself liked processions, liked them at Bournemouth and on the pier quite as much as at Chalk Farm or anywhere, she learned after a little not to be worried by his perpetual counting of the figures that made them up. There were dreadful women in particular, usually fat and in men's caps and white shoes, whom he could never let alone – not that *she* cared; it was not the great world, the world of Cocker's and Ladle's and Thrupp's, but it offered an endless field to his faculties of memory, philosophy, and frolic. She had never accepted him so much, never arranged so successfully for making him chatter while she carried on secret conversations. Her talks were with herself; and if they both practised a great thrift, she had quite mastered that of merely spending words enough to keep him imperturbably and continuously going.

He was charmed with the panorama, not knowing – or at any rate not at all showing that he knew – what far other images peopled her mind than the women in the navy caps and the shopboys in the blazers. His observations on these types, his general interpretation of the show, brought home to her the prospect of Chalk Farm. She wondered sometimes that he should have derived so little illumination, during his period, from the society at Cocker's. But one evening, as their holiday cloudlessly waned, he gave her such a proof of his quality as might have made her ashamed of her small reserves. He brought out something that, in all his overflow, he had been able to keep back till other matters were disposed of. It was the announcement that he was at last ready to marry – that he saw his way. A rise at Chalk Farm had been offered him; he was to be taken into the business, bringing with him a capital the estimation of which by other parties constituted the handsomest recognition yet made of the head on his shoulders. Therefore their waiting was over – it could be a question of a near date. They would settle this date before going back, and he meanwhile had his eye on a sweet little home. He would take her to see it on their first Sunday.

19

HIS having kept this great news for the last, having had such a card up his sleeve and not floated it out in the current of his chatter and the luxury of their leisure, was one of those incalculable strokes by which he could still affect her; the kind of thing that reminded her of the latent force that had ejected the drunken soldier – an example of the profundity of which his promotion was the proof. She listened a while in silence, on this occasion, to the wafted strains of the music; she took it in as she had not quite done before that her future was now constituted. Mr Mudge was distinctly her fate; yet at this moment she turned her face quite away from him, showing him so long a mere quarter of her cheek that she at last again heard his voice. He couldn't see a pair of tears that were partly the reason of her delay to give him the assurance he required; but he expressed at a venture the hope that she had had her fill of Cocker's.

She was finally able to turn back. 'Oh, quite. There's nothing going on. No one comes but the Americans at Thrupp's, and *they* don't do much. They don't seem to have a secret in the world.'

'Then the extraordinary reason you've been giving me for holding on there has ceased to work?'

She thought a moment. 'Yes, that one. I've seen the thing through – I've got them all in my pocket.'

'So you're ready to come?'

For a little, again, she made no answer. 'No, not yet, all the same. I've still got a reason – a different one.'

He looked her all over as if it might have been something she kept in her mouth or her glove or under her jacket – something she was even sitting upon. 'Well, I'll have it, please.'

'I went out the other night and sat in the Park with a gentleman,' she said at last.

Nothing was ever seen like his confidence in her; and she wondered a little now why it didn't irritate her. It only gave her ease and space, as she felt, for telling him the whole truth that no one knew. It had arrived at present at her really wanting to do that, and yet to do it not in the least for Mr Mudge, but altogether and only for herself. This truth filled out for her there the whole experience she was about to relinquish, suffused and coloured it as a picture that she should keep and that, describe it as she might, no one but herself would ever really see. Moreover she had no desire whatever to make Mr Mudge jealous; there would be no amusement in it, for the amusement she had lately known had spoiled her for lower pleasures. There were even no materials for it. The odd thing was that she never doubted that, properly handled, his passion was poisonable; what had happened was that he had cannily selected a partner with no poison to distil. She read then and there that she should never interest herself in anybody as to whom some other sentiment, some superior view, wouldn't be sure to interfere, for him, with jealousy. 'And what did you get out of that?' he asked with a concern that was not in the least for his honour.

'Nothing but a good chance to promise him I wouldn't forsake him. He's one of my customers.'

'Then it's for him not to forsake *you*.'

'Well, he won't. It's all right. But I must just keep on as long as he may want me.'

'Want you to sit with him in the Park?'

'He may want me for that – but I shan't. I rather liked it, but once, under the circumstances, is enough. I can do better for him in another manner.'

'And what manner, pray?'

'Well, elsewhere.'

'Elsewhere? – I *say*!'

This was an ejaculation used also by Captain Everard, but, oh, with what a different sound! 'You needn't "say" – there's nothing to be said. And yet you ought perhaps to know.'

'Certainly I ought. But *what* – up to now?'

'Why, exactly what I told him. That I would do anything for him.'

'What do you mean by "anything"?'

'Everything.'

Mr Mudge's immediate comment on this statement was to draw from his pocket a crumpled paper containing the remains of half a pound of 'sundries'. These sundries had figured conspicuously in his prospective sketch of their tour, but it was only at the end of three days that they had defined themselves unmistakably as chocolate-creams. 'Have another? – *that* one,' he said. She had another, but not the one he indicated, and then he continued: 'What took place afterwards?'

'Afterwards?'

'What did you do when you had told him you would do everything?'

'I simply came away.'

'Out of the Park?'

'Yes, leaving him there. I didn't let him follow me.'

'Then what did you let him do?'

'I didn't let him do anything.'

Mr Mudge considered an instant. 'Then what did you go there for?' His tone was even slightly critical.

'I didn't quite know at the time. It was simply to be with him, I suppose – just once. He's in danger, and I wanted him to know I know it. It makes meeting him – at Cocker's, for it's that I want to stay on for – more interesting.'

'It makes it mighty interesting for *me*!' Mr Mudge freely declared. 'Yet he didn't follow you?' he asked. '*I* would!'

'Yes, of course. That was the way you began, you know. You're awfully inferior to him.'

'Well, my dear, you're not inferior to anybody. You've got a cheek! What is he in danger of?'

'Of being found out. He's in love with a lady – and it isn't right – and *I've* found him out.'

'That'll be a look-out for *me*!' Mr Mudge joked. 'You mean she has a husband?'

'Never mind what she has! They're in awful danger, but his is the worst, because he's in danger from her too.'

'Like me from you – the woman *I* love? If he's in the same funk as me—'

'He's in a worse one. He's not only afraid of the lady – he's afraid of other things.'

Mr Mudge selected another chocolate-cream. 'Well, I'm only afraid of one! But how in the world can you help this party?'

'I don't know – perhaps not at all. But so long as there's a chance—'

'You won't come away?'

'No, you've got to wait for me.'

Mr Mudge enjoyed what was in his mouth. 'And what will he give you?'

'Give me?'

'If you do help him.'

'Nothing. Nothing in all the wide world.'

'Then what will he give *me*?' Mr Mudge inquired. 'I mean for waiting.'

The girl thought a moment; then she got up to walk. 'He never heard of you,' she replied.

'You haven't mentioned me?'

'We never mention anything. What I've told you is just what I've found out.'

Mr Mudge, who had remained on the bench, looked up at her; she often preferred to be quiet when he proposed to walk, but now that he seemed to wish to sit she had a desire to move. 'But you haven't told me what *he* has found out.'

She considered her lover. 'He'd never find *you*, my dear!'

Her lover, still on his seat, appealed to her in something of the attitude in which she had last left Captain Everard, but the impression was not the same. 'Then where do I come in?'

'You don't come in at all. That's just the beauty of it!' – and with this she turned to mingle with the multitude collected round the band. Mr Mudge presently overtook her and drew her arm into his own with a quiet force that expressed the serenity of possession; in consonance with which it was only when they parted for the night at her door that he referred again to what she had told him.

'Have you seen him since?'

'Since the night in the Park? No, not once.'

'Oh, what a cad!' said Mr Mudge.

20

It was not till the end of October that she saw Captain Everard again, and on that occasion – the only one of all the series on which hindrance had been so utter – no communication with him proved possible. She had made out, even from the cage, that it was a charming golden day: a patch of hazy autumn sunlight lay across the sanded floor and also, higher up, quickened into brightness a row of ruddy bottled syrups. Work was slack and the place in general empty; the town, as they said in the cage, had not waked up, and the feeling of the day likened itself to something that in happier conditions she would have thought of romantically as St Martin's summer. The counter-clerk had gone to his dinner; she herself was busy with arrears of postal jobs, in the midst of which she became aware that Captain Everard had apparently been in the shop a minute and that Mr Buckton had already seized him.

He had, as usual, half a dozen telegrams; and when he saw that she saw him and their eyes met, he gave, on bowing to her, an exaggerated laugh in which she read a new consciousness. It was a confession of awkwardness; it seemed to tell her that of course he knew he ought better to have kept his head, ought to have been clever enough to wait, on some pretext, till he should have found her free. Mr Buckton was a long time with him, and her attention was soon demanded by other visitors; so that nothing passed between them but the fulness of their silence. The look she took from him was his greeting, and the other one a simple sign of the eyes sent her before going out. The only token they exchanged, therefore, was his tacit assent to her wish that, since they couldn't attempt a certain frankness, they should attempt nothing at all. This was her intense preference; she could be as still and cold as any one when that was the sole solution.

Yet, more than any contact hitherto achieved, these counted instants struck her as marking a step: they were built so – just in the mere flash – on the recognition of his now definitely knowing what it was she would do for him. The 'anything, anything' she had uttered in the Park went to and fro between them and under the poked-out chins that interposed. It had all at last even put on the air of their not needing now clumsily to manoeuvre to converse: their former little postal make-believes, the intense implications of questions and answers and change, had become in the light of the personal fact, of their having had their moment, a possibility comparatively poor. It was as if they had met for all time – it exerted on their being in presence again an influence so prodigious. When she watched herself, in the memory of that night, walk away from him as if she were making an end, she found something too pitiful in the primness of such a gait. Hadn't she precisely established on the part of each a consciousness that could end only with death?

It must be admitted that, in spite of this brave margin, an irritation, after he had gone, remained with her; a sense that presently became one with a still sharper hatred of Mr Buckton, who, on her friend's withdrawal, had retired with the telegrams to the sounder and left her the other work. She knew indeed she should have a chance to see them, when she would, on file; and she was divided, as the day went on, between the two impressions of all that was lost and all that was re-asserted. What beset her above all, and as she had almost never known it before, was the desire to bound straight out, to overtake the autumn afternoon before it passed away for ever and hurry off to the Park and perhaps be with him there again on a bench. It became, for an hour, a fantastic vision with her that he might just have gone to sit and wait for her. She could almost hear him, through the tick of the sounder, scatter with his stick, in his impatience, the fallen leaves of October. Why should such a vision seize her at this particular moment with such a shake? There was a time – from four to five – when she could have cried with happiness and rage.

Business quickened, it seemed, towards five, as if the town did wake up; she had therefore more to do, and she went through it with little sharp stampings and jerkings: she made the crisp postal-orders fairly snap while she breathed to herself: 'It's the last day – the last day!' The last day of what? She couldn't have told. All she knew now was that if she *were* out of the cage she wouldn't in the least have minded, this time, its not yet being dark. She would have gone straight towards Park Chambers and have hung about there till no matter when. She would have waited, stayed, rung, asked, have gone in, sat on the stairs. What the day was the last of was probably, to her strained inner sense, the group of golden ones, of any occasion for seeing the hazy sunshine slant at that angle into the smelly shop, of any range of chances for his wishing still to repeat to her the two words that, in the Park, she had scarcely let him bring out. 'See here – see here!' – the sound of these two words had been with her perpetually; but it was in her ears today without mercy, with a loudness that grew and grew. What was it they then expressed? what was it he had wanted her to see? She seemed, whatever it was, perfectly to see it now – to see that if she should just chuck the whole thing, should have a great and beautiful courage, he would somehow make everything up to her. When the clock struck five she was on the very point of saying to Mr Buckton that she was deadly ill and rapidly getting worse. This announcement was on her lips, and she had quite composed the pale, hard face she would offer him: 'I can't stop – I must go home. If I feel better, later on, I'll come back. I'm very sorry, but I *must* go.' At that instant Captain Everard once more stood there, producing in her agitated spirit, by his real presence, the strangest, quickest revolution. He stopped her off without knowing it, and by the time he had been a minute in the shop she felt that she was saved.

That was from the first minute what she called it to herself. There were again other persons with whom she was occupied, and again the situation could only be expressed by their silence. It was expressed, in fact, in a larger phrase than ever yet, for her eyes now spoke to him with a kind of supplication. 'Be quiet, be quiet!' they pleaded; and they saw his own reply: 'I'll do whatever you say; I won't even look at you – see, see!' They kept conveying thus, with the friendliest liberality, that they wouldn't look, quite positively wouldn't. What she was to see was that he hovered at the other end of the counter, Mr Buckton's end, surrendered himself again to that frustration. It quickly proved so great indeed that what she was to see further was how he turned away before he was attended to, and hung off, waiting, smoking, looking about the shop; how he went over to Mr Cocker's own counter and appeared to price things, gave in fact presently two or three orders and put down money, stood there a long time with his back to her, considerately abstaining from any glance round to see if she were free. It at last came to pass in this way that he had remained in the shop longer than she had ever yet known him to do, and that, nevertheless, when he did turn about she could see him time himself – she was freshly taken up – and cross straight to her postal subordinate, whom some one else had released. He had in his hand all this while neither letters nor telegrams, and now that he was close to her – for she was close to the counter-clerk – it brought her heart into her mouth merely to see him look at her neighbour and open his lips. She was too nervous to bear it. He asked for a Post-Office Guide, and the young man whipped out a new one; whereupon he said that he wished not to purchase, but only to consult one a moment; with which, the copy kept on loan being produced, he once more wandered off.

What was he doing to her? What did he want of her? Well, it was just the aggravation of his 'See here!' She felt at this moment strangely and portentously afraid of him – had in her ears the hum of a sense that, should it come to that kind of tension, she must fly on the spot to Chalk Farm. Mixed with her dread and with her reflection was the idea that, if he wanted her so much as he seemed to show, it might be after all simply to do for him the 'anything' she had promised, the 'everything' she had thought it so fine to bring out to Mr Mudge. He might want her to help him, might have some particular appeal; though, of a truth, his manner didn't denote that – denoted, on the contrary, an embarrassment, an indecision, something of a desire not so much to be helped as to be treated rather more nicely than she had treated him the other time. Yes, he considered quite probably that he had help rather to offer than to ask for. Still, none the less, when he again saw her free he continued to keep away from her; when he came back with his *Guide* it was Mr Buckton he caught – it was from Mr Buckton he obtained half-a-crown's-worth of stamps.

After asking for the stamps he asked, quite as a second thought, for a postal-order for ten shillings. What did he want with so many stamps when he wrote so few letters? How could he enclose a postal-order in a telegram? She expected him, the next thing, to go into the corner and make up one of his telegrams – half a dozen of them – on purpose to prolong his presence. She had so completely stopped looking at him that she could only guess his movements – guess even where his eyes rested. Finally she saw him make a dash that might have been towards the nook where the forms were hung; and at this she suddenly felt that she couldn't keep it up. The counter-clerk had just taken a telegram from a slavey, and, to give herself something to cover her, she snatched it out of his hand. The gesture was so violent that he gave her an odd look, and she also perceived that Mr Buckton noticed it. The latter personage, with a quick stare at her, appeared for an instant to wonder whether his snatching it in *his* turn mightn't be the thing she would least like, and she anticipated this practical criticism by the frankest glare she had ever given him. It sufficed: this time it paralysed him; and she sought with her trophy the refuge of the sounder.

21

IT was repeated the next day; it went on for three days; and at the end of that time she knew what to think. When, at the beginning, she had emerged from her temporary shelter Captain Everard had quitted the shop and he had not come again that evening, as it had struck her he possibly might – might all the more easily that there were numberless persons who came, morning and afternoon, numberless times, so that he wouldn't necessarily have attracted attention. The second day it was different and yet on the whole worse. His access to her had become possible – she felt herself even reaping the fruit of her yesterday's glare at Mr Buckton; but transacting his business with him didn't simplify – it could, in spite of the rigour of circumstance, feed so her new conviction. The rigour was tremendous, and his telegrams – not, now, mere pretexts for getting at her – were apparently genuine; yet the conviction had taken but a night to develop. It could be simply enough expressed; she had had the glimmer of it the day before in her idea that he needed no more help than she had already given; that it was help he himself was prepared to render. He had come up to town but for three or four days; he had been absolutely obliged to be absent after the other time; yet he would, now that he was face to face with her, stay on as much longer as she liked. Little by little it was thus clarified, though from the first flash of his reappearance she had read into it the real essence.

That was what the night before, at eight o'clock, her hour to go, had made her hang back and dawdle. She did last things or pretended to do them; to be in the cage had suddenly become her safety, and she was literally afraid of the alternate self who might be waiting outside. *He* might be waiting; it was he who was her alternate self, and of him she was afraid. The most extraordinary change had taken place in her from the moment of her catching the impression he seemed to have returned on purpose to give her. Just before she had done so, on that bewitched afternoon, she had seen herself approach, without a scruple, the porter at Park Chambers; then, as the effect of the rush of a consciousness quite altered, she had, on at last quitting Cocker's, gone straight home for the first time since her return from Bournemouth. She had passed his door every night for weeks, but nothing would have induced her to pass it now. This change was the tribute of her fear – the result of a change in himself as to which she needed no more explanation than his mere face vividly gave her; strange though it was to find an element of deterrence in the object that she regarded as the most beautiful in the world. He had taken it from her in the Park that night that she wanted him not to propose to her to sup; but he had put away the lesson by this time – he practically proposed supper every time he looked at her. This was what, for that matter, mainly filled the three days. He came in twice on each of these, and it was as if he came in to give her a chance to relent. That was, after all, she said to herself in the intervals, the most that he did. There were ways, she fully recognized, in which he spared her, and other particular ways as to which she meant that her silence should be full, to him, of exquisite pleading. The most particular of all was his not being outside, at the corner, when she quitted the place for the night. This he might so easily have been – so easily if he hadn't been so nice. She continued to recognize in his forbearance the fruit of her dumb supplication, and the only compensation he found for it was the harmless freedom of being able to appear to say: 'Yes, I'm in town only for three or four days, but, you know, I *would* stay on.' He struck her as calling attention each day, each hour, to the rapid ebb of time; he exaggerated to the point of putting it that there were only two days more, that there was at last, dreadfully, only one.

There were other things still that he struck her as doing with a special intention; as to the most marked of which – unless indeed it were the most obscure – she might well have marvelled that it didn't seem to her more horrid. It was either the frenzy of her imagination or the disorder of his baffled passion that gave her once or twice the vision of his putting down redundant money – sovereigns not concerned with the little payments he was perpetually making – so that she might give him some sign of helping him to slip them over to her. What was most extraordinary in this impression was the amount of excuse that, with some incoherence, she found for him. He wanted to pay her because there was nothing to pay her for. He wanted to offer her things that he knew she wouldn't take. He wanted to show her how much he respected her by giving her the supreme chance to show *him* she was respectable. Over the driest transactions, at any rate, their eyes had out these questions. On the third day he put in a telegram that had evidently something of the same point as the stray sovereigns – a message that was, in the first place, concocted, and that, on a second thought, he took back from her before she had stamped it. He had given her time to read it, and had only then bethought himself that he had better not send it. If it was not to Lady Bradeen at Twindle – where she knew her ladyship then to be – this was because an address to Doctor Buzzard at Brickwood was just as good, with the added merit of its not giving away quite so much a person whom he had still, after all, in a manner to consider. It was of course most complicated, only half lighted; but there was, discernibly enough, a scheme of communication in which Lady Bradeen at Twindle and Dr Buzzard at Brickwood were, within limits, one and the same person. The words he had shown her and then taken back consisted, at all events, of the brief but vivid phrase: 'Absolutely impossible.' The point was not that she should transmit it; the point was just that she should see it. What was absolutely impossible was that before he had settled something at Cocker's he should go either to Twindle or to Brickwood.

The logic of this, in turn, for herself, was that she could lend herself to no settlement so long as she so intensely knew. What she knew was that he was, almost under peril of life, clenched in a situation: therefore how could she also know where a poor girl in the P.O. might really stand? It was more and more between them that if he might convey to her that he was free, that everything she had seen so deep into was a closed chapter, her own case might become different for her, she might understand and meet him and listen. But he could convey nothing of the sort, and he only fidgeted and floundered in his want of power. The chapter wasn't in the least closed, not for the other party; and the other party had a pull, somehow and somewhere: this his whole attitude and expression confessed, at the same time that they entreated her not to remember and not to mind. So long as she did remember and did mind he could only circle about and go and come, doing futile things of which he was ashamed. He was ashamed of his two words to Dr Buzzard, and went out of the shop as soon as he had crumpled up the paper again and thrust it into his pocket. It had been an abject little exposure of dreadful, impossible passion. He appeared in fact to be too ashamed to come back. He had left town again, and a first week elapsed, and a second. He had had naturally to return to the real mistress of his fate; she had insisted – she knew how, and he couldn't put in another hour. There was always a day when she called time. It was known to our young friend moreover that he had now been despatching telegrams from other offices. She knew at last so much, that she had quite lost her earlier sense of merely guessing. There were no shades of distinctness – it all bounced out.

22

EIGHTEEN days elapsed, and she had begun to think it probable she should never see him again. He too then understood now: he had made out that she had secrets and reasons and impediments, that even a poor girl at the P.O. might have her complications. With the charm she had cast on him lightened by distance he had suffered a final delicacy to speak to him, had made up his mind that it would be only decent to let her alone. Never so much as during these latter days had she felt the precariousness of their relation – the happy, beautiful, untroubled original one, if it could only have been restored, – in which the public servant and the casual public only were concerned. It hung at the best by the merest silken thread, which was at the mercy of any accident and might snap at any minute. She arrived by the end of the fortnight at the highest sense of actual fitness, never doubting that her decision was now complete. She would just give him a few days more to come back to her on a proper impersonal basis – for even to an embarrassing representative of the casual public a public servant with a conscience did owe something, – and then would signify to Mr Mudge that she was ready for the little home. It had been visited, in the further talk she had had with him at Bournemouth, from garret to cellar, and they had especially lingered, with their respectively darkened brows, before the niche into which it was to be broached to her mother that she was to find means to fit.

He had put it to her more definitely than before that his calculations had allowed for that dingy presence, and he had thereby marked the greatest impression he had ever made on her. It was a stroke superior even again to his handling of the drunken soldier. What she considered that, in the face of it, she hung on at Cocker's for, was something that she could only have described as the common fairness of a last word. Her actual last word had been, till it should be superseded, that she wouldn't abandon her other friend, and it stuck to her, through thick and thin, that she was still at her post and on her honour. This other friend had shown so much beauty of conduct already that he would surely, after all, just re-appear long enough to relieve her, to give her something she could take away. She saw it, caught it, at times, his parting present; and there were moments when she felt herself sitting like a beggar with a hand held out to an almsgiver who only fumbled. She hadn't taken the sovereigns, but she *would* take the penny. She heard, in imagination, on the counter, the ring of the copper. 'Don't put yourself out any longer,' he would say, 'for so bad a case. You've done all there is to be done. I thank and acquit and release you. Our lives take us. I don't know much – though I have really been interested – about yours; but I suppose you've got one. Mine, at any rate, will take *me* – and where it will. Heigh-ho! Good-bye.' And then once more, for the sweetest, faintest flower of all: 'Only, I say – see here!' She had framed the whole picture with a squareness that included also the image of how again she would decline to 'see there', decline, as she might say, to see anywhere or anything. Yet it befell that just in the fury of this escape she saw more than ever.

He came back one night with a rush, near the moment of their closing, and showed her a face so different and new, so upset and anxious, that almost anything seemed to look out of it but clear recognition. He poked in a telegram very much as if the simple sense of pressure, the distress of extreme haste, had blurred the remembrance of where in particular he was. But as she met his eyes a light came; it broke indeed on the spot into a positive, conscious glare. That made up for everything, for it was an instant proclamation of the celebrated 'danger'; it seemed to pour out in a flood. 'Oh yes, here it is – it's upon me at last! Forget, for God's sake, my having worried or bored you, and just help me, just *save* me, by getting this off without the loss of a second!' Something grave had clearly occurred, a crisis declared itself. She recognized immediately the person to whom the telegram was addressed – the Miss Dolman, of Parade Lodge, to whom Lady Bradeen had wired, at Dover, on the last occasion, and whom she had then, with her recollection of previous arrangements, fitted into a particular setting. Miss Dolman had figured before and not figured since, but she was now the subject of an imperative appeal. 'Absolutely necessary to see you. Take last train Victoria if you can catch it. If not, earliest morning, and answer me direct either way.'

'Reply paid?' said the girl. Mr Buckton had just departed, and the counter-clerk was at the sounder. There was no other representative of the public, and she had never yet, as it seemed to her, not even in the street or in the Park, been so alone with him.

'Oh yes, reply paid, and as sharp as possible, please.'

She affixed the stamps in a flash. 'She'll catch the train!' she then declared to him breathlessly, as if she could absolutely guarantee it.

'I don't know – I hope so. It's awfully important. So kind of you. Awfully sharp, please.' It was wonderfully innocent now, his oblivion of all but his danger. Anything else that had ever passed between them was utterly out of it. Well, she had wanted him to be impersonal!

There was less of the same need therefore, happily, for herself; yet she only took time, before she flew to the sounder, to gasp at him: 'You're in trouble?'

'Horrid, horrid – there's a row!' But they parted, on it, in the next breath; and as she dashed at the sounder, almost pushing, in her violence, the counter-clerk off the stool, she caught the bang with which, at Cocker's door, in his further precipitation, he closed the apron of the cab into which he had leaped. As he rushed off to some other precaution suggested by his alarm, his appeal to Miss Dolman flashed straight away.

But she had not, on the morrow, been in the place five minutes before he was with her again, still more discomposed and quite, now, as she said to herself, like a frightened child coming to its mother. Her companions were there, and she felt it to be remarkable how, in the presence of his agitation, his mere scared, exposed nature, she suddenly ceased to mind. It came to her as it had never come to her before that with absolute directness and assurance they might carry almost anything off. He had nothing to send – she was sure he had been wiring all over, – and yet his business was evidently huge. There was nothing but that in his eyes – not a glimmer of reference or memory. He was almost haggard with anxiety, and had clearly not slept a wink. Her pity for him would have given her any courage, and she seemed to know at last why she had been such a fool. 'She didn't come?' she panted.

'Oh yes, she came; but there has been some mistake. We want a telegram.'

'A telegram?'

'One that was sent from here ever so long ago. There was something in it that has to be recovered. Something very, *very* important, please – we want it immediately.'

He really spoke to her as if she had been some strange young woman at Knightsbridge or Paddington; but it had no other effect on her than to give her the measure of his tremendous flurry. Then it was that, above all, she felt how much she had missed in the gaps and blanks and absent answers – how much she had had to dispense with: it was black darkness now, save for this little wild red flare. So much as that she saw and possessed. One of the lovers was quaking somewhere out of town, and the other was quaking just where he stood. This was vivid enough, and after an instant she knew it was all she wanted. She wanted no detail, no fact – she wanted no nearer vision of discovery or shame. 'When was your telegram? Do you mean you sent it from here?' She tried to do the young woman at Knightsbridge.

'Oh yes, from here – several weeks ago. Five, six, seven' – he was confused and impatient, – 'don't you remember?'

'Remember?' she could scarcely keep out of her face, at the word, the strangest of smiles.

But the way he didn't catch what it meant was perhaps even stranger still. 'I mean, don't you keep the old ones?'

'For a certain time.'

'But how long?'

She thought; she *must* do the young woman, and she knew exactly what the young woman would say and, still more, wouldn't. 'Can you give me the date?'

'Oh God, no! It was some time or other in August – toward

the end. It was to the same address as the one I gave you last night.'

'Oh!' said the girl, knowing at this the deepest thrill she had ever felt. It came to her there, with her eyes on his face, that she held the whole thing in her hand, held it as she held her pencil, which might have broken at that instant in her tightened grip. This made her feel like the very fountain of fate, but the emotion was such a flood that she had to press it back with all her force. That was positively the reason, again, of her flute-like Paddington tone. 'You can't give us anything a little nearer?' Her 'little' and her 'us' came straight from Paddington. These things were no false note for him – his difficulty absorbed them all. The eyes with which he pressed her, and in the depths of which she read terror and rage and literal tears, were just the same he would have shown any other prim person.

'I don't know the date. I only know the thing went from here, and just about the time I speak of. It wasn't delivered, you see. We've got to recover it.'

23

SHE was as struck with the beauty of his plural pronoun as she had judged he might be with that of her own; but she knew now so well what she was about that she could almost play with him and with her new-born joy. 'You say "about the time you speak of". But I don't think you speak of an exact time – *do* you?'

He looked splendidly helpless. 'That's just what I want to find out. Don't you keep the old ones? – can't you look it up?'

Our young lady – still at Paddington – turned the question over. 'It wasn't delivered?'

'Yes, it *was*; yet, at the same time, don't you know? it wasn't.' He just hung back, but he brought it out. 'I mean it was intercepted, don't you know? and there was something in it.' He paused again and, as if to further his quest and woo and supplicate success and recovery, even smiled with an effort at the agreeable that was almost ghastly and that turned the knife in her tenderness. What must be the pain of it all, of the open gulf and the throbbing fever, when this was the mere hot breath? 'We want to get what was in it – to know what it was.'

'I see – I see.' She managed just the accent they had at Paddington when they stared like dead fish. 'And you have no clue?'

'Not at all – I've the clue I've just given you.'

'Oh, the last of August?' If she kept it up long enough she would make him really angry.

'Yes, and the address, as I've said.'

'Oh, the same as last night?'

He visibly quivered, as if with a gleam of hope; but it only poured oil on her quietude, and she was still deliberate. She ranged some papers. 'Won't you look?' he went on.

'I remember your coming,' she replied.

He blinked with a new uneasiness; it might have begun to come to him, through her difference, that he was somehow different himself. 'You were much quicker then, you know!'

'So were you – you must do me that justice,' she answered with a smile. 'But let me see. Wasn't it Dover?'

'Yes, Miss Dolman –'

'Parade Lodge, Parade Terrace?'

'Exactly – thank you so awfully much!' He began to hope again. 'Then you *have* it – the other one?'

She hesitated afresh; she quite dangled him. 'It was brought by a lady?'

'Yes; and she put in by mistake something wrong. That's what we've got to get hold of!'

Heavens! what was he going to say? – flooding poor Paddington with wild betrayals! She couldn't too much, for her joy, dangle him, yet she couldn't either, for his dignity, warm or control or check him. What she found herself doing was just to treat herself to the middle way. 'It was intercepted?'

'It fell into the wrong hands. But there's something in it,' he continued to blurt out, 'that *may* be all right. That is, if it's wrong, don't you know? It's all right if it's wrong,' he remarkably explained.

What *was* he, on earth, going to say? Mr Buckton and the counter-clerk were already interested; no one *would* have the decency to come in; and she was divided between her particular terror for him and her general curiosity. Yet she already saw with what brilliancy she could add, to carry the thing off, a little false knowledge to all her real. 'I quite understand,' she said with benevolent, with almost patronizing quickness. 'The lady has forgotten what she did put.'

'Forgotten most wretchedly, and it's an immense inconvenience. It has only just been found that it didn't get there; so that if we could immediately have it –'

'Immediately?'

'Every minute counts. You *have*,' he pleaded, 'surely got them on file.'

'So that you can see it on the spot?'

'Yes, please – this very minute.' The counter rang with his knuckles, with the knob of his stick, with his panic of alarm. 'Do, *do* hunt it up!' he repeated.

'I dare say we could get it for you,' the girl sweetly returned.

'Get it?' – he looked aghast. 'When?'

'Probably by tomorrow.'

'Then it isn't here?' – his face was pitiful.

She caught only the uncovered gleams that peeped out of the blackness, and she wondered what complication, even among the most supposable, the very worst, could be bad enough to account for the degree of his terror. There were twists and turns, there were places where the screw drew blood, that she couldn't guess. She was more and more glad she didn't want to. 'It has been sent on.'

'But how do you know if you don't look?'

She gave him a smile that was meant to be, in the absolute irony of its propriety, quite divine. 'It was August 23rd, and we have nothing later here than August 27th.'

Something leaped into his face. '27th – 23rd? Then you're sure? You know?'

She felt she scarce knew what – as if she might soon be

pounced upon for some lurid connection with a scandal. It was the queerest of all sensations, for she had heard, she had read, of these things, and the wealth of her intimacy with them at Cocker's might be supposed to have schooled and seasoned her. This particular one that she had really quite lived with was, after all, an old story; yet what it had been before was dim and distant beside the touch under which she now winced. Scandal? – it had never been but a silly word. Now it was a great palpable surface, and the surface was, somehow, Captain Everard's wonderful face. Deep down in his eyes was a picture, the vision of a great place like a chamber of justice, where, before a watching crowd, a poor girl, exposed but heroic, swore with a quavering voice to a document, proved an *alibi*, supplied a link. In this picture she bravely took her place. 'It was the 23rd.'

'Then can't you get it this morning – or some time today?'

She considered, still holding him with her look, which she then turned on her two companions, who were by this time unreservedly enlisted. She didn't care – not a scrap, and she glanced about for a piece of paper. With this she had to recognize the rigour of official thrift – a morsel of blackened blotter was the only loose paper to be seen. 'Have you got a card?' she said to her visitor. He was quite away from Paddington now, and the next instant, with a pocket-book in his hand, he had whipped a card out. She gave no glance at the name on it – only turned it to the other side. She continued to hold him, she felt at present, as she had never held him; and her command of her colleagues was, for the moment, not less marked. She wrote something on the back of the card and pushed it across to him.

He fairly glared at it. 'Seven, nine, four –'

'Nine, six, one' – she obligingly completed the number. 'Is it right?' she smiled.

He took the whole thing in with a flushed intensity; then there broke out in him a visibility of relief that was simply a tremendous exposure. He shone at them all like a tall lighthouse, embracing even, for sympathy, the blinking young men. 'By all the powers – it's wrong!' And without another look, without a word of thanks, without time for anything or anybody, he turned on them the broad back of his great stature, straightened his triumphant shoulders, and strode out of the place.

She was left confronted with her habitual critics. 'If it's wrong it's all right!' she extravagantly quoted to them.

The counter-clerk was really awe-stricken. 'But how did you know, dear?'

'I remembered, love!'

Mr Buckton, on the contrary, was rude. 'And what game is that, miss?'

No happiness she had ever known came within miles of it, and some minutes elapsed before she could recall herself sufficiently to reply that it was none of his business.

24

If life at Cocker's, with the dreadful drop of August, had lost something of its savour, she had not been slow to infer that a heavier blight had fallen on the graceful industry of Mrs Jordan. With Lord Rye and Lady Ventnor and Mrs Bubb all out of town, with the blinds down on all the homes of luxury, this ingenious woman might well have found her wonderful taste left quite on her hands. She bore up, however, in a way that began by exciting much of her young friend's esteem; they perhaps even more frequently met as the wine of life flowed less free from other sources, and each, in the lack of better diversion, carried on with more mystification for the other an intercourse that consisted not a little of peeping out and drawing back. Each waited for the other to commit herself, each profusely curtained for the other the limits of low horizons. Mrs Jordan was indeed probably the more reckless skirmisher; nothing could exceed her frequent incoherence unless it was indeed her occasional bursts of confidence. Her account of her private affairs rose and fell like a flame in the wind – sometimes the bravest bonfire and sometimes a handful of ashes. This our young woman took to be an effect of the position, at one moment and another, of the famous door of the great world. She had been struck in one of her ha'penny volumes with the translation of a French proverb according to which a door had to be either open or shut; and it seemed a part of the precariousness of Mrs Jordan's life that hers mostly managed to be neither. There had been occasions when it appeared to gape wide – fairly to woo her across its threshold; there had been others, of an order distinctly disconcerting, when it was all but banged in her face. On the whole, however, she had evidently not lost heart; these still belonged to the class of things in spite of which she looked well. She intimated that the profits of her trade had swollen so as to float her through any state of the tide, and she had, beside this, a hundred profundities and explanations.

She rose superior, above all, on the happy fact that there were always gentlemen in town and that gentlemen were her greatest admirers; gentlemen from the City in especial – as to whom she was full of information about the passion and pride excited in such breasts by the objects of her charming commerce. The City men *did*, in short, go in for flowers. There was a certain type of awfully smart stockbroker – Lord Rye called them Jews and 'bounders', but she didn't care – whose extravagance, she more than once threw out, had really, if one had any conscience, to be forcibly restrained. It was not perhaps a pure love of beauty: it was a matter of vanity and a sign of business; they wished to crush their rivals, and that was one of their weapons. Mrs Jordan's shrewdness was extreme; she knew, in any case, her customer – she dealt, as she said, with all sorts; and it was, at the worst, a race for her – a race even in the dull months – from one set of chambers to another. And then, after all, there were also still the ladies; the ladies of stockbroking circles were perpetually up and down. They were not quite perhaps Mrs Bubb or Lady Ventnor; but you couldn't tell the difference unless you quarrelled with them, and then you knew it only by their making-up sooner. These ladies formed the branch of her subject on which she most swayed in the breeze; to that degree that her confidant had ended with an inference or two tending to banish regret for opportunities not embraced. There were indeed tea-gowns that Mrs Jordan described – but tea-gowns were not the whole of respectability, and it was odd that a clergyman's widow should sometimes speak as if she almost thought so. She came back, it was true, unfailingly, to Lord Rye, never, evidently, quite losing sight of him even on the longest excursions. That he was kindness itself had become in fact the very moral it all pointed – pointed in strange flashes of the poor woman's nearsighted eyes. She launched at her young friend many portentous looks, solemn heralds of some extraordinary communication. The communication itself, from week to week, hung fire; but it was to the facts over which it hovered that she owed her power of going on. 'They *are*, in one way *and* another,' she often emphasized, 'a tower of strength'; and as the allusion was to the aristocracy, the girl could quite wonder why, if they were so in 'one' way, they should require to be so in two. She thoroughly knew, however, how many ways Mrs Jordan counted in. It all meant simply that her fate was pressing her close. If that fate was to be sealed at the matrimonial altar it was perhaps not remarkable that she shouldn't came all at once to the scratch of overwhelming a mere telegraphist. It would necessarily present to such a person a prospect of regretful sacrifice. Lord Rye – if it *was* Lord Rye – wouldn't be 'kind' to a nonentity of that sort, even though people quite as good had been.

One Sunday afternoon in November they went, by arrangement, to church together; after which – on the inspiration of the moment; the arrangement had not included it – they proceeded to Mrs Jordan's lodging in the region of Maida Vale. She had raved to her friend about her service of predilection; she was excessively 'high', and had more than once wished to introduce the girl to the same comfort and privilege. There was a thick brown fog, and Maida Vale tasted of acrid smoke; but they had been sitting among chants and incense and wonderful music, during which, though the effect of such things on her mind was great, our young lady had indulged in a series of reflections but indirectly related to them. One of these was the result of Mrs Jordan's having said to her on the way, and with a certain fine significance, that Lord Rye had been for some time in town. She had spoken as if it were a circumstance to which little required to be added – as if the bearing of such an item on her life might easily be grasped. Perhaps it was the wonder of whether Lord Rye wished to marry her that made her guest, with thoughts straying to that quarter, quite determine that some other nuptials also should take place at St Julian's. Mr Mudge was still an attendant at his Wesleyan chapel, but this was the least of her worries – it had never even vexed her enough for her to so much as name it to Mrs Jordan. Mr Mudge's form of worship was one of several things – they made up in superiority and beauty for what they wanted in number – that she had long ago settled he should take from her, and she had now moreover for the first time definitely established her own. Its principal feature was that it was to be the same as that of Mrs Jordan and Lord Rye; which was indeed very much what she said to her hostess as they sat together later on. The brown fog was in this hostess's little parlour, where it acted as a postponement of the question of there being, besides, anything else than the teacups and a pewter pot, and a very black little fire, and a paraffin lamp without a shade. There was at any rate no sign of a flower; it was not for herself Mrs Jordan gathered sweets. The girl waited till they had had a cup of tea – waited for the announcement that she fairly believed her friend had, this time, possessed herself of her formally at last to make; but nothing came, after the interval, save a little poke at the fire, which was like the clearing of a throat for a speech.

25

'I THINK you must have heard me speak of Mr Drake?' Mrs Jordan had never looked so queer, nor her smile so suggestive of a large benevolent bite.

'Mr Drake? Oh yes; isn't he a friend of Lord Rye?'

'A great and trusted friend. Almost – I may say – a loved friend.'

Mrs Jordan's 'almost' had such an oddity that her companion was moved, rather flippantly perhaps, to take it up. 'Don't people as good as love their friends when they "trust" them?'

It pulled up a little the eulogist of Mr Drake. 'Well, my dear, I love *you* –'

'But you don't trust me?' the girl unmercifully asked.

Again Mrs Jordan paused – still she looked queer. 'Yes,' she replied with a certain austerity; 'that's exactly what I'm about to give you rather a remarkable proof of.' The sense of its being remarkable was already so strong that, while she bridled a little, this held her auditor in a momentary muteness of submission. 'Mr Drake has rendered his lordship, for several years, services that his lordship has highly appreciated and that make it all the more – a – unexpected that they should, perhaps a little suddenly, separate.'

'Separate?' Our young lady was mystified, but she tried to be interested; and she already saw that she had put the saddle on the wrong horse. She had heard something of Mr Drake, who was a member of his lordship's circle – the member with whom, apparently, Mrs Jordan's avocations had most happened to throw her. She was only a little puzzled at the 'separation'. 'Well, at any rate,' she smiled, 'if they separate as friends –!'

'Oh, his lordship takes the greatest interest in Mr Drake's future. He'll do anything for him; he has in fact just done a great deal. There *must*, you know, be changes –!'

'No one knows it better than I,' the girl said. She wished to draw her interlocutress out. 'There will be changes enough for me.'

'You're leaving Cocker's?'

The ornament of that establishment waited a moment to answer, and then it was indirect. 'Tell me what *you're* doing.'

'Well, what will you think of it?'

'Why, that you've found the opening you were always so sure of.'

Mrs Jordan, on this, appeared to muse with embarrassed intensity. 'I was always sure, yes – and yet I often wasn't!'

'Well, I hope you're sure now. Sure, I mean, of Mr Drake.'

'Yes, my dear, I think I may say I *am*. I kept him going till I was.'

'Then he's yours?'

'My very own.'

'How nice! And awfully rich?' our young woman went on.

Mrs Jordan showed promptly enough that she loved for higher things. 'Awfully handsome – six foot two. And he *has* put by.'

'Quite like Mr Mudge, then!' that gentleman's friend rather desperately exclaimed.

'Oh, not *quite*!' Mr Drake's was ambiguous about it, but the name of Mr Mudge had evidently given her some sort of stimulus. 'He'll have more opportunity now, at any rate. He's going to Lady Bradeen.'

'To Lady Bradeen?' This was bewilderment. '"Going –"?'

The girl had seen, from the way Mrs Jordan looked at her, that the effect of the name had been to make her let something out. 'Do you know her?'

She hesitated; then she found her feet. 'Well, you'll remember I've often told you that if you have grand clients, I have them too.'

'Yes,' said Mrs Jordan; 'but the great difference is that you hate yours, whereas I really love mine. *Do* you know Lady Bradeen?' she pursued.

'Down to the ground! She's always in and out.'

Mrs Jordan's foolish eyes confessed, in fixing themselves on this sketch, to a degree of wonder and even of envy. But she bore up and, with a certain gaiety, 'Do you hate *her*?' she demanded.

Her visitor's reply was prompt. 'Dear no! – not nearly so much as some of them. She's too outrageously beautiful.'

Mrs Jordan continued to gaze. 'Outrageously?'

'Well, yes; deliciously.' What was really delicious was Mrs Jordan's vagueness. 'You don't know her – you've not seen her?' her guest lightly continued.

'No, but I've heard a great deal about her.'

'So have I!' our young lady exclaimed.

Mrs Jordan looked an instant as if she suspected her good

faith or at least her seriousness. 'You know some friend –?'

'Of Lady Bradeen's? Oh yes – I know one.'

'Only one?'

The girl laughed out. 'Only one – but he's so intimate.'

Mrs Jordan just hesitated. 'He's a gentleman?'

'Yes, he's not a lady.'

Her interlocutress appeared to muse. 'She's immensely surrounded.'

'She *will* be – with Mr Drake!'

Mrs Jordan's gaze became strangely fixed. 'Is she *very* good-looking?'

'The handsomest person I know.'

Mrs Jordan continued to contemplate. 'Well, *I* know some beauties.' Then, with her odd jerkiness, 'Do you think she looks *good*?' she inquired.

'Because that's not always the case with the good-looking?' – the other took it up. 'No, indeed, it isn't: that's one thing Cocker's has taught me. Still, there are some people who have everything. Lady Bradeen, at any rate, has enough: eyes and a nose and a mouth, a complexion, a figure –'

'A figure?' Mrs Jordan almost broke in.

'A figure, a head of hair!' The girl made a little conscious motion that seemed to let the hair all down, and her companion watched the wonderful show. 'But Mr Drake *is* another –?'

'Another?' – Mrs Jordan's thoughts had to come back from a distance.

'Of her ladyship's admirers. He's "going", you say, to her?'

At this Mrs Jordan really faltered. 'She has engaged him.'

'Engaged him?' – our young woman was quite at sea.

'In the same capacity as Lord Rye.'

'And was Lord Rye engaged?'

26

Mrs Jordan looked away from her now – looked, she thought, rather injured and, as if trifled with, even a little angry. The mention of Lady Bradeen had frustrated for a while the convergence of our heroine's thoughts; but with this impression of her old friend's combined impatience and diffidence they began again to whirl round her, and continued it till one of them appeared to dart at her, out of the dance, as if with a sharp peck. It came to her with a lively shock, with a positive sting, that Mr Drake was – could it be possible? With the idea she found herself afresh on the edge of laughter, of a sudden and strange perversity of mirth. Mr Drake loomed, in a swift image, before her; such a figure as she had seen in open doorways of houses in Cocker's quarter – majestic, middle-aged, erect, flanked on either side by a footman and taking the name of a visitor. Mr Drake then verily *was* a person who opened the door! Before she had time, however, to recover from the effect of her evocation, she was offered a vision which quite engulphed it. It was communicated to her somehow that the face with which she had seen it rise prompted Mrs Jordan to dash, at a venture, at something that might attenuate criticism. 'Lady Bradeen is re-arranging – she's going to be married.'

'Married?' The girl echoed it ever so softly, but there it was at last.

'Didn't you know it?'

She summoned all her sturdiness. 'No, she hasn't told me.'

'And her friends – haven't they?'

'I haven't seen any of them lately. I'm not so fortunate as *you*.'

Mrs Jordan gathered herself. 'Then you haven't even heard of Lord Bradeen's death?'

Her comrade, unable for a moment to speak, gave a slow headshake. 'You know it from Mr Drake?' It was better surely not to learn things at all than to learn them by the butler.

'She tells him everything.'

'And he tells *you* – I see.' Our young lady got up; recovering her muff and her gloves, she smiled. 'Well, I haven't, unfortunately, any Mr Drake. I congratulate you with all my heart. Even without your sort of assistance, however, there's a trifle here and there that I do pick up. I gather that if she's to marry any one, it must quite necessarily be my friend.'

Mrs Jordan was now also on her feet. 'Is Captain Everard your friend?'

The girl considered, drawing on a glove. 'I saw, at one time, an immense deal of him.'

Mrs Jordan looked hard at the glove, but she had not, after all, waited for that to be sorry it was not cleaner. 'What time was that?'

'It must have been the time you were seeing so much of Mr Drake.' She had now fairly taken it in: the distinguished person Mrs Jordan was to marry would answer bells and put on coals and superintend, at least, the cleaning of boots for the other distinguished person whom *she* might – well, whom she might have had, if she had wished, so much more to say to. 'Good-bye,' she added; 'good-bye.'

Mrs Jordan, however, again taking her muff from her, turned it over, brushed it off, and thoughtfully peeped into it. 'Tell me this before you go. You spoke just now of your own changes. Do you mean that Mr Mudge –?'

'Mr Mudge has had great patience with me – he has brought me at last to the point. We're to be married next month and have a nice little home. But he's only a grocer, you know' – the girl met her friend's intent eyes – 'so that I'm afraid that, with the set you've got into, you won't see your way to keep up our friendship.'

Mrs Jordan for a moment made no answer to this; she only held the muff up to her face, after which she gave it back. 'You don't like it. I see, I see.'

To her guest's astonishment there were tears now in her eyes. 'I don't like what?' the girl asked.

'Why, my engagement. Only, with your great cleverness,' the poor lady quavered out, 'you put it in your own way. I mean that you'll cool off. You already *have* –!' And on this, the next instant, her tears began to flow. She succumbed to them and collapsed; she sank down again, burying her face and trying to smother her sobs.

Her young friend stood there, still in some rigour, but taken much by surprise even if not yet fully moved to pity. 'I don't put anything in any "way", and I'm very glad you're suited. Only, you know, you did put to *me* so splendidly what, even for me, if I had listened to you, it might lead to.'

Mrs Jordan kept up a mild, thin, weak wail; then, drying her eyes, as feebly considered this reminder. 'It has led to my not starving!' she faintly gasped.

Our young lady, at this, dropped into the place beside her, and now, in a rush, the small, silly misery was clear. She took her hand as a sign of pitying it, then, after another instant, confirmed this expression with a consoling kiss. They sat there together; they looked out, hand in hand, into the damp, dusky, shabby little room and into the future, of no such very different suggestion, at last accepted by each. There was no definite utterance, on either side, of Mr Drake's position in the great world, but the temporary collapse of his prospective bride threw all further necessary light; and what our heroine saw and felt for in the whole business was the vivid reflection of her own dreams and delusions and her own return to reality. Reality, for the poor things they both were, could only be ugliness and obscurity, could never be the escape, the rise. She pressed her friend – she had tact enough for that – with no other personal question, brought on no need of further revelations, only just continued to hold and comfort her and to acknowledge by stiff little forbearances the common element in their fate. She felt indeed magnanimous in such matters; for if it was very well, for condolence or re-assurance, to suppress just then invidious shrinkings, she yet by no means saw herself sitting down, as she might say, to the same table with Mr Drake. There would luckily, to all appearances, be little question of tables; and the circumstance that, on their peculiar lines, her friend's interests would still attach themselves to Mayfair flung over Chalk Farm the first radiance it had shown. Where was one's pride and one's passion when the real way to judge of one's luck was by making not the wrong, but the right, comparison? Before she had again gathered herself to go she felt very small and cautious and thankful. 'We shall have our own house,' she said, 'and you must come very soon and let me show it you.'

'*We* shall have our own too,' Mrs Jordan replied; 'for don't you know, he makes it a condition that he sleeps out?'

'A condition?' – the girl felt out of it.

'For any new position. It was on that he parted with Lord Rye. His lordship can't meet it; so Mr Drake has given him up.'

'And all for you?' – our young woman put it as cheerfully as possible.

'For me and Lady Bradeen. Her ladyship's too glad to get him at any price. Lord Rye, out of interest in us, has in fact quite *made* her take him. So, as I tell you, he will have his own establishment.'

Mrs Jordan, in the elation of it, had begun to revive; but there was nevertheless between them rather a conscious pause – a pause in which neither visitor nor hostess brought out a hope or an invitation. It expressed in the last resort that, in spite of submission and sympathy, they could now, after all, only look at each other across the social gulf. They remained together, as if it would be indeed their last chance, still sitting, though awkwardly, quite close, and feeling also – and this most unmistakably – that there was one thing more to go into. By the time it came to the surface, moreover, our young friend had recognized the whole of the main truth, from which she even drew again a slight irritation. It was not the main truth perhaps that most signified; but after her momentary effort, her embarrassment and her tears, Mrs Jordan had begun to sound afresh – and even without speaking – the note of a social connection. She hadn't really let go of it that she was marrying into society. Well, it was a harmless compensation, and it was all that the prospective bride of Mr Mudge had to leave with her.

27

THIS young lady at last rose again, but she lingered before going. 'And has Captain Everard nothing to say to it?'

'To what, dear?'

'Why, to such questions – the domestic arrangements, things in the house.'

'How *can* he, with any authority, when nothing in the house is his?'

'Not his?' The girl wondered, perfectly conscious of the appearance she thus conferred on Mrs Jordan of knowing, in comparison with herself, so tremendously much about it. Well, there were things she wanted so to get at that she was willing at last, though it hurt her, to pay for them with humiliation. 'Why are they not his?'

'Don't you know, dear, that he has nothing?'

'Nothing?' It was hard to see him in such a light, but Mrs Jordan's power to answer for it had a superiority that began, on the spot, to grow. 'Isn't he rich?'

Mrs Jordan looked immensely, looked both generally and particularly, informed. 'It depends on what you call –! Not, at any rate, in the least as *she* is. What does he bring? Think what she has. And then, my love, his debts.'

'His debts?' His young friend was fairly betrayed into helpless innocence. She could struggle a little, but she had to let herself go; and if she had spoken frankly she would have said: 'Do tell me, for I don't know so much about him as *that*!' As she didn't speak frankly she only said: 'His debts are nothing – when she so adores him.'

Mrs Jordan began to fix her again, and now she saw that she could only take it all. That was what it had come to: his having sat with her there, on the bench and under the trees, in the summer darkness, and put his hand on her, making her know what he would have said if permitted; his having returned to her afterwards, repeatedly, with supplicating eyes and a fever in his blood; and her having, on her side, hard and pedantic, helped by some miracle and with her impossible condition, only answered him, yet supplicating back, through the bars of the cage, – all simply that she might hear of him, now for ever lost, only through Mrs Jordan, who touched him through Mr Drake, who reached him through Lady Bradeen. 'She adores him – but of course that wasn't all there was about it.'

The girl met her eyes a minute, then quite surrendered. 'What was there else about it?'

'Why, don't you know?' – Mrs Jordan was almost compassionate.

Her interlocutress had, in the cage, sounded depths, but there was a suggestion here somehow of an abyss quite measureless. 'Of course I know that she would never let him alone.'

'How *could* she – fancy! – when he had so compromised her?'

The most artless cry they had ever uttered broke, at this, from the younger pair of lips. '*Had* he so –?'

'Why, don't you know the scandal?'

Our heroine thought, recollected; there was something, whatever it was, that she knew, after all, much more of than Mrs Jordan. She saw him again as she had seen him come that morning to recover the telegram – she saw him as she had seen him leave the shop. She perched herself a moment on this. 'Oh, there was nothing public.'

'Not exactly public – no. But there was an awful scare and an awful row. It was all on the very point of coming out. Something was lost – something was found.'

'Ah yes,' the girl replied, smiling as if with the revival of a blurred memory; 'something was found.'

'It all got about – and there was a point at which Lord Bradeen had to act.'

'Had to – yes. But he didn't.'

Mrs Jordan was obliged to admit it. 'No, he didn't. And then, luckily for them, he died.'

'I didn't know about his death,' her companion said.

'It was nine weeks ago, and most sudden. It has given them a prompt chance.'

'To get married' – this was a wonder – 'within nine weeks?'

'Oh, not immediately, but – in all the circumstances – very quietly and, I assure you, very soon. Every preparation's made. Above all, she holds him.'

'Oh yes, she holds him!' our young friend threw off. She had this before her again a minute; then she continued: 'You mean through his having made her talked about?'

'Yes, but not only that. She has still another pull.'

'Another,'

Mrs Jordan hesitated. 'Why, he was *in* something.'

Her comrade wondered. 'In what?'

'I don't know. Something bad. As I tell you, something was found.'

The girl stared. 'Well?'

'It would have been very bad for him. But she helped him some way – she recovered it, got hold of it. It's even said she stole it!'

Our young woman considered afresh. 'Why, it was what was found that precisely saved him.'

Mrs Jordan, however, was positive. 'I beg your pardon. I happen to know.'

Her disciple faltered but an instant. 'Do you mean through Mr Drake. Do they tell *him* these things?'

'A good servant,' said Mrs Jordan, now thoroughly superior and proportionately sententious, 'doesn't need to be told! Her ladyship saved – as a woman so often saves! – the man she loves.'

This time our heroine took longer to recover herself, but she found a voice at last. 'Ah well – of course I don't know! The great thing was that he got off. They seem then, in a manner,' she added, 'to have done a great deal for each other.'

'Well, it's she that has done most. She has him tight.'

'I see, I see. Good-bye.' The women had already embraced, and this was not repeated; but Mrs Jordan went down with her guest to the door of the house. Here again the younger lingered, reverting, though three or four other remarks had on the way passed between them, to Captain Everard and Lady Bradeen. 'Did you mean just now that if she hadn't saved him, as you call it, she wouldn't hold him so tight?'

'Well, I daresay.' Mrs Jordan, on the door-step, smiled with a reflection that had come to her; she took one of her big bites of the brown gloom. 'Men always dislike one when they have done one an injury.'

'But what injury had he done her?'

'The one I've mentioned. He *must* marry her, you know.'

'And didn't he want to?'

'Not before.'

'Not before she recovered the telegram?'

Mrs Jordan was pulled up a little. 'Was it a telegram?'

The girl hesitated. 'I thought you said so. I mean whatever it was.'

'Yes, whatever it was, I don't think she saw *that*.'

'So she just nailed him?'

'She just nailed him.' The departing friend was now at the bottom of the little flight of steps; the other was at the top, with a certain thickness of fog. 'And when am I to think of you in your little home? – next month?' asked the voice from the top.

'At the very latest. And when am I to think of you in yours?'

'Oh, even sooner. I feel, after so much talk with you about it, as if I were already there!' Then '*Good*-bye' came out of the fog.

'Good-*bye*!' went into it. Our young lady went into it also, in the opposed quarter, and presently, after a few sightless turns, came out on the Paddington canal. Distinguishing vaguely what the low parapet enclosed, she stopped close to it and stood a while, very intently, but perhaps still sightlessly, looking down on it. A policeman, while she remained, strolled past her; then, going his way a little further and half lost in the atmosphere, paused and watched her. But she was quite unaware – she was full of her thoughts. They were too numerous to find a place just here, but two of the number may at least be mentioned. One of these was that, decidedly, her little home must be not for next month, but for next week; the other, which came indeed as she resumed her walk and went her way, was that it was strange such a matter should be at last settled for her by Mr Drake.

THE SIEGE OF LONDON

PART ONE

1

THAT solemn piece of upholstery, the curtain of the Comédie Française, had fallen upon the first act of the piece, and our two Americans had taken advantage of the interval to pass out of the huge, hot theatre, in company with the other occupants of the stalls. But they were among the first to return, and they beguiled the rest of the intermission with looking at the house, which had lately been cleansed of its historic cobwebs and ornamented with frescos illustrative of the classic drama. In the month of September the audience at the Théâtre Français is comparatively thin, and on this occasion the drama – *L'Aventurière* of Emile Augier – had no pretensions to novelty. Many of the boxes were empty, others were occupied by persons of provincial or nomadic appearance. The boxes are far from the stage, near which our spectators were placed; but even at a distance Rupert Waterville was able to appreciate certain details. He was fond of appreciating details, and when he went to the theatre he looked about him a good deal, making use of a dainty but remarkably powerful glass. He knew that such a course was wanting in true distinction, and that it was indelicate to level at a lady an instrument which was often only less injurious in effect than a double-barrelled pistol; but he was always very curious, and he was sure, in any case, that at that moment, at that antiquated play – so he was pleased to qualify the masterpiece of an Academician – he would not be observed by any one he knew. Standing up therefore with his back to the stage, he made the circuit of the boxes, while several other persons, near him, performed the same operation with even greater coolness.

'Not a single pretty woman,' he remarked at last to his friend; an observation which Littlemore, sitting in his place and staring with a bored expression at the new-looking curtain, received in perfect silence. He rarely indulged in these optical excursions; he had been a great deal in Paris and had ceased to care about it, or wonder about it, much; he fancied that the French capital could have no more surprises for him, though it had had a good many in former days. Waterville was still in the stage of surprise; he suddenly expressed this emotion. 'By Jove!' he exclaimed; 'I beg your pardon – I beg *her* pardon – there is, after all, a woman that may be called' – he paused a little, inspecting her – 'a kind of beauty!'

'What kind?' Littlemore asked, vaguely.

'An unusual kind – an indescribable kind.' Littlemore was not heeding his answer, but he presently heard himself appealed to. 'I say, I wish very much you would do me a favor.'

'I did you a favor in coming here,' said Littlemore. 'It's insufferably hot, and the play is like a dinner that has been dressed by the kitchen-maid. The actors are all *doublures*.'

'It's simply to answer me this: is *she* respectable, now?' Waterville rejoined, inattentive to his friend's epigram.

Littlemore gave a groan, without turning his head. 'You are always wanting to know if they are respectable. What on earth can it matter?'

'I have made such mistakes – I have lost all confidence,' said poor Waterville, to whom European civilization had not ceased to be a novelty, and who during the last six months had found himself confronted with problems long unsuspected. Whenever he encountered a very nice-looking woman, he was sure to discover that she belonged to the class represented by the heroine of M. Augier's drama; and whenever his attention rested upon a person of a florid style of attraction, there was the strongest probability that she would turn out to be a countess. The countesses looked so superficial and the others looked so exclusive. Now Littlemore distinguished at a glance; he never made mistakes.

'Simply for looking at them, it doesn't matter, I suppose,' said Waterville, ingenuously, answering his companion's rather cynical inquiry.

'You stare at them all alike,' Littlemore went on, still without moving; 'except indeed when I tell you that they are not respectable – then your attention acquires a fixedness!'

'If your judgement is against this lady, I promise never to look at her again. I mean the one in the third box from the passage, in white, with the red flowers,' he added, as Littlemore slowly rose and stood beside him. 'The young man is leaning forward. It is the young man that makes me doubt of her. Will you have the glass?'

Littlemore looked about him without concentration. 'No, I thank you, my eyes are good enough. The young man's a very good young man,' he added in a moment.

'Very indeed; but he's several years younger than she. Wait till she turns her head.'

She turned it very soon – she apparently had been speaking to the *ouvreuse*, at the door of the box – and presented her face to the public – a fair, well-drawn face, with smiling eyes, smiling lips, ornamented over the brow with delicate rings of black hair and, in each ear, with the sparkle of a diamond sufficiently large to be seen across the Théâtre Français. Littlemore looked at her; then, abruptly, he gave an exclamation. 'Give me the glass!'

'Do you know her?' his companion asked, as he directed the little instrument.

Littlemore made no answer; he only looked in silence; then he handed back the glass. 'No, she's not respectable,' he said. And he dropped into his seat again. As Waterville remained standing, he added, 'Please sit down; I think she saw me.'

'Don't you want her to see you?' asked Waterville the interrogator, taking his seat.

Littlemore hesitated. 'I don't want to spoil her game.' By this time the *entr'acte* was at an end; the curtain rose again.

It had been Waterville's idea that they should go to the theatre. Littlemore, who was always for not doing a thing, had recommended that, the evening being lovely, they should simply sit and smoke at the door of the Grand Café, in a decent part of the Boulevard. Nevertheless Rupert Waterville enjoyed the second act even less than he had done the first, which he thought heavy. He began to wonder whether his companion would wish to stay to the end; a useless line of speculation, for now that he had got to the theatre, Littlemore's objection to doing things would certainly keep him from going. Waterville also wondered what he knew about the lady in the box. Once or twice he glanced at his friend, and then he saw that Littlemore was not following the play. He was thinking of something else; he was thinking of that woman. When the curtain fell again he sat in his place, making way for his neighbors, as usual, to edge past him, grinding his knees – his legs were long – with their own protuberances. When the two men were alone in the stalls, Littlemore said: 'I think I should like to see her again, after all.' He spoke as if Waterville might have known all about her. Waterville was conscious of not doing so, but as there was evidently a good deal to know, he felt that he should lose nothing by being a little discreet. So, for the moment, he asked no questions; he only said –

'Well, here's the glass.'

Littlemore gave him a glance of good-natured compassion. 'I don't mean that I want to stare at her with that beastly thing. I mean – to see her – as I used to see her.'

'How did you use to see her?' asked Waterville, bidding farewell to discretion.

'On the back piazza, at San Diego.' And as his interlocutor, in receipt of this information, only stared, he went on – 'Come out where we can breathe, and I'll tell you more.'

They made their way to the low and narrow door, more worthy of a rabbit-hutch than of a great theatre, by which you pass from the stalls of the Comédie to the lobby, and as Littlemore went first, his ingenuous friend, behind him, could see that he glanced up at the box in the occupants of which they were interested. The more interesting of these had her back to the house; she was apparently just leaving the box, after her companion; but as she had not put on her mantle it was evident that they were not quitting the theatre. Littlemore's pursuit of fresh air did not lead him into the street; he had passed his arm into Waterville's, and when they reached that fine frigid staircase which ascends to the Foyer, he began silently to mount it. Littlemore was averse to active pleasures, but his friend reflected that now at least he had launched himself – he was going to look for the lady whom, with a monosyllable, he appeared to have classified. The young man resigned himself for the moment to asking no questions, and the two strolled together into the shining saloon where Houdon's admirable statue of Voltaire, reflected in a dozen mirrors, is gaped at by visitors obviously less acute than the genius expressed in those living features. Waterville knew that Voltaire was very witty; he had read *Candide*, and had already had several opportunities of appreciating the statue. The Foyer was not crowded; only a dozen groups were scattered over the polished floor, several others having passed out to the balcony which overhangs the square of the Palais Royal. The windows were open, the brilliant lights of Paris made the dull summer evening look like an anniversary or a revolution; a murmur of voices seemed to come up from the streets, and even in the Foyer one heard the slow click of the horses and the rumble of the crookedly-driven fiacres on the hard, smooth asphalt. A lady and a gentleman, with their backs to our friends, stood before the image of Voltaire; the lady was dressed in white, including a white bonnet. Littlemore felt, as so many persons feel in that spot, that the scene was conspicuously Parisian, and he gave a mysterious laugh.

'It seems comical to see her here! The last time was in New Mexico.'

'In New Mexico?'

'At San Diego.'

'Oh, on the back piazza,' said Waterville, putting things together. He had not been aware of the position of San Diego, for if on the occasion of his lately being appointed to a subordinate diplomatic post in London, he had been paying a good deal of attention to European geography, he had rather neglected that of his own country.

They had not spoken loud, and they were not standing near her; but suddenly, as if she had heard them, the lady in white turned round. Her eye caught Waterville's first, and in that glance he saw that if she had heard them it was not because they were audible but because she had extraordinary quickness of ear. There was no recognition in it – there was none, at first, even when it rested lightly upon George Littlemore. But recognition flashed out a moment later, accompanied with a delicate increase of color and a quick extension of her apparently constant smile. She had turned completely round; she stood there in sudden friendliness, with parted lips, with a hand, gloved to the elbow, almost imperiously offered. She was even prettier than at a distance. 'Well, I declare!' she exclaimed; so loud that every one in the room appeared to feel personally addressed. Waterville was surprised; he had not been prepared, even after the mention of the back piazza, to find her an American. Her companion turned round as she spoke; he was a fresh, lean young man, in evening dress; he kept his hands in his pockets; Waterville imagined that he at any rate was not an American. He looked very grave – for such a fair, festive young man – and gave Waterville and Littlemore, though his height was not superior to theirs, a narrow, vertical glance. Then he turned back to the statue of Voltaire, as if it had been, after all, among his premonitions that the lady he was attending would recognize people he didn't know, and didn't even, perhaps, care to know. This possibly confirmed slightly Littlemore's assertion that she was not respectable. The young man was, at least; consummately so. 'Where in the world did you drop from?' the lady inquired.

'I have been here some time,' Littlemore said, going forward, rather deliberately, to shake hands with her. He smiled a little, but he was more serious than she; he kept his eye on her own as if she had been just a trifle dangerous; it was the manner in which a duly discreet person would have approached some glossy, graceful animal which had an occasional trick of biting.

'Here in Paris, do you mean?'

'No; here and there – in Europe generally.'

'Well, it's queer I haven't met you.'

'Better late than never!' said Littlemore. His smile was a little fixed.

'Well, you look very natural,' the lady went on.

'So do you – or very charming – it's the same thing,' Littlemore answered, laughing, and evidently wishing to be easy.

It was as if, face to face, and after a considerable lapse of time, he had found her more imposing than he expected when, in the stalls below, he determined to come and meet her. As he spoke, the young man who was with her gave up his inspection of Voltaire and faced about, listlessly, without looking either at Littlemore or at Waterville.

'I want to introduce you to my friend,' she went on. 'Sir Arthur Demesne – Mr Littlemore. Mr Littlemore – Sir Arthur Demesne. Sir Arthur Demesne is an Englishman – Mr Littlemore is a countryman of mine, an old friend. I haven't seen him for years. For how long? Don't let's count! – I wonder you knew me,' she continued, addressing Littlemore. 'I'm fearfully changed.' All this was said in a clear, gay tone, which was the more audible as she spoke with a kind of caressing slowness. The two men, to do honor to her introduction, silently exchanged a glance; the Englishman, perhaps, colored a little. He was very conscious of his companion. 'I haven't introduced you to many people yet,' she remarked.

'Oh, I don't mind,' said Sir Arthur Demesne.

'Well, it's queer to see you!' she exclaimed, looking still at Littlemore. 'You have changed, too – I can see that.'

'Not where you are concerned.'

'That's what I want to find out. Why don't you introduce your friend? I see he's dying to know me!'

Littlemore proceeded to this ceremony; but he reduced it to its simplest elements, merely glancing at Rupert Waterville, and murmuring his name.

'You didn't tell him *my* name,' the lady cried, while Waterville made her a formal salutation. 'I hope you haven't forgotten it!'

Littlemore gave her a glance which was intended to be more penetrating than what he had hitherto permitted himself; if it had been put into words it would have said, 'Ah, but *which* name?'

She answered the unspoken question, putting out her hand, as she had done to Littlemore, 'Happy to make your acquaintance, Mr Waterville. I'm Mrs Headway – perhaps you've heard of me. If you've ever been in America you must have heard of me. Not so much in New York, but in the Western cities. You *are* an American? Well, then, we are all compatriots – except Sir Arthur Demesne. Let me introduce you to Sir Arthur. Sir Arthur Demesne, Mr Waterville – Mr Waterville, Sir Arthur Demesne. Sir Arthur Demesne is a member of Parliament; don't he look young?' She waited for no answer to this question, but suddenly asked another, as she moved her bracelets back over her long, loose gloves. 'Well, Mr Littlemore, what are you thinking of?'

He was thinking that he must indeed have forgotten her name, for the one that she had pronounced awakened no association. But he could hardly tell her that.

'I'm thinking of San Diego.'

'The back piazza, at my sister's? Oh, don't; it was too horrid. She has left now. I believe every one has left.'

Sir Arthur Demesne drew out his watch with the air of a man who could take no part in these domestic reminiscences; he appeared to combine a generic self-possession with a degree of individual shyness. He said something about its being time they should go back to their seats, but Mrs Headway paid no attention to the remark. Waterville wished her to linger; he felt in looking at her as if he had been looking at a charming picture. Her low-growing hair, with its fine dense undulations, was of a shade of blackness that has now become rare; her complexion had the bloom of a white flower; her profile, when she turned her head, was as pure and fine as the outline of a cameo.

'You know this is the first theatre,' she said to Waterville, as if she wished to be sociable. 'And this is Voltaire, the celebrated writer.'

'I'm devoted to the Comédie Française,' Waterville answered, smiling.

'Dreadfully bad house; we didn't hear a word,' said Sir Arthur.

'Ah, yes, the boxes!' murmured Waterville.

'I'm rather disappointed,' Mrs Headway went on. 'But I want to see what becomes of that woman.'

'Doña Clorinde? Oh, I suppose they'll shoot her; they generally shoot the women, in French plays,' Littlemore said.

'It will remind me of San Diego!' cried Mrs Headway.

'Ah, at San Diego the women did the shooting.'

'They don't seem to have killed you!' Mrs Headway rejoined, archly.

'No, but I am riddled with wounds.'

'Well, this is very remarkable,' the lady went on, turning to Houdon's statue. 'It's beautifully modelled.'

'You are perhaps reading M. de Voltaire,' Littlemore suggested.

'No; but I've purchased his works.'

'They are not proper reading for ladies,' said the young Englishman, severely, offering his arm to Mrs Headway.

'Ah, you might have told me before I had bought them!' she exclaimed, in exaggerated dismay.

'I couldn't imagine you would buy a hundred and fifty volumes.'

'A hundred and fifty? I have only bought two.'

'Perhaps two won't hurt you?' said Littlemore with a smile.

She darted him a reproachful ray. 'I know what you mean, – that I'm too bad already. Well, bad as I am, you must come and see me.' And she threw him the name of her hotel, as she walked away with her Englishman. Waterville looked after the latter with a certain interest; he had heard of him in London, and had seen his portrait in 'Vanity Fair'.

It was not yet time to go down, in spite of this gentleman's saying so, and Littlemore and his friend passed out on the balcony of the Foyer. 'Headway – Headway? Where the deuce did she get that name?' Littlemore asked, as they looked down into the animated dusk.

'From her husband, I suppose,' Waterville suggested.

'From her husband? From which? The last was named Beck.'

'How many has she had? Waterville inquired, anxious to hear how it was that Mrs Headway was not respectable.

'I haven't the least idea. But it wouldn't be difficult to find out, as I believe they are all living. She was Mrs Beck – Nancy Beck – when I knew her.'

'Nancy Beck!' cried Waterville, aghast. He was thinking of

her delicate profile, like that of a pretty Roman empress. There was a great deal to be explained.

Littlemore explained it in a few words before they returned to their places, admitting indeed that he was not yet able to elucidate her present situation. She was a memory of his Western days; he had seen her last some six years before. He had known her very well and in several places; the circle of her activity was chiefly the Southwest. This activity was of a vague character, except in the sense that it was exclusively social. She was supposed to have a husband, one Philadelphus Beck, the editor of a Democratic newspaper, the *Dakotah Sentinel*; but Littlemore had never seen him – the pair were living apart – and it was the impression at San Diego that matrimony, for Mr and Mrs Beck, was about played out. He remembered now to have heard afterwards that she was getting a divorce. She got divorces very easily, she was so taking in court. She had got one or two before from a man whose name he had forgotten, and there was a legend that even these were not the first. She had been exceedingly divorced! When he first met her in California, she called herself Mrs Grenville, which he had been given to understand was not an appellation acquired in matrimony, but her parental name, resumed after the dissolution of an unfortunate union. She had had these episodes – her unions were all unfortunate – and had borne half a dozen names. She was a charming woman, especially for New Mexico; but she had been divorced too often – it was a tax on one's credulity; she must have repudiated more husbands than she had married.

At San Diego she was staying with her sister, whose actual spouse (she, too, had been divorced), the principal man of the place, kept a bank (with the aid of a six-shooter), and who had never suffered Nancy to want for a home during her unattached periods. Nancy had begun very young; she must be about thirty-seven today. That was all he meant by her not being respectable. The chronology was rather mixed; her sister at least had once told him that there was one winter when she didn't know herself *who* was Nancy's husband. She had gone in mainly for editors – she esteemed the journalistic profession.

They must all have been dreadful ruffians, for her own amiability was manifest. It was well known that whatever she had done she had done in self-defence. In fine, she had done things; that was the main point now! She was very pretty, good-natured and clever, and quite the best company in those parts. She was a genuine product of the far West – a flower of the Pacific slope; ignorant, audacious, crude, but full of pluck and spirit, of natural intelligence, and of a certain intermittent, haphazard good taste. She used to say that she only wanted a chance – apparently she had found it now. At one time, without her, he didn't see how he could have put up with the life. He had started a cattle-ranch, to which San Diego was the nearest town, and he used to ride over to see her. Sometimes he stayed there for a week; then he went to see her every evening. It was horribly hot; they used to sit on the back piazza. She was always as attractive, and very nearly as well-dressed, as they had just beheld her. As far as appearance went, she might have been transplanted at an hour's notice from that dusty old settlement to the city by the Seine.

'Some of those Western women are wonderful,' Littlemore said. 'Like her, they only want a chance.'

He had not been in love with her – there never was anything of that sort between them. There might have been of course; but as it happened there was not. Headway apparently was the successor of Beck; perhaps there had been others between. She was in no sort of 'society'; she only had a local reputation ('the elegant and accomplished Mrs Beck,' the newspapers called her – the other editors, to whom she wasn't married), though, indeed, in that spacious civilization the locality was large. She knew nothing of the East, and to the best of his belief at that period had never seen New York. Various things might have happened in those six years, however; no doubt she had 'come up'. The West was sending us everything (Littlemore spoke as a New Yorker); no doubt it would send us at last our brilliant women. This little woman used to look quite over the head of New York; even in those days she thought and talked of Paris, which there was no prospect of her knowing; that was the way she had got on in New Mexico. She had had her ambition, her presentiments; she had known she was meant for better things. Even at San Diego she had prefigured her little Sir Arthur; every now and then a wandering Englishman came within her range. They were not all baronets and M.P.'s, but they were usually a change from the editors. What she was doing with her present acquisition he was curious to see. She was certainly – if he had any capacity for that state of mind, which was not too apparent – making him happy. She looked very splendid; Headway had probably made a 'pile', an achievement not to be imputed to any of the others. She didn't accept money – he was sure she didn't accept money.

On their way back to their seats Littlemore, whose tone had been humorous, but with that strain of the pensive which is inseparable from retrospect, suddenly broke into audible laughter.

'The modelling of a statue and the works of Voltaire!' he exclaimed, recurring to two or three things she had said. 'It's comical to hear her attempt those flights, for in New Mexico she knew nothing about modelling.'

'She didn't strike me as affected,' Waterville rejoined, feeling a vague impulse to take a considerate view of her.

'Oh, no; she's only – as she says – fearfully changed.'

They were in their places before the play went on again, and they both gave another glance at Mrs Headway's box. She leaned back, slowly fanning herself, and evidently watching Littlemore, as if she had been waiting to see him come in. Sir Arthur Demesne sat beside her, rather gloomily, resting a round pink chin upon a high stiff collar; neither of them seemed to speak.

'Are you sure she makes him happy?' Waterville asked.

'Yes – that's the way those people show it.'

'But does she go about alone with him that way? Where's her husband?'

'I suppose she has divorced him.'

'And does she want to marry the baronet?' Waterville asked, as if his companion were omniscient.

It amused Littlemore for the moment to appear so. 'He wants to marry her, I guess.'

'And be divorced, like the others?'

'Oh, no; this time she has got what she wants,' said Littlemore, as the curtain rose.

He suffered three days to elapse before he called at the Hôtel Meurice, which she had designated, and we may occupy this interval in adding a few words to the story we have taken from his lips. George Littlemore's residence in the far West had been of the usual tentative sort – he had gone there to replenish a pocket depleted by youthful extravagance. His first attempts had failed; the days were passing away when a fortune was to be picked up even by a young man who might be supposed to have inherited from an honorable father, lately removed, some of those fine abilities, mainly dedicated to the importation of tea, to which the elder Mr Littlemore was indebted for the power of leaving his son well off. Littlemore had dissipated his patrimony, and he was not quick to discover his talents, which, consisting chiefly of an unlimited faculty for smoking and horse-breaking, appeared to lie in the direction of none of the professions called liberal. He had been sent to Harvard to have his aptitudes cultivated, but here they took such a form that repressions had been found more necessary than stimulus – repression embodied in an occasional sojourn in one of the lovely villages of the Connecticut valley. Rustication saved him, perhaps, in the sense that it detached him; it destroyed his ambitions, which had been foolish. At the age of thirty, Littlemore had mastered none of the useful arts, unless we include in the number the great art of indifference. He was roused from his indifference by a stroke of good luck. To oblige a friend who was even in more pressing need of cash than himself, he had purchased for a moderate sum (the proceeds of a successful game of poker) a share in a silver-mine which the disposer, with unusual candor, admitted to be destitute of metal. Littlemore looked into his mine and recognized the truth of the contention, which, however, was demolished some two years later by a sudden revival of curiosity on the part of one of the other shareholders. This gentleman, convinced that a silver-mine without silver is as rare as an effect without a cause, discovered the sparkle of the precious element deep down in the reasons of things. The discovery was agreeable to Littlemore, and was the beginning of a fortune which, through several dull years and in many rough places, he had repeatedly despaired of, and which a man whose purpose was never very keen did not perhaps altogether deserve. It was before he saw himself successful that he had made the acquaintance of the lady now established at the Hôtel Meurice. Today he owned the largest share in his mine, which remained perversely productive, and which enabled him to buy, among other things, in Montana, a cattle-ranch of much finer proportions than the dry acres near San Diego. Ranches and mines encourage security, and the consciousness of not having to watch the sources of his income too anxiously (an obligation which for a man of his disposition spoils everything) now added itself to his usual coolness. It was not that this same coolness had not been considerably tried. To take only one – the principal – instance: he had lost his wife after only a twelvemonth of marriage, some three years before the date at which we meet him. He was more than forty when he encountered and wooed a young girl of twenty-three, who, like himself, had consulted all the probabilities in expecting a succession of happy years. She left him a small daughter, now intrusted to the care of his only sister, the wife of an English squire and mistress of a dull park in Hampshire. This lady, Mrs Dolphin by name, had captivated her landowner during a journey in which Mr Dolphin had promised himself to examine the institutions of the United States. The institution on which he reported most favorably was the pretty girls of the larger towns, and he returned to New York a year or two later to marry Miss Littlemore, who, unlike her brother, had not wasted her patrimony. Her sister-in-law, married many years later, and coming to Europe on this occasion, had died in London – where she flattered herself the doctors were infallible – a week after the birth of her little girl; and poor Littlemore, though relinquishing his child for the moment, remained in these disappointing countries, to be within call of the Hampshire nursery. He was rather a noticeable man, especially since his hair and mustache had turned white. Tall and strong, with a good figure and a bad carriage, he looked capable but indolent, and was usually supposed to have an importance of which he was far from being conscious. His eye was at once keen and quiet, his smile dim and dilatory, but exceedingly genuine. His principal occupation today was doing nothing, and he did it with a sort of artistic perfection. This faculty excited real envy on the part of Rupert Waterville, who was ten years younger than he, and who had too many ambitions and anxieties – none of them very important, but making collectively a considerable incubus – to be able to wait for inspiration. He thought it a great accomplishment, he hoped some day to arrive at it; it made a man so independent; he had his resources within his own breast. Littlemore could sit for a whole evening, without utterance or movement, smoking cigars and looking absently at his finger-nails. As every one knew that he was a good fellow and had made his fortune, this dull behaviour could not well be attributed to stupidity or to moroseness. It seemed to imply a fund of reminiscence, an experience of life which had left him hundreds of things to think about. Waterville felt that if he could make a good use of these present years, and keep a sharp look-out for experience, he too, at forty-five, might have time to look at his finger-nails. He had an idea that such contemplations – not of course in their literal, but in their symbolic intensity – were a sign of a man of the world. Waterville, reckoning possibly without an ungrateful Department of State, had also an idea that he had embraced the diplomatic career. He was the junior of the two Secretaries who render the *personnel* of the United States Legation in London exceptionally numerous, and was at present enjoying his annual leave of absence. It became a diplomatist to be inscrutable, and though he had by no means, as a whole, taken Littlemore as his model – there were much better ones in the diplomatic body in London – he thought he looked inscrutable when of an evening, in Paris, after he had been asked what he would like to do, he replied that he should like to do nothing, and simply sat for an interminable time in front of the Grand Café, on the Boulevard de la Madeleine (he was very fond of cafés), ordering a succession of *demi-tasses*. It was very rarely that Littlemore cared even to go to the theatre, and the visit to the Comédie Française, which we have described, had been undertaken at Waterville's instance. He had seen *Le Demi-Monde* a few nights before, and had been told that *L'Aventurière* would show him a particular treatment of the same subject – the justice to be meted out to unscrupulous women who attempt to thrust themselves into honorable families. It seemed to him that in both of these cases the ladies had deserved their fate, but he wished it might have been brought about by a little less lying on the part of the representatives of honor. Littlemore and he, without being intimate, were very good friends, and spent much of their time together. As it turned out, Littlemore was very glad he had gone to the theatre, for he found himself much interested in this new incarnation of Nancy Beck.

2

HIS delay in going to see her was nevertheless calculated; there were more reasons for it than it is necessary to mention. But when he went, Mrs Headway was at home, and Littlemore was not surprised to see Sir Arthur Demesne in her sitting-room. There was something in the air which seemed to indicate that this gentleman's visit had already lasted a certain time. Littlemore thought it probable that, given the circumstances, he would now bring it to a close; he must have learned from their hostess that Littlemore was an old and familiar friend. He might of course have definite rights – he had every appearance of it; but the more definite they were the more gracefully he could afford to waive them. Littlemore made these reflections while Sir Arthur Demesne sat there looking at him without giving any sign of departure. Mrs Headway was very gracious – she had the manner of having known you a hundred years; she scolded Littlemore extravagantly for not having been to see her sooner, but this was only a form of the gracious. By daylight she looked a little faded; but she had an expression which could never fade. She had the best rooms in the hotel, and an air of extreme opulence and prosperity; her courier sat outside, in the ante-chamber, and she evidently knew how to live. She attempted to include Sir Arthur in the conversation, but though the young man remained in his place, he declined to be included. He smiled, in silence; but he was evidently uncomfortable. The conversation, therefore, remained superficial – a quality that, of old, had by no means belonged to Mrs Headway's interviews with her friends. The Englishman looked at Littlemore with a strange, perverse expression which Littlemore, at first, with a good deal of private amusement, simply attributed to jealousy.

'My dear Sir Arthur, I wish very much you would go,' Mrs Headway remarked, at the end of a quarter of an hour.

Sir Arthur got up and took his hat. 'I thought I should oblige you by staying.'

'To defend me against Mr Littlemore? I've known him since I was a baby – I know the worst he can do.' She fixed her charming smile for a moment on her retreating visitor, and she added, with much unexpectedness, 'I want to talk to him about my past!'

'That's just what I want to hear,' said Sir Arthur, with his hand on the door.

'We are going to talk American; you wouldn't understand us! – He speaks in the English style,' she explained, in her little sufficient way, as the baronet, who announced that at all events he would come back in the evening, let himself out.

'He doesn't know about your past?' Littlemore inquired, trying not to make the question sound impertinent.

'Oh, yes; I've told him everything; but he doesn't understand. The English are so peculiar; I think they are rather stupid. He has never heard of a woman being –' But here Mrs Headway checked herself, while Littlemore filled out the blank. 'What are you laughing at? It doesn't matter,' she went on; 'there are more things in the world than those people have heard of. However, I like them very much; at least I like him. He's such a gentleman; do you know what I mean? Only, he stays too long, and he isn't amusing. I'm very glad to see you, for a change.'

'Do you mean I'm not a gentleman?' Littlemore asked.

'No, indeed; you used to be, in New Mexico. I think you were the only one – and I hope you are still. That's why I recognized you the other night; I might have cut you, you know.'

'You can still, if you like. It's not too late.'

'Oh, no; that's not what I want. I want you to help me.'

'To help you?'

Mrs Headway fixed her eyes for a moment on the door. 'Do you suppose that man is there still?'

'That young man – your poor Englishman?'

'No; I mean Max. Max is my courier,' said Mrs Headway, with a certain impressiveness.

'I haven't the least idea. I'll see, if you like.'

'No; in that case I should have to give him an order, and I don't know what in the world to ask him to do. He sits there for hours; with my simple habits I afford him no employment. I am afraid I have no imagination.'

'The burden of grandeur,' said Littlemore.

'Oh yes, I'm very grand. But on the whole I like it. I'm only afraid he'll hear. I talk so very loud; that's another thing I'm trying to get over.'

'Why do you want to be different?'

'Well, because everything else is different,' Mrs Headway rejoined, with a little sigh. 'Did you hear that I'd lost my husband?' she went on, abruptly.

'Do you mean – a – Mr –?' and Littlemore paused, with an effect that did not seem to come home to her.

'I mean Mr Headway,' she said, with dignity. 'I've been through a good deal since you saw me last: marriage, and death, and trouble, and all sorts of things.'

'You had been through a good deal of marriage before that,' Littlemore ventured to observe.

She rested her eyes on him with soft brightness, and without a change of color. 'Not so much – not so much –'

'Not so much as might have been thought.'

'Not so much as was reported. I forget whether I was married when I saw you last.'

'It was one of the reports,' said Littlemore. 'But I never saw Mr Beck.'

'You didn't lose much; he was a simple *wretch!* I have done certain things in my life which I have never understood; no wonder others can't understand them. But that's all over! Are you sure Max doesn't hear?' she asked, quickly.

'Not at all sure. But if you suspect him of listening at the keyhole, I would send him away.'

'I don't think he does that. I am always rushing to the door.'

'Then he doesn't hear. I had no idea you had so many secrets. When I parted with you, Mr Headway was in the future.'

'Well, now he's in the past. He was a pleasant man – I can understand my doing that. But he only lived a year. He had neuralgia of the heart; he left me very well off.' She mentioned these various facts as if they were quite of the same order.

'I'm glad to hear it; you used to have expensive tastes.'

'I have plenty of money,' said Mrs Headway. 'Mr Headway had property at Denver, which has increased immensely in value. After his death I tried New York. But I don't like New York.' Littlemore's hostess uttered this last sentence in a tone which was the *résumé* of a social episode. 'I mean to live in Europe – I like Europe,' she announced; and the manner of the announcement had a touch of prophecy, as the other words had had a reverberation of history.

Littlemore was very much struck with all this, and he was greatly entertained with Mrs Headway. 'Are you travelling with that young man?' he inquired, with the coolness of a person who wishes to make his entertainment go as far as possible.

She folded her arms as she leaned back in her chair. 'Look here, Mr Littlemore,' she said. 'I'm about as good-natured as I used to be in America, but I know a great deal more. Of course I ain't travelling with that young man; he's only a friend.'

'He isn't a lover?' asked Littlemore, rather cruelly.

'Do people travel with their lovers? I don't want you to laugh at me – I want you to help me.' She fixed her eyes on him with an air of tender remonstrance that might have touched him; she looked so gentle and reasonable. 'As I tell you, I have taken a great fancy to this old Europe; I feel as if I should never go back. But I want to see something of the life. I think it would suit me – if I could get started a little. Mr Littlemore,' she added, in a moment – 'I may as well be frank, for I ain't at all ashamed. I want to get into society. That's what I'm after!'

Littlemore settled himself in his chair, with the feeling of a man who, knowing that he will have to pull, seeks to obtain a certain leverage. It was in a tone of light jocosity, almost of encouragement, however, that he repeated: 'Into society? It seems to me you are in it already, with baronets for your adorers.'

'That's just what I want to know!' she said, with a certain eagerness. 'Is a baronet much?'

'So they are apt to think. But I know very little about it.'

'Ain't you in society yourself?'

'I? Never in the world! Where did you get that idea? I care no more about society than about that copy of the *Figaro*.'

Mrs Headway's countenance assumed for a moment a look of extreme disappointment, and Littlemore could see that, having heard of his silver-mine and his cattle-ranch, and knowing that he was living in Europe, she had hoped to find him immersed in the world of fashion. But she speedily recovered herself. 'I don't believe a word of it. You know you're a gentleman – you can't help yourself.'

'I may be a gentleman, but I have none of the habits of one.' Littlemore hesitated a moment, and then he added – 'I lived too long in the great Southwest.'

She flushed quickly; she instantly understood – understood even more than he had meant to say. But she wished to make use of him, and it was of more importance that she should appear forgiving – especially as she had the happy consciousness of being so, than that she should punish a cruel speech. She could afford, however, to be lightly ironical. 'That makes no difference – a gentleman is always a gentleman.'

'Not always,' said Littlemore, laughing.

'It's impossible that, through your sister, you shouldn't know something about European society,' said Mrs Headway.

At the mention of his sister, made with a studied lightness of reference which he caught as it passed, Littlemore was unable to repress a start. 'What in the world have you got to do with my sister?' he would have liked to say. The introduction of this lady was disagreeable to him; she belonged to quite another order of ideas, and it was out of the question that Mrs Headway should ever make her acquaintance – if this was what, as that lady would have said – she was 'after'. But he took advantage of a side-issue. 'What do you mean by European society? One can't talk about that. It's a very vague phrase.'

'Well, I mean English society – I mean the society your sister lives in – that's what I mean,' said Mrs Headway, who was quite prepared to be definite. 'I mean the people I saw in London last May – the people I saw at the opera and in the park, the people who go to the Queen's drawing-rooms. When I was in London I stayed at that hotel on the corner of Piccadilly – that looking straight down St James's Street – and I spent hours together at the window looking at the people in the carriages. I had a carriage of my own, and when I was not at my window I was driving all round. I was all alone; I saw every one, but I knew no one – I had no one to tell me. I didn't know Sir Arthur then – I only met him a month ago at Homburg. He followed me to Paris – that's how he came to be my guest.' Serenely, prosaically, without any of the inflation of vanity, Mrs Headway made this last assertion; it was as if she were used to being followed, or as if a gentleman one met at Homburg would inevitably follow. In the same tone she went on: 'I attracted a good deal of attention in London – I could easily see that.'

'You'll do that wherever you go,' Littlemore said, insufficiently enough, as he felt.

'I don't want to attract so much; I think it's vulgar,' Mrs Headway rejoined, with a certain soft sweetness which seemed to denote the enjoyment of a new idea. She was evidently open to new ideas.

'Every one was looking at you the other night at the theatre,' Littlemore continued. 'How can you hope to escape notice?'

'I don't want to escape notice – people have always looked

at me, and I suppose they always will. But there are different ways of being looked at, and I know the way I want. I mean to have it, too!' Mrs Headway exclaimed. Yes, she was very definite.

Littlemore sat there, face to face with her, and for some time he said nothing. He had a mixture of feelings, and the memory of other places, other hours, was stealing over him. There had been of old a very considerable absence of interposing surfaces between these two – he had known her as one knew people only in the great Southwest. He had liked her extremely, in a town where it would have been ridiculous to be difficult to please. But his sense of this fact was somehow connected with Southwestern conditions; his liking for Nancy Beck was an emotion of which the proper setting was a back piazza. She presented herself here on a new basis – she appeared to desire to be classified afresh. Littlemore said to himself that this was too much trouble; he had taken her in that way – he couldn't begin at this time of day to take her in another way. He asked himself whether she were going to be a bore. It was not easy to suppose Mrs Headway capable of this offence; but she might become tiresome if she were bent upon being different. It made him rather afraid when she began to talk about European society, about his sister, about things being vulgar. Littlemore was a very good fellow, and he had at least the average human love of justice; but there was in his composition an element of the indolent, the sceptical, perhaps even the brutal, which made him desire to preserve the simplicity of their former terms of intercourse. He had no particular desire to see a woman rise again, as the mystic process was called; he didn't believe in women's rising again. He believed in their not going down; thought it perfectly possible and eminently desirable, but held it was much better for society that they should not endeavor, as the French say, to *mêler les genres*. In general, he didn't pretend to say what was good for society – society seemed to him in rather a bad way; but he had a conviction on this particular point. Nancy Beck going in for the great prizes, that spectacle might be entertaining for a simple spectator; but it would be a nuisance, an embarrassment, from the moment anything more than contemplation should be expected of him. He had no wish to be rough, but it might be well to show her that he was not to be humbugged.

'Oh, if there's anything you want you'll have it,' he said in answer to her last remark. 'You have always had what you want.'

'Well, I want something new this time. Does your sister reside in London?'

'My dear lady, what do you know about my sister?' Littlemore asked. 'She's not a woman you would care for.'

Mrs Headway was silent a moment. 'You don't respect me!' she exclaimed suddenly in a loud, almost gay tone of voice. If Littlemore wished, as I say, to preserve the simplicity of their old terms of intercourse, she was apparently willing to humor him.

'Ah, my dear Mrs Beck ...!' he cried, vaguely, protestingly, and using her former name quite by accident. At San Diego he had never thought whether he respected her or not; that never came up.

'That's a proof of it – calling me by that hateful name! Don't you believe I'm married? I haven't been fortunate in my names,' she added, pensively.

'You make it very awkward when you say such mad things. My sister lives most of the year in the country; she is very simple, rather dull, perhaps a trifle narrow-minded. You are very clever, very lively, and as wide as all creation. That's why I think you wouldn't like her.'

'You ought to be ashamed to run down your sister!' cried Mrs Headway. 'You told me once – at San Diego – that she was the nicest woman you knew. I made a note of that, you see. And you told me she was just my age. So that makes it rather uncomfortable for you, if you won't introduce me!' And Littlemore's hostess gave a pitiless laugh. 'I'm not in the least afraid of her being dull. It's very distinguished to be dull. I'm ever so much too lively.'

'You are indeed, ever so much! But nothing is more easy than to know my sister,' said Littlemore, who knew perfectly that what he said was untrue. And then, as a diversion from this delicate topic, he suddenly asked, 'Are you going to marry Sir Arthur?'

'Don't you think I've been married about enough?'

'Possibly; but this is a new line, it would be different. An Englishman – that's a new sensation.'

'If I should marry, it would be a European,' said Mrs Headway calmly.

'Your chance is very good; they are all marrying Americans.'

'He would have to be some one fine, the man I should marry now. I have a good deal to make up for! That's what I want to know about Sir Arthur; all this time you haven't told me.'

'I have nothing in the world to tell – I have never heard of him. Hasn't he told you himself?'

'Nothing at all; he is very modest. He doesn't brag, nor make himself out anything great. That's what I like him for: I think it's in such good taste. I like good taste!' exclaimed Mrs Headway. 'But all this time,' she added, 'you haven't told me you would help me.'

'How can I help you? I'm no one, I have no power.'

'You can help me by not preventing me. I want you to promise not to prevent me.' She gave him her fixed, bright gaze again; her eyes seemed to look far into his.

'Good Lord, how could I prevent you?'

'I'm not sure that you could. But you might try.'

'I'm too indolent, and too stupid,' said Littlemore jocosely.

'Yes,' she replied, musing as she still looked at him. 'I think you are too stupid. But I think you are also too kind,' she added more graciously. She was almost irresistible when she said such a thing as that.

They talked for a quarter of an hour longer, and at last – as if she had had scruples – she spoke to him of his own marriage, of the death of his wife, matters to which she alluded more felicitously (as he thought) than to some other points. 'If you have a little girl you ought to be very happy; that's what I should like to have. Lord, I should make her a nice woman! Not like me – in another style!' When he rose to leave her, she told him that he must come and see her very often; she was to be some weeks longer in Paris; he must bring Mr Waterville.

'Your English friend won't like that – our coming very often,' Littlemore said, as he stood with his hand on the door.

'I don't know what he has got to do with it,' she answered, staring.

'Neither do I. Only he must be in love with you.'

'That doesn't give him any right. Mercy, if I had had to put myself out for all the men that have been in love with me!'

'Of course you would have had a terrible life! Even doing as you please, you have had rather an agitated one. But your young Englishman's sentiments appear to give him the right to sit there, after one comes in, looking blighted and bored. That might become very tiresome.'

'The moment he becomes tiresome I send him away. You can trust me for that.'

'Oh,' said Littlemore, 'it doesn't matter, after all.' He remembered that it would be very inconvenient to him to have undisturbed possession of Mrs Headway.

She came out with him into the antechamber. Mr Max, the courier, was fortunately not there. She lingered a little; she appeared to have more to say.

'On the contrary, he likes you to come,' she remarked in a moment; 'he wants to study my friends.'

'To study them?'

'He wants to find out about me, and he thinks they may tell him something. Some day he will ask you right out, "What sort of a woman is she, any way?"'

'Hasn't he found out yet?'

'He doesn't understand me,' said Mrs Headway, surveying the front of her dress. 'He has never seen any one like me.'

'I should imagine not!'

'So he will ask you, as I say.'

'I will tell him you are the most charming woman in Europe.'

'That ain't a description! Besides, he knows it. He wants to know if I'm respectable.'

'He's very curious!' Littlemore cried, with a laugh.

She grew a little pale; she seemed to be watching his lips. 'Mind you tell him,' she went on with a smile that brought none of her color back.

'Respectable? I'll tell him you're adorable!'

Mrs Headway stood a moment longer. 'Ah, you're no use!' she murmured. And she suddenly turned away and passed back into her sitting-room, slowly drawing her far-trailing skirts.

3

'*Elle ne se doute de rien!*' Littlemore said to himself as he walked away from the hotel; and he repeated the phrase in talking about her to Waterville. 'She wants to be right,' he added; 'but she will never really succeed; she has begun too late, she will never be more than half-right. However, she won't know when she's wrong, so it doesn't signify!' And then he proceeded to assert that in some respects she would remain incurable; she had no delicacy; no discretion, no shading; she was a woman who suddenly said to you, 'You don't respect me!' As if that were a thing for a woman to say!

'It depends upon what she meant by it.' Waterville liked to see the meanings of things.

'The more she meant by it the less she ought to say it!' Littlemore declared.

But he returned to the Hôtel Meurice, and on the next occasion he took Waterville with him. The Secretary of Legation, who had not often been in close quarters with a lady of this ambiguous quality, was prepared to regard Mrs Headway as a very curious type. He was afraid she might be dangerous; but, on the whole, he felt secure. The object of his devotion at present was his country, or at least the Department of State; he had no intention of being diverted from that allegiance. Besides, he had his ideal of the attractive woman – a person pitched in a very much lower key than this shining, smiling, rustling, chattering daughter of the Territories. The woman he should care for would have repose, a certain love of privacy – she would sometimes let one alone. Mrs Headway was personal, familiar, intimate; she was always appealing or accusing, demanding explanations and pledges, saying things one had to answer. All this was accompanied with a hundred smiles and radiations and other natural graces, but the general effect of it was slightly fatiguing. She had certainly a great deal of charm, an immense desire to please, and a wonderful collection of dresses and trinkets; but she was eager and preoccupied, and it was impossible that other people should share her eagerness. If she wished to get into society, there was no reason why her bachelor visitors should wish to see her there; for it was the absence of the usual social incumbrances which made her drawing-room attractive. There was no doubt whatever that she was several women in one, and she ought to content herself with that sort of numerical triumph. Littlemore said to Waterville that it was stupid of her to wish to scale the heights; she ought to know how much more she was in her place down below. She appeared vaguely to irritate him; even her fluttering attempts at self-culture – she had become a great critic, and handled many of the productions of the age with a bold, free touch – constituted a vague invocation, an appeal for sympathy which was naturally annoying to a man who disliked the trouble of revising old decisions, consecrated by a certain amount of reminiscence that might be called tender. She had, however, one palpable charm; she was full of surprises. Even Waterville was obliged to confess that an element of the unexpected was not to be excluded from his conception of the woman who should have an ideal repose. Of course there were two kinds of surprises, and only one of them was thoroughly pleasant, though Mrs Headway dealt impartially in both. She had the sudden delights, the odd exclamations, the queer curiosities of a person who has grown up in a country where everything is new and many things ugly, and who, with a natural turn for the arts and amenities of life, makes a tardy acquaintance with some of the finer usages, the higher pleasures. She was provincial – it was easy to see that she was provincial; that took no great cleverness. But what was Parisian enough – if to be Parisian was the measure of success – was the way she picked up ideas and took a hint from every circumstance. 'Only give me time, and I shall know all I have need of,' she said to Littlemore, who watched her progress with a mixture of admiration and sadness. She delighted to speak of herself as a poor little barbarian who was trying to pick up a few crumbs of knowledge, and this habit took great effect from her delicate face, her perfect dress and the brilliancy of her manners.

One of her surprises was that after that first visit she said no more to Littlemore about Mrs Dolphin. He did her perhaps the grossest injustice; but he had quite expected her to bring up this lady whenever they met. 'If she will only leave Agnes alone, she may do what she will,' he said to Waterville, expressing his relief. 'My sister would never look at her, and it would be very awkward to have to tell her so.' She expected assistance; she made him feel that simply by the way she looked at him; but for the moment she demanded no definite service. She held her tongue, but she waited, and her patience itself was a kind of admonition. In the way of society, it must be confessed, her privileges were meagre, Sir Arthur Demesne and her two compatriots being, so far as the latter could discover, her only visitors. She might have had other friends, but she held her head very high, and liked better to see no one than not to see the best company. It was evident that she flattered herself that she produced the effect of being, not neglected, but fastidious. There were plenty of Americans in Paris, but in this direction she failed to extend her acquaintance; the nice people wouldn't come and see her, and nothing would have induced her to receive the others. She had the most exact conception of the people she wished to see and to avoid. Littlemore expected every day that she would ask him why he didn't bring some of his friends, and he had his answer ready. It was a very poor one, for it consisted simply of a conventional assurance that he wished to keep her for himself. She would be sure to retort that this was very 'thin', as, indeed, it was; but the days went by without her calling him to account. The little American colony in Paris is rich in amiable women, but there were none to whom Littlemore could make up his mind to say that it would be a favor to him to call on Mrs Headway. He shouldn't like them the better for doing so, and he wished to like those of whom he might ask a favor. Except, therefore, that he occasionally spoke of her as a little Western woman, very pretty and rather queer, who had formerly been a great chum of his, she remained unknown in the *salons* of the Avenue Gabriel and the streets that encircle the Arch of Triumph. To ask the men to go and see her, without asking the ladies, would only accentuate the fact that he didn't ask the ladies; so he asked no one at all. Besides, it was true – just a little – that he wished to keep her to himself, and he was fatuous enough to believe that she cared much more for him than for her Englishman. Of course, however, he would never dream of marrying her, whereas the Englishman apparently was immersed in that vision. She hated her past; she used to announce that very often, talking of it as if it were an appendage of the same order as a dishonest courier, or even an inconvenient protrusion of drapery. Therefore, as Littlemore was part of her past, it might have been supposed that she would hate him too, and wish to banish him, with all the images he recalled, from her sight. But she made an exception in his favor, and if she disliked their old relations as a chapter of her own history, she seemed still to like them as a chapter of his. He felt that she clung to him, that she believed he could help her and in the long run would. It was to the long run that she appeared little by little to have attuned herself.

She succeeded perfectly in maintaining harmony between Sir Arthur Demesne and her American visitors, who spent much less time in her drawing-room. She had easily persuaded him that there were no grounds for jealousy, and that they had no wish, as she said, to crowd him out; for it was ridiculous to be jealous of two persons at once, and Rupert Waterville, after he had learned the way to her hospitable apartment, appeared there as often as his friend Littlemore. The two, indeed, usually came together, and they ended by relieving their competitor of a certain sense of responsibility. This amiable and excellent but somewhat limited and slightly pretentious young man, who had not yet made up his mind, was sometimes rather oppressed with the magnitude of his undertaking, and when he was alone with Mrs Headway the tension of his thoughts occasionally became quite painful. He was very slim and straight, and looked taller than his height; he had the prettiest, silkiest hair, which waved away from a large white forehead, and he was endowed with a nose of the so-called Roman model. He looked younger than his years (in spite of those last two attributes), partly on account of the delicacy of his complexion and the almost childlike candor of his round blue eye. He was diffident and self-conscious; there were certain letters he could not pronounce. At the same time he had the manners of a young man who had been brought up to fill a considerable place in the world, with whom a certain correctness had become a habit, and who, though he might occasionally be a little awkward about small things, would be sure to acquit himself honorably in great ones. He was very simple, and he believed himself very serious; he had the blood of a score of Warwickshire squires in his veins; mingled in the last instance with the somewhat paler fluid which animated the long-necked daughter of a banker who had expected an earl for his son-in-law, but who had consented to regard Sir Baldwin Demesne as the least insufficient of baronets. The boy, the only one, had come into his title at five years of age; his mother, who disappointed her auriferous sire a second time when poor Sir Baldwin broke his neck in the hunting field, watched over him with a tenderness that burned as steadily as a candle shaded by a transparent hand. She never admitted, even to herself, that he was not the cleverest of men; but it took all her own cleverness, which was much greater than his, to maintain this appearance. Fortunately he was not wild, so that he would never marry an actress or a governess, like two or three of the young men who had been at Eton with him. With this ground of nervousness the less, Lady Demesne awaited with an air of confidence his promotion to some high office. He represented in Parliament the Conservative instincts and vote of a red-roofed market town, and sent regularly to his bookseller for all the new publications on economical subjects, for he was determined that his political attitude should have a firm statistical basis. He was not conceited; he was only misinformed – misinformed, I mean, about himself. He thought himself indispensable in the scheme of things – not as an individual, but as an institution. This conviction, however, was too sacred to betray itself by vulgar assumptions. If he was a little man in a big place, he never strutted nor talked loud; he merely felt it as a kind of luxury that he had a large social circumference. It was like sleeping in a big bed; one didn't toss about the more, but one felt a greater freshness.

He had never seen anything like Mrs Headway; he hardly knew by what standard to measure her. She was not like an English lady – not like those at least with whom he had been accustomed to converse; and yet it was impossible not to see that she had a standard of her own. He suspected that she was provincial, but as he was very much under the charm he compromised matters by saying to himself that she was only foreign. It was of course provincial to be foreign; but this was, after all, a peculiarity which she shared with a great many nice people. He was not wild, and his mother had flattered herself that in this all-important matter he would not be perverse; but it was all the same most unexpected that he should have taken a fancy to an American widow, five years older than himself, who knew no one and who sometimes didn't appear to understand exactly who he was. Though he disapproved of it, it was precisely her foreignness that pleased him; she seemed to be as little as possible of his own race and creed; there was not a touch of Warwickshire in her composition. She was like an Hungarian or a Pole, with the difference that he could almost understand her language. The unfortunate young man was fascinated, though he had not yet admitted to himself that he was in love. He would be very slow and deliberate in such a position, for he was deeply conscious of its importance. He was a young man who had arranged his life; he had determined to marry at thirty-two. A long line of ancestors was watching him; he hardly knew what they would think of Mrs Headway. He hardly knew what he thought himself; the only thing he was absolutely sure of was that she made the time pass as it passed in no other pursuit. He was vaguely uneasy; he was by no means sure it was right the time should pass like that. There was nothing to show for it but the fragments of Mrs Headway's conversation, the peculiarities of her accent, the sallies of her wit, the audacities of her fancy, her mysterious allusions to her past. Of course he knew that she had a past; she was not a young girl, she was a widow – and widows are essentially an expression of an accomplished fact. He was not jealous of her antecedents, but he wished to understand them, and it was here that the difficulty occurred. The subject was illumined with fitful flashes, but it never placed itself before him as a general picture. He asked her a good many questions, but her answers were so startling that, like sudden luminous points, they seemed to intensify the darkness round their edges. She had apparently spent her life in an inferior province of an inferior country; but it didn't follow from this that she herself had been low. She had been a lily among thistles; and there was something romantic in a man in his position taking an interest in such a woman. It pleased Sir Arthur to believe he was romantic; that had been the case with several of his ancestors, who supplied a precedent without which he would perhaps not have ventured to trust himself. He was the victim of perplexities from which a single spark of direct perception would have saved him. He took everything in the literal sense; he had not a grain of humor. He sat there vaguely waiting for something to happen, and not committing himself by rash declarations. If he was in love, it was in his own way, reflectively, inexpressively, obstinately. He was waiting for the formula which would justify his conduct and Mrs Headway's peculiarities. He hardly knew where it would come from; you might have thought from his manner that he would discover it in one of the elaborate *entrées* that were served to the pair when Mrs Headway consented to dine with him at Bignon's or the Café Anglais; or in one of the numerous bandboxes that arrived from the Rue de la Paix, and from which she often lifted the lid in the presence of her admirer. There were moments when he got weary of waiting in vain, and at these moments the arrival of her American friends (he often wondered that she had so few), seemed to lift the mystery from his shoulders and give him a chance to rest. This formula – she herself was not yet able to give it, for she was not aware how much ground it was expected to cover. She talked about her past, because she thought it the best thing to do; she had a shrewd conviction that it was better to make a good use of it than to attempt to efface it. To efface it was impossible, though that was what she would have preferred. She had no objection to telling fibs, but now that she was taking a new departure, she wished to tell only those that were necessary. She would have been delighted if it had been possible to tell none at all. A few, however, were indispensable, and we need not attempt to estimate more closely the ingenious rearrangements of fact with which she entertained and mystified Sir Arthur. She knew of course that as a product of fashionable circles she was nowhere, but she might have great success as a child of nature.

4

RUPERT WATERVILLE, in the midst of intercourse in which every one perhaps had a good many mental reservations, never forgot that he was in a representative position, that he was responsible, official; and he asked himself more than once how far it was permitted to him to countenance Mrs Headway's pretensions to being an American lady typical even of the newer phases. In his own way he was as puzzled as poor Sir Arthur, and indeed he flattered himself that he was as particular as any Englishman could be. Suppose that after all this free association Mrs Headway should come over to London and ask at the Legation to be presented to the Queen? It would be so awkward to refuse her – of course they would have to refuse her – that he was very careful about making tacit promises. She might construe anything as a tacit promise – he knew how the smallest gestures of diplomatists were studied and interpreted. It was his effort therefore to be really the diplomatist in his relations with this attractive but dangerous woman. The party of four used often to dine together – Sir Arthur pushed his confidence so far – and on these occasions Mrs Headway, availing herself of one of the privileges of a lady, even at the most expensive restaurant – used to wipe her glasses with her napkin. One evening, when after polishing a goblet she held it up to the light, giving it, with her head on one side, the least glimmer of a wink, he said to himself as he watched her that she looked like a modern bacchante. He noticed at this moment that the baronet was gazing at her too, and he wondered if the same idea had come to him. He often wondered what the baronet thought; he had devoted first and last a good deal of speculation to the baronial class. Littlemore, alone, at this moment, was not observing Mrs Headway; he never appeared to observe her, though she often observed him. Waterville asked himself among other things why Sir Arthur had not brought his own friends to see her, for Paris during the several weeks that now elapsed was rich in English visitors. He wondered whether she had asked him and he had refused; he would have liked very much to know whether she had asked him. He explained his curiosity to Littlemore, who, however, took very little interest in it. Littlemore said, nevertheless, that he had no doubt she had asked him; she never would be deterred by false delicacy.

'She has been very delicate with you,' Waterville replied. 'She hasn't been at all pressing of late.'

'It is only because she has given me up; she thinks I'm a brute.'

'I wonder what she thinks of me,' Waterville said, pensively.

'Oh, she counts upon you to introduce her to the Minister. It's lucky for you that our representative here is absent.'

'Well,' Waterville rejoined, 'the Minister has settled two or three difficult questions, and I suppose he can settle this one. I shall do nothing but by the orders of my chief.' He was very fond of talking about his chief.

'She does me injustice,' Littlemore added in a moment. 'I have spoken to several people about her.'

'Ah; but what have you told them?'

'That she lives at the Hôtel Meurice; and that she wants to know nice people.'

'They are flattered, I suppose, at your thinking them nice, but they don't go,' said Waterville.

'I spoke of her to Mrs Bagshaw, and Mrs Bagshaw has promised to go.'

'Ah,' Waterville murmured; 'you don't call Mrs Bagshaw nice? Mrs Headway won't see her.'

'That's exactly what she wants, – to be able to cut some one!'

Waterville had a theory that Sir Arthur was keeping Mrs Headway as a surprise – he meant perhaps to produce her during the next London season. He presently, however, learned as much about the matter as he could have desired to know. He had once offered to accompany his beautiful compatriot to the Museum of the Luxembourg and tell her a little about the modern French school. She had not examined this collection, in spite of her determination to see everything remarkable (she carried her *Murray* in her lap even when she went to see the great tailor in the Rue de la Paix, to whom, as she said, she had given no end of points); for she usually went to such places with Sir Arthur, and Sir Arthur was indifferent to the modern painters of France. 'He says there are much better men in England. I must wait for the Royal Academy, next year. He seems to think one can wait for anything, but I'm not so good at waiting as he. I can't afford to wait – I've waited long enough.' So much as this Mrs Headway said on the occasion of her arranging with Rupert Waterville that they should some day visit the Luxembourg together. She alluded to the Englishman as if he were her husband or her brother, her natural protector and companion.

'I wonder if she knows how that sounds?' Waterville said to himself. 'I don't believe she would do it if she knew how it sounds.' And he made the further reflection that when one arrived from San Diego there was no end to the things one had to learn: it took so many things to make a well-bred woman. Clever as she was, Mrs Headway was right in saying that she couldn't afford to wait. She must learn quickly. She wrote to Waterville one day to propose that they should go to the Museum on the morrow; Sir Arthur's mother was in Paris, on her way to Cannes, where she was to spend the winter. She was only passing through, but she would be there three days and he would naturally give himself up to her. She appeared to have the properest ideas as to what a gentleman would propose to do for his mother. She herself, therefore, would be free, and she named the hour at which she should expect him to call for her. He was punctual to the appointment, and they drove across the river in the large high-hung barouche in which she constantly rolled about Paris. With Mr Max on the box – the courier was ornamented with enormous whiskers – this vehicle had an appearance of great respectability, though Sir Arthur assured her – she repeated this to her other friends – that in London, next year, they would do the thing much better for her. It struck her other friends of course that the baronet was prepared to be very consistent, and this on the whole was what Waterville would have expected of him. Littlemore simply remarked that at San Diego she drove herself about in a rickety buggy, with muddy wheels, and with a mule very often in the shafts. Waterville felt something like excitement as he asked himself whether the baronet's mother would now consent to know her. She must of course be aware that it was a woman who was keeping her son in Paris at a season when English gentlemen were most naturally employed in shooting partridges.

'She is staying at the Hôtel du Rhin, and I have made him feel that he mustn't leave her while she is here,' Mrs Headway said, as they drove up the narrow Rue de Seine. 'Her name is Lady Demesne, but her full title is the Honorable Lady Demesne, as she's a Baron's daughter. Her father used to be a banker, but he did something or other for the Government – the Tories, you know, they call them – and so he was raised to the peerage. So you see one *can* be raised! She has a lady with her as a companion.' Waterville's neighbor gave him this information with a seriousness that made him smile; he wondered whether she thought he didn't know how a Baron's daughter was addressed. In that she was very provincial; she had a way of exaggerating the value of her intellectual acquisitions and of assuming that others had been as ignorant as she. He noted, too, that she had ended by suppressing poor Sir Arthur's name altogether, and designating him only by a sort of conjugal pronoun. She had been so much, and so easily, married, that she was full of these misleading references to gentlemen.

5

THEY walked through the gallery of the Luxembourg, and except that Mrs Headway looked at everything at once and at nothing long enough, talked, as usual, rather too loud, and bestowed too much attention on the bad copies that were being made of several indifferent pictures, she was a very agreeable companion and a grateful recipient of knowledge. She was very quick to understand, and Waterville was sure that before she left the gallery she knew something about the French school. She was quite prepared to compare it critically with London exhibitions of the following year. As Littlemore and he had remarked more than once, she was a very odd mixture. Her conversation, her personality, were full of little joints and seams, all of them very visible, where the old and the new had been pieced together. When they had passed through the different rooms of the palace Mrs Headway proposed that instead of returning directly they should take a stroll in the adjoining gardens, which she wished very much to see and was sure she should like. She had quite seized the difference between the old Paris and the new, and felt the force of the romantic associations of the Latin quarter as perfectly as if she had enjoyed all the benefits of modern culture. The autumn sun was warm in the alleys and terraces of the Luxembourg; the masses of foliage above them, clipped and squared, rusty with ruddy patches, shed a thick lacework over the white sky, which was streaked with the palest blue. The beds of flowers near the palace were of the vividest yellow and red, and the sunlight rested on the smooth gray walls of those parts of its basement that looked south; in front of which, on the long green benches, a row of brown-cheeked nurses, in white caps and aprons, sat offering nutrition to as many bundles of white drapery. There were other white caps wandering in the broad paths, attended by little brown French children; the small, straw-seated chairs were piled and stacked in some places and disseminated in others. An old lady in black, with white hair fastened over each of her temples by a large black comb, sat on the edge of a stone bench (too high for her delicate length), motionless, staring straight before her and holding a large door-key; under a tree a priest was reading – you could see his lips move at a distance; a young soldier, dwarfish and red-legged, strolled past with his hands in his pockets, which were very much distended. Waterville sat down with Mrs Headway on the straw-bottomed chairs, and she presently said, 'I like this; it's even better than the pictures in the gallery. It's more of a picture.'

'Everything in France is a picture – even things that are ugly,' Waterville replied. 'Everything makes a subject.'

'Well, I like France!' Mrs Headway went on, with a little incongruous sigh. Then, suddenly, from an impulse even more inconsequent than her sigh, she added, 'He asked me to go and see her, but I told him I wouldn't. She may come and see me if she likes.' This was so abrupt that Waterville was slightly confounded; but he speedily perceived that she had returned by a short cut to Sir Arthur Demesne and his honorable mother. Waterville liked to know about other people's affairs, but he did not like this taste to be imputed to him; and therefore, though he was curious to see how the old lady, as he called her, would treat his companion, he was rather displeased with the latter for being so confidential. He had never imagined he was so intimate with her as that. Mrs Headway, however, had a manner of taking intimacy for granted; a manner which Sir Arthur's mother at least would be sure not to like. He pretended to wonder a little what she was talking about, but she scarcely explained. She only went on, through untraceable transitions: 'The least she can do is to come. I have been very kind to her son. That's not a reason for my going to her – it's a reason for her coming to me. Besides, if she doesn't like what I've done, she can leave me alone. I want to get into European society, but I want to get in in my own way. I don't want to run after people; I want them to run after me. I guess they will, some day!' Waterville listened to this with his eyes on the ground; he felt himself blushing a little. There was something in Mrs Headway that shocked and mortified him, and Littlemore had been right in saying that she had a deficiency of shading. She was terribly distinct; her motives, her impulses, her desires were absolutely glaring. She needed to see, to hear, her own thoughts. Vehement thought, with Mrs Headway, was inevitably speech, though speech was not always thought, and now she had suddenly become vehement. 'If she does once come then, ah, then, I shall be too perfect with her; I sha'n't let her go! But she must take the first step. I confess, I hope she'll be nice.'

'Perhaps she won't,' said Waterville perversely.

'Well, I don't care if she isn't. He has never told me anything about her; never a word about any of his own belongings. If I wished, I might believe he's ashamed of them.'

'I don't think it's that.'

'I know it isn't. I know what it is. It's just modesty. He doesn't want to brag – he's too much of a gentleman. He doesn't want to dazzle me – he wants me to like him for himself. Well, I do like him,' she added in a moment. 'But I shall like him still better if he brings his mother. They shall know that in America.'

'Do you think it will make an impression in America?' Waterville asked, smiling.

'It will show them that I am visited by the British aristocracy. They won't like that.'

'Surely they grudge you no innocent pleasure,' Waterville murmured, smiling still.

'They grudge me common politeness – when I was in New York! Did you ever hear how they treated me, when I came on from the West?'

Waterville stared; this episode was quite new to him. His companion had turned towards him; her pretty head was tossed back like a flower in the wind; there was a flush in her cheek, a sharper light in her eye. 'Ah! my dear New Yorkers, they're incapable of rudeness!' cried the young man.

'You're one of them, I see. But I don't speak of the men. The men were well enough – though they did allow it.'

'Allow what, Mrs Headway?' Waterville was quite in the dark.

She wouldn't answer at once; her eyes, glittering a little, were fixed upon absent images. 'What did you hear about me over there? Don't pretend you heard nothing.'

He had heard nothing at all; there had not been a word about Mrs Headway in New York. He couldn't pretend, and he was obliged to tell her this. 'But I have been away,' he added, 'and in America I didn't go out. There's nothing to go out for in New York – only little boys and girls.'

'There are plenty of old women! They decided I was improper. I'm very well known in the West – I'm known from Chicago to San Francisco – if not personally (in all cases), at least by reputation. People can tell you out there. In New York they decided I wasn't good enough. Not good enough for New York! What do you say to that?' And she gave a sweet little laugh. Whether she had struggled with her pride before making this avowal, Waterville never knew. The crudity of the avowal seemed to indicate that she had no pride, and yet there was a spot in her heart which, as he now perceived, was intensely sore and had suddenly begun to throb. 'I took a house for the winter – one of the handsomest houses in the place – but I sat there all alone. They didn't think me proper. Such as you see me here, I wasn't a success! I tell you the truth, at whatever cost. Not a decent woman came to see me!'

Waterville was embarrassed; diplomatist as he was, he hardly knew what line to take. He could not see what need there was of her telling him the truth, though the incident appeared to have been most curious, and he was glad to know the facts on the best authority. It was the first he knew of this remarkable woman's having spent a winter in his native city – which was virtually a proof of her having come and gone in complete obscurity. It was vain for him to pretend that he had been a good deal away, for he had been appointed to his post in London only six months before, and Mrs Headway's social failure preceded that event. In the midst of these reflections he had an inspiration. He attempted neither to explain, to minimize, nor to apologize; he ventured simply to lay his hand for an instant on her own and to explain, as tenderly as possible, 'I wish *I* had known you were there!'

'I had plenty of men – but men don't count. If they are not a positive help, they're a hindrance, and the more you have, the worse it looks. The women simply turned their backs.'

'They were afraid of you – they were jealous,' Waterville said.

'It's very good of you to try and explain it away; all I know is, not one of them crossed my threshold. You needn't try and tone it down; I know perfectly how the case stands. In New York, if you please, I was a failure!'

'So much the worse for New York!' cried Waterville, who, as he afterwards said to Littlemore, had got quite worked up.

'And now you know why I want to get into society over here?' She jumped up and stood before him; with a dry, hard smile she looked down at him. Her smile itself was an answer to her question; it expressed an urgent desire for revenge. There was an abruptness in her movements which left Waterville quite behind; but as he still sat there, returning her glance, he felt that he at last, in the light of that smile, the flash of that almost fierce question, understood Mrs Headway.

She turned away, to walk to the gate of the garden, and he went with her, laughing vaguely, uneasily, at her tragic tone. Of course she expected him to help her to her revenge; but his female relations, his mother and his sisters, his innumerable cousins, had been a party to the slight she suffered, and he reflected as he walked along that after all they had been right. They had been right in not going to see a woman who could chatter that way about her social wrongs; whether Mrs Headway were respectable or not, they had a corrected instinct, for at any rate she was vulgar. European society might let her in, but European society would be wrong. New York, Waterville said to himself with a glow of civic pride, was quite capable of taking a higher stand in such a matter than London. They went some distance without speaking; at last he said, expressing honestly the thought which at that moment was uppermost in his mind, 'I hate that phrase, "getting into society". I don't think one ought to attribute to one's self that sort of ambition.

One ought to assume that one is in society – that one *is* society – and to hold that if one has good manners, one has, from the social point of view, achieved the great thing. The rest regards others.'

For a moment she appeared not to understand; then she broke out: 'Well, I suppose I haven't good manners; at any rate, I'm not satisfied! Of course, I don't talk right – I know that very well. But let me get where I want to first – then I'll look after my expressions. If I once get there, I shall be perfect!' she cried with a tremor of passion. They reached the gate of the garden and stood a moment outside, opposite to the low arcade of the Odéon, lined with bookstalls at which Waterville cast a slightly wistful glance, waiting for Mrs Headway's carriage, which had drawn up at a short distance. The whiskered Max had seated himself within, and on the tense, elastic cushions had fallen into a doze. The carriage got into motion without his awaking; he came to his senses only as it stopped again. He started up, staring; then, without confusion, he proceeded to descend.

'I have learned it in Italy – they say the *siesta*,' he remarked with an agreeable smile, holding the door open to Mrs Headway.

'Well, I should think you had!' this lady replied, laughing amicably as she got into the vehicle, whither Waterville followed her. It was not a surprise to him to perceive that she spoiled her courier; she naturally would spoil her courier. But civilization begins at home, said Waterville; and the incident threw an ironical light upon her desire to get into society. It failed, however, to divert her thoughts from the subject she was discussing with Waterville, for as Max ascended the box and the carriage went on its way, she threw out another little note of defiance. 'If once I'm right over here, I can snap my fingers at New York! You'll see the faces those women will make.'

Waterville was sure his mother and sisters would make no faces; but he felt afresh, as the carriage rolled back to the Hôtel Meurice, that now he understood Mrs Headway. As they were about to enter the court of the hotel a closed carriage passed before them, and while a few moments later he helped his companion to alight, he saw that Sir Arthur Desmesne had descended from the other vehicle. Sir Arthur perceived Mrs Headway, and instantly gave his hand to a lady seated in the *coupé*. This lady emerged with a certain slow impressiveness, and as she stood before the door of the hotel – a woman still young and fair, with a good deal of height, gentle, tranquil, plainly dressed, yet distinctly imposing – Waterville saw that the baronet had brought his mother to call upon Nancy Beck. Mrs Headway's triumph had begun; the Dowager Lady Demesne had taken the first step. Waterville wondered whether the ladies in New York, notified by some magnetic wave, were distorting their features. Mrs Headway, quickly conscious of what had happened, was neither too prompt to appropriate the visit, nor too slow to acknowledge it. She just paused, smiling at Sir Arthur.

'I wish to introduce my mother – she wants very much to know you.' He approached Mrs Headway; the lady had taken his arm. She was at once simple and circumspect; she had all the resources of an English matron.

Mrs Headway, without advancing a step, put out her hands as if to draw her visitor quickly closer. 'I declare, you're too sweet!' Waterville heard her say.

He was turning away, as his own business was over; but the young Englishman, who had surrendered his mother to the embrace, as it might now almost be called, of their hostess, just checked him with a friendly gesture. 'I daresay I sha'n't see you again – I'm going away.'

'Good-by, then,' said Waterville. 'You return to England?'

'No; I go to Cannes with my mother.'

'You remain at Cannes?'

'Till Christmas very likely.'

The ladies, escorted by Mr Max, had passed into the hotel, and Waterville presently quitted his interlocutor. He smiled as he walked away reflecting that this personage had obtained a concession from his mother only at the price of a concession.

The next morning he went to see Littlemore, from whom he had a standing invitation to breakfast, and who, as usual, was smoking a cigar and looking through a dozen newspapers. Littlemore had a large apartment and an accomplished cook; he got up late and wandered about his room all the morning, stopping from time to time to look out of his windows which overhung the Place de la Madeleine. They had not been seated many minutes at breakfast when Waterville announced that Mrs Headway was about to be abandoned by Sir Arthur, who was going to Cannes.

'That's no news to me,' Littlemore said. 'He came last night to bid me good-by.'

'To bid you good-by? He was very civil all of a sudden.'

'He didn't come from civility – he came from curiosity. Having dined here, he had a pretext for calling.'

'I hope his curiosity was satisfied,' Waterville remarked, in the manner of a person who could enter into such a sentiment.

Littlemore hesitated. 'Well. I suspect not. He sat here some time, but we talked about everything but what he wanted to know.'

'And what did he want to know?'

'Whether I know anything against Nancy Beck.'

Waterville stared. 'Did he call her Nancy Beck?'

'We never mentioned her; but I saw what he wanted, and that he wanted me to lead up to her – only I wouldn't do it.'

'Ah, poor man!' Waterville murmured.

'I don't see why you pity him,' said Littlemore. 'Mrs Beck's admirers were never pitied.'

'Well, of course he wants to marry her.'

'Let him do it, then. I have nothing to say to it.'

'He believes there's something in her past that's hard to swallow.'

'Let him leave it alone, then.'

'How can he, if he's in love with her?' Waterville asked, in the tone of a man who could enter into that sentiment too.

'Ah, my dear fellow, he must settle it himself. He has no right, at any rate, to ask me such a question. There was a moment, just as he was going, when he had it on his tongue's end. He stood there in the doorway, he couldn't leave me – he was going to plump out with it. He looked at me straight, and

I looked straight at him; we remained that way for almost a minute. Then he decided to hold his tongue, and took himself off.'

Waterville listened to this little description with intense interest. 'And if he had asked you, what would you have said?'

'What do you think?'

'Well, I suppose you would have said that his question wasn't fair?'

'That would have been tantamount to admitting the worst.'

'Yes,' said Waterville, thoughtfully, 'you couldn't do that. On the other hand, if he had put it to you on your honor whether she were a woman to marry, it would have been very awkward.'

'Awkward enough. Fortunately, he has no business to put things to me on my honor. Moreover, nothing has passed between us to give him the right to ask me questions about Mrs Headway. As she is a great friend of mine, he can't pretend to expect me to give confidential information about her.'

'You don't think she's a woman to marry, all the same,' Waterville declared. 'And if a man were to ask you that, you might knock him down, but it wouldn't be an answer.'

'It would have to serve,' said Littlemore. He added in a moment, 'There are certain cases where it's a man's duty to commit perjury.'

Waterville looked grave. 'Certain cases?'

'Where a woman's honor is at stake.'

'I see what you mean. That's of course if he has been himself concerned –'.

'Himself or another. It doesn't matter.'

'I think it does matter. I don't like perjury,' said Waterville. 'It's a delicate question.'

They were interrupted by the arrival of the servant with a second course, and Littlemore gave a laugh as he helped himself. 'It would be a joke to see her married to that superior being!'

'It would be a great responsibility.'

'Responsibility or not, it would be very amusing.'

'Do you mean to assist her, then?'

'Heaven forbid! But I mean to bet on her.'

Waterville gave his companion a serious glance; he thought him strangely superficial. The situation, however, was difficult, and he laid down his fork with a little sigh.

PART TWO

6

THE Easter holidays that year were unusually genial; mild, watery sunshine assisted the progress of the spring. The high, dense hedges, in Warwickshire, were like walls of hawthorn imbedded in banks of primrose, and the finest trees in England, springing out of them with a regularity which suggested conservative principles, began to cover themselves with a kind of green downiness. Rupert Waterville, devoted to his duties and faithful in attendance at the Legation, had had little time to enjoy that rural hospitality which is the great invention of the English people and the most perfect expression of their character. He had been invited now and then – for in London he commended himself to many people as a very sensible young man – but he had been obliged to decline more proposals than he accepted. It was still, therefore, rather a novelty to him to stay at one of those fine old houses, surrounded with hereditary acres, which from the first of his coming to England he had thought of with such curiosity and such envy. He proposed to himself to see as many of them as possible, but he disliked to do things in a hurry, or when his mind was preoccupied, as it was so apt to be, with what he believed to be business of importance. He kept the country-houses in reserve; he would take them up in their order, after he should have got a little more used to London. Without hesitation, however, he had accepted the invitation to Longlands; it had come to him in a simple and familiar note, from Lady Demesne, with whom he had no acquaintance. He knew of her return from Cannes, where she had spent the whole winter, for he had seen it related in a Sunday newspaper; yet it was with a certain surprise that he heard from her in these informal terms. 'Dear Mr Waterville,' she wrote, 'my son tells me that you will perhaps be able to come down here on the 17th, to spend two or three days. If you can, it will give us much pleasure. We can promise you the society of your charming countrywoman, Mrs Headway.'

He had seen Mrs Headway; she had written to him a fortnight before from an hotel in Cork Street, to say that she had arrived in London for the season and should be very glad to see him. He had gone to see her, trembling with the fear that she would break ground about her presentation; but he was agreeably surprised to observe that she neglected this topic. She had spent the winter in Rome, travelling directly from that city to England, with just a little stop in Paris, to buy a few clothes. She had taken much satisfaction in Rome, where she made many friends; she assured him that she knew half the Roman nobility. 'They are charming people; they have only one fault, they stay too long,' she said. And, in answer to his inquiring glance, 'I mean when they come to see you,' she explained. 'They used to come every evening, and they wanted to stay till the next day. They were all princes and counts. I used to give them cigars, &c. I knew as many people as I wanted,' she added, in a moment, discovering perhaps in Waterville's eye the traces of that sympathy with which six months before he had listened to her account of her discomfiture in New York. 'There were lots of English; I knew all the English, and I mean to visit them here. The Americans waited to see what the English would do, so as to do the opposite. Thanks to that, I was spared some precious specimens. There are, you know, some fearful ones. Besides, in Rome, society doesn't matter, if you have a feeling for the ruins and the Campagna; I had an immense feeling for the Campagna. I was always mooning round in some damp old temple. It reminded me a good deal of the country round San Diego – if it hadn't been for the temples. I liked to think it all over, when I was driving round; I was always brooding over the past.' At this moment, however, Mrs Headway had dismissed the past; she was prepared to give herself up wholly to the actual. She wished Waterville to advise her as to how she should live – what she should do. Should she stay at a hotel or should she take a house? She guessed she had better take a house, if she could find a nice one. Max wanted to look for one, and she didn't know but she'd let him; he got her such a nice one in

Rome. She said nothing about Sir Arthur Demesne, who, it seemed to Waterville, would have been her natural guide and sponsor; he wondered whether her relations with the baronet had come to an end. Waterville had met him a couple of times since the opening of Parliament, and they had exchanged twenty words, none of which, however, had reference to Mrs Headway. Waterville had been recalled to London just after the incident of which he was witness in the court of the Hôtel Meurice; and all he knew of its consequence was what he had learned from Littlemore, who, on his way back to America where he had suddenly ascertained that there were reasons for his spending the winter, passed through the British capital. Littlemore had reported that Mrs Headway was enchanted with Lady Demesne, and had no words to speak of her kindness and sweetness. 'She told me she liked to know her son's friends, and I told her I liked to know my friends' mothers,' Mrs Headway had related. 'I should be willing to be old if I could be like that,' she had added, oblivious for the moment that she was at least as near to the age of the mother as to that of the son. The mother and son, at any rate, had retired to Cannes together, and at this moment Littlemore had received letters from home which caused him to start for Arizona. Mrs Headway had accordingly been left to her own devices, and he was afraid she had bored herself, though Mrs Bagshaw had called upon her. In November she had travelled to Italy, not by way of Cannes.

'What do you suppose she'll do in Rome?' Waterville had asked; his imagination failing him here, for he had not yet trodden the Seven Hills.

'I haven't the least idea. And I don't care!' Littlemore added in a moment. Before he left London he mentioned to Waterville that Mrs Headway, on his going to take leave of her in Paris, had made another, and a rather unexpected, attack. 'About the society business – she said I must really do something – she couldn't go on in that way. And she appealed to me in the name – I don't think I quite know how to say it.'

'I should be very glad if you would try,' said Waterville, who was constantly reminding himself that Americans in Europe were, after all, in a manner, to a man in his position, as the sheep to the shepherd.

'Well, in the name of the affection that we had formerly entertained for each other.'

'The affection?'

'So she was good enough to call it. But I deny it all. If one had to have an affection for every woman one used to sit up "evenings" with—!' And Littlemore paused, not defining the result of such an obligation. Waterville tried to imagine what it would be; while his friend embarked for New York, without telling him how, after all, he had resisted Mrs Headway's attack.

At Christmas, Waterville knew of Sir Arthur's return to England, and believed that he also knew that the baronet had not gone down to Rome. He had a theory that Lady Demesne was a very clever woman – clever enough to make her son do what she preferred and yet also make him think it his own choice. She had been politic, accommodating, about going to see Mrs Headway; but, having seen her and judged her, she had determined to break the thing off. She had been sweet and kind, as Mrs Headway said, because for the moment that was easiest; but she had made her last visit on the same occasion as her first. She had been sweet and kind, but she had set her face as a stone, and if poor Mrs Headway, arriving in London for the season, expected to find any vague promises redeemed, she would taste of the bitterness of shattered hopes. He had made up his mind that, shepherd as he was, and Mrs Headway one of his sheep, it was none of his present duty to run about after her, especially as she could be trusted not to stray too far. He saw her a second time, and she still said nothing about Sir Arthur. Waterville, who always had a theory, said to himself that she was waiting, that the baronet had not turned up. She was also getting into a house; the courier had found her in Chesterfield Street, Mayfair, a little gem, which was to cost her what jewels cost. After all this, Waterville was greatly surprised at Lady Demesne's note, and he went down to Longlands with much the same impatience with which, in Paris, he would have gone, if he had been able, to the first night of a new comedy.

It seemed to him that, through a sudden stroke of good fortune, he had received a *billet d'auteur*.

It was agreeable to him to arrive at an English country-house at the close of the day. He liked the drive from the station in the twilight, the sight of the fields and copses and cottages, vague and lonely in contrast to his definite, lighted goal; the sound of the wheels on the long avenue, which turned and wound repeatedly without bringing him to what he reached however at last – the wide, gray front, with a glow in its scattered windows and a sweep of still firmer gravel up to the door. The front at Longlands, which was of this sober complexion, had a grand, pompous air; it was attributed to the genius of Sir Christopher Wren. There were wings which came forward in a semicircle, with statues placed at intervals on the cornice; so that in the flattering dusk it looked like an Italian palace, erected through some magical evocation in an English park. Waterville had taken a late train, which left him but twenty minutes to dress for dinner. He prided himself considerably on the art of dressing both quickly and well; but this operation left him no time to inquire whether the apartment to which he had been assigned befitted the dignity of a Secretary of Legation. On emerging from his room he found there was an ambassador in the house, and this discovery was a check to uneasy reflections. He tacitly assumed that he would have had a better room if it had not been for the ambassador, who was of course counted first. The large, brilliant house gave an impression of the last century and of foreign taste, of light colors, high, vaulted ceilings, with pale mythological frescos, gilded doors, surmounted by old French panels, faded tapestries and delicate damasks, stores of ancient china, among which great jars of pink roses were conspicuous. The people in the house had assembled for dinner in the principal hall, which was animated by a fire of great logs, and the company was so numerous that Waterville was afraid he was the last. Lady Demesne gave him a smile and a touch of her hand; she was very tranquil, and, saying nothing in particular, treated him as if he had been a constant visitor. Waterville was not sure whether he liked this or hated it; but these alternatives mattered equally little to his hostess, who looked at her guests as if to see whether the number were right. The master of the house was talking to a lady before the fire; when he caught sight of Waterville across the room, he waved him 'how d'ye do,' with an air of being delighted to see him. He had never had that air in Paris, and Waterville had a chance to observe, what he had often heard, to how much greater advantage the English appear in their country houses. Lady Demesne turned to him again, with her sweet vague smile, which looked as if it were the same for everything.

'We are waiting for Mrs Headway,' she said.

'Ah, she has arrived?' Waterville had quite forgotten her.

'She came at half-past five. At six she went to dress. She has had two hours.'

'Let us hope that the results will be proportionate,' said Waterville, smiling.

'Oh, the results; I don't know,' Lady Demesne murmured, without looking at him; and in these simple words Waterville saw the confirmation of his theory that she was playing a deep game. He wondered whether he should sit next to Mrs Headway at dinner, and hoped, with due deference to this lady's charms, that he should have something more novel. The results of a toilet which she had protracted through two hours were presently visible. She appeared on the staircase which descended to the hall, and which, for three minutes, as she came down rather slowly, facing the people beneath, placed her in considerable relief. Waterville, as he looked at her, felt that this was a moment of importance for her: it was virtually her entrance into English society. Mrs Headway entered English society very well, with her charming smile upon her lips and with the trophies of the Rue de la Paix trailing behind her. She made a portentous rustling as she moved. People turned their eyes toward her; there was soon a perceptible diminution of talk, though talk had not been particularly audible. She looked very much alone, and it was rather pretentious of her to come down last, though it was possible that this was simply because, before her glass, she had been unable to please herself. For she evidently felt the importance of the occasion, and Waterville was sure that her heart was beating. She was very valiant, however; she smiled more intensely, and advanced like a woman who was used to being looked at. She had at any rate the support of knowing that she was pretty; for nothing on this occasion was wanting to her prettiness, and the determination to succeed, which might have made her hard, was veiled in the virtuous consciousness that she had neglected nothing. Lady Demesne went forward to meet her; Sir Arthur took no notice of her; and presently Waterville found himself proceeding to dinner with the wife of an ecclesiastic, to whom Lady Demesne had presented him for this purpose when the hall was almost empty. The rank of this ecclesiastic in the hierarchy he learned early on the morrow; but in the mean time it seemed to him strange, somehow, that in England ecclesiastics should have wives. English life, even at the end of a year, was full of those surprises. The lady, however, was very easily accounted for; she was in no sense a violent exception, and there had been no need of the Reformation to produce her. Her name was Mrs April; she was wrapped in a large lace shawl; to eat her dinner she removed but one glove, and the other gave Waterville at moments an odd impression that the whole repast, in spite of its great completeness, was something of the picnic order. Mrs Headway was opposite, at a little distance; she had been taken in, as Waterville learned from his neighbor, by a general, a gentleman with a lean, aquiline face and a cultivated whisker, and she had on the other side a smart young man of an identity less definite. Poor Sir Arthur sat between two ladies much older than himself, whose names, redolent of history, Waterville had often heard, and had associated with figures more romantic. Mrs Headway gave Waterville no greeting; she evidently had not seen him till they were seated at table, when she simply stared at him with a violence of surprise that for a moment almost effaced her smile. It was a copious and well-ordered banquet, but as Waterville looked up and down the table he wondered whether some of its elements might not be a little dull. As he made this reflection he became conscious that he was judging the affair much more from Mrs Headway's point of view than from his own. He knew no one but Mrs

April, who, displaying an almost motherly desire to give him information, told him the names of many of their companions; in return for which he explained to her that he was not in that set. Mrs Headway got on in perfection with her general; Waterville watched her more than he appeared to do, and saw that the general, who evidently was a cool hand, was drawing her out. Waterville hoped she would be careful. He was a man of fancy, in his way, and as he compared her with the rest of the company he said to himself that she was a very plucky little woman, and that her present undertaking had a touch of the heroic. She was alone against many, and her opponents were a very serried phalanx; those who were there represented a thousand others. They looked so different from her that to the eye of the imagination she stood very much on her merits. All those people seemed so completely made up, so unconscious of effort, so surrounded with things to rest upon; the men with their clean complexions, their well-hung chins, their cold, pleasant eyes, their shoulders set back, their absence of gesture; the women, several very handsome, half strangled in strings of pearls, with smooth plain tresses, seeming to look at nothing in particular, supporting silence as if it were as becoming as candlelight, yet talking a little, sometimes, in fresh, rich voices. They were all wrapped in a community of ideas, of traditions; they understood each other's accents, even each other's variations. Mrs Headway, with all her prettiness, seemed to transcend these variations; she looked foreign, exaggerated; she had too much expression; she might have been engaged for the evening. Waterville remarked, moreover, that English society was always looking out for amusement and that its transactions were conducted on a cash basis. If Mrs Headway were amusing enough she would probably succeed, and her fortune – if fortune there was – would not be a hindrance.

In the drawing-room, after dinner, he went up to her, but she gave him no greeting. She only looked at him with an expression he had never seen before – a strange, bold expression of displeasure.

'Why have you come down here?' she asked. 'Have you come to watch me?'

Waterville colored to the roots of his hair. He knew it was terribly little like a diplomatist; but he was unable to control his blushes. Besides, he was shocked, he was angry, and in addition he was mystified. 'I came because I was asked,' he said.

'Who asked you?'

'The same person that asked you, I suppose – Lady Demesne.'

'She's an old cat!' Mrs Headway exclaimed, turning away from him.

He turned away from her as well. He didn't know what he had done to deserve such treatment. It was a complete surprise; he had never seen her like that before. She was a very vulgar woman; that was the way people talked, he supposed, at San Diego. He threw himself almost passionately into the conversation of the others, who all seemed to him, possibly a little by contrast, extraordinarily genial and friendly. He had not, however, the consolation of seeing Mrs Headway punished for her rudeness, for she was not in the least neglected. On the contrary, in the part of the room where she sat the group was denser, and every now and then it was agitated with unanimous laughter. If she should amuse them, he said to himself, she would succeed, and evidently she was amusing them.

7

If she was strange, he had not come to the end of her strangeness. The next day was a Sunday and uncommonly fine; he was down before breakfast, and took a walk in the park, stopping to gaze at the thin-legged deer, scattered like pins on a velvet cushion over some of the remoter slopes, and wandering along the edge of a large sheet of ornamental water, which had a temple, in imitation of that of Vesta, on an island in the middle. He thought at this time no more about Mrs Headway; he only reflected that these stately objects had for more than a hundred years furnished a background to a great deal of family history. A little more reflection would perhaps have suggested to him that Mrs Headway was possibly an incident of some importance in the history of a family. Two or three ladies failed to appear at breakfast; Mrs Headway was one of them.

'She tells me she never leaves her room till noon,' he heard Lady Demesne say to the general, her companion of the previous evening, who had asked about her. 'She takes three hours to dress.'

'She's a monstrous clever woman!' the general exclaimed.

'To do it in three hours?'

'No, I mean the way she keeps her wits about her.'

'Yes; I think she's very clever,' said Lady Demesne, in a tone in which Waterville flattered himself that he saw more meaning than the general could see. There was something in this tall, straight, deliberate woman, who seemed at once benevolent and distant, that Waterville admired. With her delicate surface, her conventional mildness, he could see that she was very strong; she had set her patience upon a height, and she carried it like a diadem. She had very little to say to Waterville, but every now and then she made some inquiry of him that showed she had not forgotten him. Demesne himself was apparently in excellent spirits, though there was nothing bustling in his deportment, and he only went about looking very fresh and fair, as if he took a bath every hour or two, and very secure against the unexpected. Waterville had less conversation with him than with his mother; but the young man had found occasion to say to him the night before, in the smoking-room, that he was delighted Waterville had been able to come, and that if he was fond of real English scenery there were several things about there he should like very much to show him.

'You must give me an hour or two before you go, you know; I really think there are some things you'll like.'

Sir Arthur spoke as if Waterville would be very fastidious; he seemed to wish to attach a vague importance to him. On the Sunday morning after breakfast he asked Waterville if he should care to go to church; most of the ladies and several of the men were going.

'It's just as you please, you know; but it's rather a pretty walk across the fields, and a curious little church of King Stephen's time.'

Waterville knew what this meant; it was already a picture. Besides, he liked going to church, especially when he sat in the Squire's pew, which was sometimes as big as a boudoir. So he replied that he should be delighted. Then he added, without explaining his reason –

'Is Mrs Headway going?'

'I really don't know,' said his host, with an abrupt change of tone – as if Waterville had asked him whether the housekeeper were going.

'The English are awfully queer!' Waterville indulged mentally in this exclamation, to which since his arrival in England he had had recourse whenever he encountered a gap in the consistency of things. The church was even a better picture than Sir Arthur's description of it, and Waterville said to himself that Mrs Headway had been a great fool not to come. He knew what she was after; she wished to study English life, so that she might take possession of it, and to pass in among a hedge of bobbing rustics, and sit among the monuments of the old Demesnes, would have told her a great deal about English life. If she wished to fortify herself for the struggle she had better come to that old church. When he returned to Longlands – he had walked back across the meadows with the canon's wife, who was a vigorous pedestrian – it wanted half an hour of luncheon, and he was unwilling to go indoors. He remembered that he had not yet seen the gardens, and he wandered away in search of them. They were on a scale which enabled him to find them without difficulty, and they looked as if they had been kept up unremittingly for a century or two. He had not advanced very far between their blooming borders when he heard a voice that he recognized, and a moment after, at the turn of an alley, he came upon Mrs Headway, who was attended by the master of Longlands. She was bareheaded beneath her parasol, which she flung back, stopping short, as she beheld her compatriot.

'Oh, it's Mr Waterville come to spy me out as usual!' It

was with this remark that she greeted the slightly embarrassed young man.

'Hallo! you've come home from church,' Sir Arthur said, pulling out his watch.

Waterville was struck with his coolness. He admired it; for, after all, he said to himself, it must have been disagreeable to him to be interrupted. He felt a little like a fool, and wished he had kept Mrs April with him, to give him the air of having come for her sake.

Mrs Headway looked adorably fresh, in a toilet which Waterville, who had his ideas on such matters, was sure would not be regarded as the proper thing for a Sunday morning in an English country house: a *néglige* of white flounces and frills, interspersed with yellow ribbons – a garment which Madame de Pompadour might have worn when she received a visit from Louis XV, but would probably not have worn when she went into the world. The sight of this costume gave the finishing touch to Waterville's impression that Mrs Headway knew, on the whole, what she was about. She would take a line of her own; she would not be too accommodating. She would not come down to breakfast; she would not go to church; she would wear on Sunday mornings little elaborately informal dresses, and look dreadfully un-British and un-Protestant. Perhaps, after all, this was better. She began to talk with a certain volubility.

'Isn't this too lovely? I walked all the way from the house. I'm not much at walking, but the grass in this place is like a parlor. The whole thing is beyond everything. Sir Arthur, you ought to go and look after the Ambassador; it's shameful the way I've kept you. You didn't care about the Ambassador? You said just now you had scarcely spoken to him, and you must make it up. I never saw such a way of neglecting your guests. Is that the usual style over here? Go and take him out for a ride, or make him play a game of billiards. Mr Waterville will take me home; besides, I want to scold him for spying on me.'

Waterville sharply resented this accusation. 'I had no idea you were here,' he declared.

'We weren't hiding,' said Sir Arthur quietly. 'Perhaps you'll see Mrs Headway back to the house. I think I ought to look after old Davidoff. I believe lunch is at two.'

He left them, and Waterville wandered through the gardens with Mrs Headway. She immediately wished to know if he had come there to look after her; but this inquiry was accompanied, to his surprise, with the acrimony she had displayed the night before. He was determined not to let that pass, however; when people had treated him in that way they should not be allowed to forget it.

'Do you suppose I am always thinking of you?' he asked. 'You're out of my mind sometimes. I came here to look at the gardens, and if you hadn't spoken to me I should have passed on.'

Mrs Headway was perfectly good-natured; she appeared not even to hear his defence. 'He has got two other places,' she simply rejoined. 'That's just what I wanted to know.'

But Waterville would not be turned away from his grievance. That mode of reparation to a person whom you had insulted which consisted in forgetting that you had done so, was doubtless largely in use in New Mexico; but a person of honor demanded something more. 'What did you mean last night by accusing me of having come down here to watch you? You must excuse me if I tell you that I think you were rather rude.' The sting of this accusation lay in the fact that there was a certain amount of truth in it; yet for a moment Mrs Headway, looking very blank, failed to recognize the allusion. 'She's a barbarian, after all,' thought Waterville. 'She thinks a woman may slap a man's face and run away!'

'Oh!' cried Mrs Headway, suddenly, 'I remember, I was angry with you; I didn't expect to see you. But I didn't really care about it at all. Every now and then I am angry, like that, and I work it off on any one that's handy. But it's over in three minutes, and I never think of it again. I was angry last night; I was furious with the old woman.'

'With the old woman?'

'With Sir Arthur's mother. She has no business here, any way. In this country, when the husband dies, they're expected to clear out. She has a house of her own, ten miles from here, and she has another in Portman Square; so she's got plenty of places to live. But she sticks – she sticks to him like a plaster. All of a sudden it came over me that she didn't invite me here because she liked me, but because she suspects me. She's afraid we'll make a match, and she thinks I ain't good enough for her son. She must think I'm in a great hurry to get hold of him. I never went after him, he came after me. I should never have thought of anything if it hadn't been for him. He began it last summer at Homburg; he wanted to know why I didn't come to England; he told me I should have great success. He doesn't know much about it, any way; he hasn't got much gumption. But he's a very nice man, all the same; it's very pleasant to see him surrounded by his –' And Mrs Headway paused a moment, looking admiringly about her – 'Surrounded by all his old heirlooms. I like the old place,' she went on; 'it's beautifully mounted; I'm quite satisfied with what I've seen. I thought Lady Demesne was very friendly; she left a card on me in London, and very soon after, she wrote to me to ask me here. But I'm very quick; I sometimes see things in a flash. I saw something yesterday, when she came to speak to me at dinner-time. She saw I looked pretty, and it made her blue with rage; she hoped I would be ugly. I should like very much to oblige her; but what can one do? Then I saw that she had asked me here only because he insisted. He didn't come to see me when I first arrived – he never came near me for ten days. She managed to prevent him; she got him to make some promise. But he changed his mind after a little, and then he had to do something really polite. He called three days in succession, and he made her come. She's one of those women that resists as long as she can, and then seems to give in, while she's really resisting more than ever. She hates me like poison; I don't know what she thinks I've done. She's very underhand; she's a regular old cat. When I saw you last night at dinner, I thought she had got you here to help her.'

'To help her?' Waterville asked.

'To tell her about me. To give her information, that she can make use of against me. You may tell her what you like!'

Waterville was almost breathless with the attention he had given this extraordinary burst of confidence, and now he really felt faint. He stopped short; Mrs Headway went on a few steps, and then, stopping too, turned and looked at him. 'You're the most unspeakable woman!' he exclaimed. She seemed to him indeed a barbarian.

She laughed at him – he felt she was laughing at his expression of face – and her laugh rang through the stately gardens. 'What sort of a woman is that?'

'You've got no delicacy,' said Waterville, resolutely.

She colored quickly, though, strange to say, she appeared not to be angry. 'No delicacy?' she repeated.

'You ought to keep those things to yourself.'

'Oh, I know what you mean; I talk about everything. When I'm excited I've got to talk. But I must do things in my own way. I've got plenty of delicacy, when people are nice to me. Ask Arthur Demesne if I ain't delicate – ask George Littlemore if I ain't. Don't stand there all day; come in to lunch!' And Mrs Headway resumed her walk, while Rupert Waterville, raising his eyes for a moment, slowly overtook her. 'Wait till I get settled; then I'll be delicate,' she pursued. 'You can't be delicate when you're trying to save your life. It's very well for *you* to talk, with the whole American Legation to back you. Of course I'm excited. I've got hold of this thing, and I don't mean to let go!' Before they reached the house she told him why he had been invited to Longlands at the same time as herself. Waterville would have liked to believe that his personal attractions sufficiently explained the fact; but she took no account of this supposition. Mrs Headway preferred to think that she lived in an element of ingenious machination, and that most things that happened had reference to herself. Waterville had been asked because he represented, however modestly, the American Legation, and their host had a friendly desire to make it appear that this pretty American visitor, of whom no one knew anything, was under the protection of that establishment. 'It would start me better,' said Mrs Headway, serenely. 'You can't help yourself – you've helped to start me. If he had known the Minister he would have asked him – or the first secretary. But he don't know them.'

They reached the house by the time Mrs Headway had developed this idea, which gave Waterville a pretext more than sufficient for detaining her in the portico. 'Do you mean to say Sir Arthur told you this?' he inquired, almost sternly.

'Told me? Of course not! Do you suppose I would let him take the tone with me that I need any favors? I should like to hear him tell me that I'm in want of assistance!'

'I don't see why he shouldn't – at the pace you go yourself. You say it to every one.'

'To every one? I say it to you, and to George Littlemore – when I'm nervous. I say it to you because I like you, and to him because I'm afraid of him. I'm not in the least afraid of you, by the way. I'm all alone – I haven't got any one. I must have some comfort, mustn't I? Sir Arthur scolded me for putting you off last night – he noticed it; and that was what made me guess his idea.'

'I'm much obliged to him,' said Waterville, rather bewildered.

'So mind you answer for me. Don't you want to give me your arm, to go in?'

'You're a most extraordinary combination,' he murmured, as she stood smiling at him.

'Oh, come, don't *you* fall in love with me!' she cried, with a laugh; and, without taking his arm, passed in before him.

That evening, before he went to dress for dinner, Waterville wandered into the library, where he felt sure that he should find some superior bindings. There was no one in the room, and he spent a happy half-hour among the treasures of literature and the triumphs of old morocco. He had a great esteem for good literature; he held that it should have handsome covers. The daylight had begun to wane, but whenever, in the rich-looking dimness, he made out the glimmer of a well-gilded back, he took down the volume and carried it to one of the deep-set windows. He had just finished the inspection of a delightfully fragrant folio, and was about to carry it back to its niche, when he found himself standing face to face with

Lady Demesne. He was startled for a moment, for her tall, slim figure, her fair visage, which looked white in the high, brown room, and the air of serious intention with which she presented herself, gave something spectral to her presence. He saw her smile, however, and heard her say, in that tone of hers which was sweet almost to sadness, 'Are you looking at our books? I'm afraid they are rather dull.'

'Dull? Why, they are as bright as the day they were bound.' And he turned the glittering panels of his folio towards her.

'I'm afraid I haven't looked at them for a long time,' she murmured, going nearer to the window, where she stood looking out. Beyond the clear pane the park stretched away, with the grayness of evening beginning to hang itself on the great limbs of the oaks. The place appeared cold and empty, and the trees had an air of conscious importance, as if nature herself had been bribed somehow to take the side of county families. Lady Demesne was not an easy person to talk with; she was neither spontaneous nor abundant; she was conscious of herself, conscious of many things. Her very simplicity was conventional, though it was rather a noble convention. You might have pitied her, if you had seen that she lived in constant unrelaxed communion with certain rigid ideals. This made her at times seem tired, like a person who has undertaken too much. She gave an impression of still brightness, which was not at all brilliancy, but a carefully preserved purity. She said nothing for a moment, and there was an appearance of design in her silence, as if she wished to let him know that she had a certain business with him, without taking the trouble to announce it. She had been accustomed to expect that people would suppose things, and to be saved the trouble of explanations. Waterville made some haphazard remark about the beauty of the evening (in point of fact, the weather had changed for the worse), to which she vouchsafed no reply. Then, presently, she said, with her usual gentleness, 'I hoped I should find you here – I wish to ask you something.'

'Anything I can tell you – I shall be delighted!' Waterville exclaimed.

She gave him a look, not imperious, almost appealing, which

seemed to say – 'Please be very simple – very simple indeed.' Then she glanced about her, as if there had been other people in the room; she didn't wish to appear closeted with him, or to have come on purpose. There she was, at any rate, and she went on. 'When my son told me he should ask you to come down, I was very glad. I mean, of course, that we were delighted –' And she paused a moment. Then she added, simply, 'I want to ask you about Mrs Headway.'

'Ah, here it is!' cried Waterville within himself. More superficially, he smiled, as agreeably as possible, and said, 'Ah yes, I see!'

'Do you mind my asking you? I hope you don't mind. I haven't any one else to ask.'

'Your son knows her much better than I do.' Waterville said this without an intention of malice, simply to escape from the difficulties of his situation; but after he had said it, he was almost frightened by its mocking sound.

'I don't think he knows her. She knows him, which is very different. When I ask him about her, he merely tells me she is fascinating. She *is* fascinating,' said her ladyship, with inimitable dryness.

'So I think, myself. I like her very much,' Waterville rejoined, cheerfully.

'You are in all the better position to speak of her, then.'

'To speak well of her,' said Waterville, smiling.

'Of course, if you can. I should be delighted to hear you do that. That's what I wish – to hear some good of her.'

It might have seemed, after this, that nothing would have remained but for Waterville to launch himself in a panegyric of his mysterious countrywoman; but he was no more to be tempted into the danger than into another. 'I can only say I like her,' he repeated. 'She has been very kind to me.'

'Every one seems to like her,' said Lady Demesne, with an unstudied effect of pathos. 'She is certainly very amusing.'

'She is very good-natured; she has lots of good intentions.'

'What do you call good intentions?' asked Lady Demesne, very sweetly.

'Well, I mean that she wants to be friendly and pleasant.'

'Of course you have to defend her. She's your country-woman.'

'To defend her – I must wait till she's attacked,' said Waterville, laughing.

'That's very true. I needn't call your attention to the fact that I am not attacking her. I should never attack a person staying in this house. I only want to know something about her, and if you can't tell me, perhaps at least you can mention some one who will.'

'She'll tell you herself. Tell you by the hour!'

'What she has told my son? I shouldn't understand it. My son doesn't understand it. It's very strange. I rather hoped you might explain it.'

Waterville was silent a moment. 'I'm afraid I can't explain Mrs Headway,' he remarked at last.

'I see you admit she is very peculiar.'

Waterville hesitated again. 'It's too great a responsibility to answer you.' He felt that he was very disobliging; he knew exactly what Lady Demesne wished him to say. He was unprepared to blight the reputation of Mrs Headway to accommodate Lady Demesne; and yet, with his active little imagination, he could enter perfectly into the feelings of this tender, formal, serious woman, who – it was easy to see – had looked for her own happiness in the cultivation of duty and in extreme constancy to two or three objects of devotion chosen once for all. She must, indeed, have had a vision of things which would represent Mrs Headway as both displeasing and dangerous. But he presently became aware that she had taken his last words as a concession in which she might find help.

'You know why I ask you these things, then?'

'I think I have an idea,' said Waterville, persisting in irrelevant laughter. His laugh sounded foolish in his own ears.

'If you know that, I think you ought to assist me.' Her tone changed as she spoke these words; there was a quick tremor in it; he could see it was a confession of distress. Her distress was deep; he immediately felt that it must have been, before she made up her mind to speak to him. He was sorry for her, and determined to be very serious.

'If I could help you I would. But my position is very difficult.'

'It's not so difficult as mine!' She was going all lengths; she was really appealing to him. 'I don't imagine that you are under any obligation to Mrs Headway – you seem to me very different,' she added.

Waterville was not insensible to any discrimination that told in his favor; but these words gave him a slight shock, as if they had been an attempt at bribery. 'I am surprised that you don't like her,' he ventured to observe.

Lady Demesne looked out of the window a little. 'I don't think you are really surprised, though possibly you try to be. I don't like her, at any rate, and I can't fancy why my son should. She's very pretty, and she appears to be very clever; but I don't trust her. I don't know what has taken possession of him; it is not usual in his family to marry people like that. I don't think she's a lady. The person I should wish for him would be so very different – perhaps you can see what I mean. There's something in her history that we don't understand. My son understands it no better than I. If you could only explain to us, that might be a help. I treat you with great confidence the first time I see you; it's because I don't know where to turn. I am exceedingly anxious.'

It was very plain that she was anxious; her manner had become more vehement; her eyes seemed to shine in the thickening dusk. 'Are you very sure there is danger?' Waterville asked. 'Has he asked her to marry him, and has she consented?'

'If I wait till they settle it all, it will be too late. I have reason to believe that my son is not engaged, but he is terribly entangled. At the same time he is very uneasy, and that may save him yet. He has a great sense of honor. He is not satisfied about her past life; he doesn't know what to think of what we have been told. Even what she admits is so strange. She has been married four or five times – she has been divorced again and again – it seems so extraordinary. She tells him that in America it is different, and I daresay you have not our ideas; but really there is a limit to everything. There must have been some great irregularities – I am afraid some great scandals. It's dreadful to have to accept such things. He has not told me all this; but it's not necessary he should tell me; I know him well enough to guess.'

'Does he know that you have spoken to me?' Waterville asked.

'Not in the least. But I must tell you that I shall repeat to him anything that you may say against her.'

'I had better say nothing, then. It's very delicate. Mrs Headway is quite undefended. One may like her or not, of course. I have seen nothing of her that is not perfectly correct.'

'And you have heard nothing?'

Waterville remembered Littlemore's assertion that there were cases in which a man was bound in honor to tell an untruth, and he wondered whether this were such a case. Lady Demesne imposed herself, she made him believe in the reality of her grievance, and he saw the gulf that divided her from a pushing little woman who had lived with Western editors. She was right to wish not to be connected with Mrs Headway. After all, there had been nothing in his relations with that lady to make it incumbent on him to lie for her. He had not sought her acquaintance, she had sought his; she had sent for him to come and see her. And yet he couldn't give her away, as they said in New York; that stuck in his throat. 'I am afraid I really can't say anything. And it wouldn't matter. Your son won't give her up because I happen not to like her.'

'If he were to believe she has done wrong, he would give her up.'

'Well, I have no right to say so,' said Waterville.

Lady Demesne turned away; she was much disappointed in him. He was afraid she was going to break out – 'Why, then, do you suppose I asked you here?' She quitted her place near the window and was apparently about to leave the room. But she stopped short. 'You know something against her, but you won't say it.'

Waterville hugged his folio and looked awkward. 'You attribute things to me. I shall never say anything.'

'Of course you are perfectly free. There is some one else

who knows, I think – another American – a gentleman who was in Paris when my son was there. I have forgotten his name.'

'A friend of Mrs Headway's? I suppose you mean George Littlemore.'

'Yes – Mr Littlemore. He has a sister, whom I have met; I didn't know she was his sister till today. Mrs Headway spoke of her, but I find she doesn't know her. That itself is a proof, I think. Do you think *he* would help me?' Lady Demesne asked, very simply.

'I doubt it, but you can try.'

'I wish he had come with you. Do you think he would come?'

'He is in America at this moment, but I believe he soon comes back.'

'I shall go to his sister; I will ask her to bring him to see me. She is extremely nice; I think she will understand. Unfortunately there is very little time.'

'Don't count too much on Littlemore,' said Waterville, gravely.

'You men have no pity.'

'Why should we pity you? How can Mrs Headway hurt such a person as you?'

Lady Demesne hesitated a moment. 'It hurts me to hear her voice.'

'Her voice is very sweet.'

'Possibly. But she's horrible!'

This was too much, it seemed to Waterville; poor Mrs Headway was extremely open to criticism, and he himself had declared she was a barbarian. Yet she was not horrible. 'It's for your son to pity you. If he doesn't, how can you expect it of others?'

'Oh, but he does!' And with a majesty that was more striking even than her logic, Lady Demesne moved towards the door.

Waterville advanced to open it for her, and as she passed out he said, 'There's one thing you can do – try to like her!'

She shot him a terrible glance. 'That would be worst of all!'

8

George Littlemore arrived in London on the twentieth of May, and one of the first things he did was to go and see Waterville at the Legation, where he made known to him that he had taken for the rest of the season a house at Queen Anne's Gate, so that his sister and her husband, who, under the pressure of diminished rents, had let their own town-residence, might come up and spend a couple of months with him.

'One of the consequences of your having a house will be that you will have to entertain Mrs Headway,' Waterville said.

Littlemore sat there with his hands crossed upon his stick; he looked at Waterville with an eye that failed to kindle at the mention of this lady's name. 'Has she got into European society?' he asked, rather languidly.

'Very much, I should say. She has a house, and a carriage, and diamonds, and everything handsome. She seems already to know a lot of people; they put her name in the *Morning Post*. She has come up very quickly; she's almost famous. Every one is asking about her – you'll be plied with questions.'

Littlemore listened gravely. 'How did she get in?'

'She met a large party at Longlands, and made them all think her great fun. They must have taken her up; she only wanted a start.'

Littlemore seemed suddenly to be struck with the grotesqueness of this news, to which his first response was a burst of quick laughter. 'To think of Nancy Beck! The people here are queer people. There's no one they won't go after. They wouldn't touch her in New York.'

'Oh, New York's old-fashioned,' said Waterville; and he announced to his friend that Lady Demesne was very eager for his arrival, and wanted to make him help her prevent her son's bringing such a person into the family. Littlemore apparently was not alarmed at her ladyship's projects, and intimated, in the manner of a man who thought them rather impertinent, that he could trust himself to keep out of her way. 'It isn't a proper marriage, at any rate,' Waterville declared.

'Why not, if he loves her?'

'Oh, if that's all you want!' cried Waterville, with a degree of cynicism that rather surprised his companion. 'Would you marry her yourself?'

'Certainly, if I were in love with her.'

'You took care not to be that.'

'Yes, I did – and so Demesne had better have done. But since he's bitten –!' and Littlemore terminated his sentence in a suppressed yawn.

Waterville presently asked him how he would manage, in view of his sister's advent, about asking Mrs Headway to his house; and he replied that he would manage by simply not asking her. Upon this, Waterville declared that he was very inconsistent; to which Littlemore rejoined that it was very possible. But he asked whether they couldn't talk about something else than Mrs Headway. He couldn't enter into the young man's interest in her, and was sure to have enough of her later.

Waterville would have been sorry to give a false idea of his interest in Mrs Headway; for he flattered himself the feeling had definite limits. He had been two or three times to see her; but it was a relief to think that she was now quite independent of him. There had been no revival of that intimate intercourse which occurred during the visit to Longlands. She could dispense with assistance now; she knew herself that she was in the current of success. She pretended to be surprised at her good fortune, especially at its rapidity; but she was really surprised at nothing. She took things as they came, and, being essentially a woman of action, wasted almost as little time in elation as she would have done in despondence. She talked a great deal about Lord Edward and Lady Margaret, and about such other members of the nobility as had shown a desire to cultivate her acquaintance; professing to understand perfectly the sources of a popularity which apparently was destined to increase. 'They come to laugh at me,' she said; 'they come simply to get things to repeat. I can't open my mouth but they burst into fits. It's a settled thing that I'm an American humorist; if I say the simplest things, they begin to roar. I must express myself somehow; and indeed when I hold my tongue they think me funnier than ever. They repeat what I say to a great person, and a great person told some of them the other night that he wanted to hear me for himself. I'll do for him what I do for the others; no better and no worse. I don't know how I do it; I talk the only way I can. They tell me it isn't so much the things I say as the way I say them. Well, they're very easy to please. They don't care for me; it's only to be able to repeat Mrs Headway's "last". Every one wants to have it first; it's a regular race.' When she found what was expected of her, she undertook to supply the article in abundance; and the poor little woman really worked hard at her Americanisms. If the taste of London lay that way, she would do her best to gratify it; it was only a pity she hadn't known it before; she would have made more extensive preparations. She thought it a disadvantage, of old, to live in Arizona, in Dakotah, in the newly admitted States; but now she perceived that, as she phrased it to herself, this was the best thing that ever had happened to her. She tried to remember all the queer stories she had heard out there, and keenly regretted that she had not taken them down in writing; she drummed up the echoes of the Rocky Mountains and practised the intonations of the Pacific slope. When she saw her audience in convulsions, she said to herself that this was success, and believed that, if she had only come to London five years sooner, she might have married a duke. That would have been even a more absorbing spectacle for the London world than the actual proceedings of Sir Arthur Desmesne, who, however, lived sufficiently in the eye of society to justify the rumor that there were bets about town as to the issue of his already protracted courtship. It was food for curiosity to see a young man of his pattern – one of the few 'earnest' young men of the Tory side, with an income sufficient for tastes more marked than those by which he was known – make up to a lady several years older than himself, whose fund of Californian slang was even larger than her stock of dollars. Mrs Headway had got a good many new ideas since her arrival in London, but she also retained several old ones. The chief of these – it was now a year old – was that Sir Arthur Demesne was the most irreproachable young man in the world. There were, of course, a good many things that he was not. He was not amusing; he was not insinuating; he was not of an absolutely irrepressible ardor. She believed he was constant; but he was certainly not eager. With these things, however, Mrs Headway could perfectly dispense; she had, in particular, quite outlived the need of being amused. She had had a very exciting life, and her vision of happiness at present was to be magnificently bored. The idea of complete and uncriticised respectability filled her soul with satisfaction; her imagination prostrated itself in the presence of this virtue. She was aware that she had achieved it but ill in her own person; but she could now, at least, connect herself with it by sacred ties. She could prove in that way what was her deepest feeling. This was a religious appreciation of Sir Arthur's great quality – his smooth and rounded, his blooming, lily-like exemption from social flaws.

She was at home when Littlemore went to see her, and surrounded by several visitors, to whom she was giving a late cup of tea and to whom she introduced her compatriot. He stayed till they dispersed, in spite of the manoeuvres of a gentleman who evidently desired to oustay him, but who, whatever might have been his happy fortune on former visits, received on this occasion no encouragement from Mrs Headway. He looked at Littlemore slowly, beginning with his boots and travelling upwards, as if to discover the reason of so unexpected a preference, and then, without a salutation, left him face to face with their hostess.

'I'm curious to see what you'll do for me, now that you've got your sister with you,' Mrs Headway presently remarked, having heard of this circumstance from Rupert Waterville. 'I suppose you'll have to do something, you know. I'm sorry for you; but I don't see how you can get off. You might ask me to dine some day when she's dining out. I would come even then, I think, because I want to keep on the right side of you.'

'I call that the wrong side,' said Littlemore.

'Yes, I see. It's your sister that's on the right side. You're in rather an embarrassing position, ain't you? However, you take those things very quietly. There's something in you that exasperates me. What does your sister think of me? Does she hate me?'

'She knows nothing about you.'

'Have you told her nothing?'

'Never a word.'

'Hasn't she asked you? That shows that she hates me. She thinks I ain't creditable to America. I know all that. She wants to show people over here that, however they may be taken in by me, she knows much better. But she'll have to ask you about me; she can't go on for ever. Then what'll you say?'

'That you're the most successful woman in Europe.'

'Oh, bother!' cried Mrs Headway, with irritation.

'Haven't you got into European society?'

'Maybe I have, maybe I haven't. It's too soon to see. I can't tell this season. Every one says I've got to wait till next, to see if it's the same. Sometimes they take you up for a few weeks, and then never know you again. You've got to fasten the thing somehow – to drive in a nail.'

'You speak as if it were your coffin,' said Littlemore.

'Well, it is a kind of coffin. I'm burying my past!'

Littlemore winced at this. He was tired to death of her past. He changed the subject, and made her talk about London, a topic which she treated with a great deal of humor. She entertained him for half an hour, at the expense of most of her new acquaintances and of some of the most venerable features of the great city. He himself looked at England from the outside, as much as it was possible to do; but in the midst of her familiar allusions to people and things known to her only since yesterday, he was struck with the fact that she would never really be initiated. She buzzed over the surface of things like a fly on a window-pane. She liked it immensely; she was flattered, encouraged, excited; she dropped her confident judgements as if she were scattering flowers, and talked about her intentions, her prospects, her wishes. But she knew no more about English life than about the molecular theory. The words in which he had described her of old to Waterville came back to him; '*Elle ne se doute de rien!*' Suddenly she jumped up; she was going out to dine, and it was time to dress. 'Before you leave I want you to promise me something,' she said off-hand, but with a look which he had seen before and which meant that the point was important. 'You'll be sure to be questioned about me.' And then she paused.

'How do people know I know you?'

'You haven't bragged about it? Is that what you mean? You can be a brute when you try. They do know it, at any rate. Possibly I may have told them. They'll come to you, to ask about me. I mean from Lady Demesne. She's in an awful state – she's so afraid her son'll marry me.'

Littlemore was unable to control a laugh. 'I'm not, if he hasn't done it yet.'

'He can't make up his mind. He likes me so much, yet he thinks I'm not a woman to marry.' It was positively grotesque, the detachment with which she spoke of herself.

'He must be a poor creature if he won't marry you as you are,' Littlemore said.

This was not a very gallant form of speech; but Mrs Headway let it pass. She only replied, 'Well, he wants to be very careful, and so he ought to be!'

'If he asks too many questions, he's not worth marrying.'

'I beg your pardon – he's worth marrying whatever he does – he's worth marrying for me. And I want to marry him – that's what I want to do.'

'Is he waiting for me, to settle it?'

'He's waiting for I don't know what – for some one to come and tell him that I'm the sweetest of the sweet. Then he'll believe it. Some one who has been out there and knows all about me. Of course you're the man, you're created on purpose. Don't you remember how I told you in Paris that he wanted to ask you? He was ashamed, and he gave it up; he tried to forget me. But now it's all on again; only, meanwhile, his mother has been at him. She works at him night and day, like a weasel in a hole, to persuade him that I'm far beneath him. He's very fond of her, and he's very open to influence –

I mean from his mother, not from any one else. Except me, of course. Oh, I've influenced him, I've explained everything fifty times over. But some things are rather complicated, don't you know; and he keeps coming back to them. He wants every little speck explained. He won't come to you himself, but his mother will, or she'll send some of her people. I guess she'll send the lawyer – the family solicitor, they call him. She wanted to send him out to America to make inquiries, only she didn't know where to send. Of course I couldn't be expected to give the places, they've got to find them out for themselves. She knows all about you, and she has made the acquaintance of your sister. So you see how much I know. She's waiting for you; she means to catch you. She has an idea she can fix you – make you say what'll meet her views. Then she'll lay it before Sir Arthur. So you'll be so good as to deny everything.'

Littlemore listened to this little address attentively, but the conclusion left him staring. 'You don't mean that anything I can say will make a difference?'

'Don't be affected! You know it will as well as I.'

'You make him out a precious idiot.'

'Never mind what I make him out. I want to marry him, that's all. And I appeal to you solemnly. You can save me, as you can lose me. If you lose me, you'll be a coward. And if you say a word against me, I shall be lost.'

'Go and dress for dinner, that's your salvation,' Littlemore answered, separating from her at the head of the stairs.

9

It was very well for him to take that tone; but he felt as he walked home that he should scarcely know what to say to people who were determined, as Mrs Headway put it, to catch him. She had worked a certain spell; she had succeeded in making him feel responsible. The sight of her success, however, rather hardened his heart; he was irritated by her ascending movement. He dined alone that evening, while his sister and her husband, who had engagements every day for a month, partook of their repast at the expense of some friends. Mrs Dolphin, however, came home rather early, and immediately sought admittance to the small apartment at the foot of the staircase, which was already spoken of as Littlemore's den. Reginald had gone to a 'squash' somewhere, and she had returned without delay, having something particular to say to her brother. She was too impatient even to wait till the next morning. She looked impatient; she was very unlike George Littlemore. 'I want you to tell me about Mrs Headway,' she said, while he started slightly at the coincidence of this remark with his own thoughts. He was just making up his mind at last to speak to her. She unfastened her cloak and tossed it over a chair, then pulled off her long tight black gloves, which were not so fine as those Mrs Headway wore; all this as if she were preparing herself for an important interview. She was a small, neat woman, who had once been pretty, with a small, thin voice, a sweet, quiet manner, and a perfect knowledge of what it was proper to do on every occasion in life. She always did it, and her conception of it was so definite that failure would have left her without excuse. She was usually not taken for an American, but she made a point of being one, because she flattered herself that she was of a type which, in that nationality, borrowed distinction from its rarity. She was by nature a great conservative, and had ended by being a better Tory than her husband. She was thought by some of her old friends to have changed immensely since her marriage. She knew as much about English society as if she had invented it; had a way, usually, of looking as if she were dressed for a ride; had also thin lips and pretty teeth; and was as positive as she was amiable. She told her brother that Mrs Headway had given out that he was her most intimate friend, and she thought it rather odd he had never spoken of her. He admitted that he had known her for a long time, referred to the circumstances in which the acquaintance had sprung up, and added that he had seen her that afternoon. He sat there smoking his cigar and looking at the ceiling, while Mrs Dolphin delivered herself of a series of questions. Was it true that he liked her so much, was it true he thought her a possible woman to marry, was it not true that her antecedents had been most peculiar?

'I may as well tell you that I have a letter from Lady Demesne,' Mrs Dolphin said. 'It came to me just before I went out, and I have it in my pocket.'

She drew forth the missive, which she evidently wished to read to him; but he gave her no invitation to do so. He knew that she had come to him to extract a declaration adverse to Mrs Headway's projects, and however little satisfaction he might take in this lady's upward flight, he hated to be urged and pushed. He had a great esteem for Mrs Dolphin, who, among other Hampshire notions, had picked up that of the preponderance of the male members of a family, so that she treated him with a consideration which made his having an English sister rather a luxury. Nevertheless he was not very encouraging about Mrs Headway. He admitted once for all that she had not behaved properly – it wasn't worth while to split hairs about that – but he couldn't see that she was much worse than many other women, and he couldn't get up much feeling about her marrying or not marrying. Moreover, it was none of his business, and he intimated that it was none of Mrs Dolphin's.

'One surely can't resist the claims of common humanity!' his sister replied; and she added that he was very inconsistent. He didn't respect Mrs Headway, he knew the most dreadful things about her, he didn't think her fit company for his own flesh and blood. And yet he was willing to let poor Arthur Demesne be taken in by her!

'Perfectly willing!' Littlemore exclaimed. 'All I've got to do is not to marry her myself.'

'Don't you think we have any responsibilities, any duties?'

'I don't know what you mean. If she can succeed, she's welcome. It's a splendid sight in its way.'

'How do you mean splendid?'

'Why, she has run up the tree as if she were a squirrel!'

'It's very true that she has an audacity *à toute épreuve*. But English society has become scandalously easy. I never saw anything like the people that are taken up. Mrs Headway has had only to appear to succeed. If they think there's something bad about you they'll be sure to run after you. It's like the decadence of the Roman Empire. You can see to look at Mrs Headway that she's not a lady. She's pretty, very pretty, but she looks like a dissipated dressmaker. She failed absolutely in New York. I have seen her three times – she apparently goes everywhere. I didn't speak of her – I was wanting to see what you would do. I saw that you meant to do nothing, then this letter decided me. It's written on purpose to be shown to you; it's what she wants you to do. She wrote to me before I came to town, and I went to see her as soon as I arrived. I think it very important. I told her that if she would draw up a little statement I would put it before you as soon as we got settled. She's in real distress. I think you ought to feel for her. You ought to communicate the facts exactly as they stand. A woman has no right to do such things and come and ask to be accepted. She may make it up with her conscience, but she can't make it up with society. Last night at Lady Dovedale's I was afraid she would know who I was and come and speak to me. I was so frightened that I went away. If Sir Arthur wishes to marry her for what she is, of course he's welcome. But at least he ought to know.'

Mrs Dolphin was not excited nor voluble; she moved from point to point with a calmness which had all the air of being used to have reason on its side. She deeply desired, however, that Mrs Headway's triumphant career should be checked; she had sufficiently abused the facilities of things. Herself a party to an international marriage, Mrs Dolphin naturally wished that the class to which she belonged should close its ranks and carry its standard high.

'It seems to me that she's quite as good as the little baronet,' said Littlemore, lighting another cigar.

'As good? What do you mean? No one has ever breathed a word against him.'

'Very likely. But he's a nonentity, and she at least is somebody. She's a person, and a very clever one. Besides, she's quite as good as the women that lots of them have married. I never heard that the British gentry were so unspotted.'

'I know nothing about other cases,' Mrs Dolphin said, 'I only know about this one. It so happens that I have been brought near to it, and that an appeal has been made to me. The English are very romantic – the most romantic people in the world, if that's what you mean. They do the strangest things, from the force of passion – even those from whom you would least expect it. They marry their cooks – they marry their coachmen – and their romances always have the most miserable end. I'm sure this one would be most wretched. How can you pretend that such a woman as that is to be trusted? What I see is a fine old race – one of the oldest and most honorable in England, people with every tradition of good conduct and high principle – and a dreadful, disreputable, vulgar little woman, who hasn't an idea of what such things are, trying to force her way into it. I hate to see such things – I want to go to the rescue!'

'I don't – I don't care anything about the fine old race.'

'Not from interested motives, of course, any more than I. But surely, on artistic grounds, on grounds of decency?'

'Mrs Headway isn't indecent – you go too far. You must remember that she's an old friend of mine.' Littlemore had become rather stern; Mrs Dolphin was forgetting the consideration due, from an English point of view, to brothers.

She forgot it even a little more. 'Oh, if you are in love with her, too!' she murmured, turning away.

He made no answer to this, and the words had no sting for him. But at last, to finish the affair, he asked what in the world the old lady wanted him to do. Did she want him to go out into Piccadilly and announce to the passers-by that there was one winter when even Mrs Headway's sister didn't know who was her husband?

Mrs Dolphin answered this inquiry by reading out Lady Demesne's letter, which her brother, as she folded it up again, pronounced one of the most extraordinary letters he had ever heard.

'It's very sad – it's a cry of distress,' said Mrs Dolphin. 'The whole meaning of it is that she wishes you would come and see her. She doesn't say so in so many words, but I can read between the lines. Besides, she told me she would give anything to see you. Let me assure you it's your duty to go.'

'To go and abuse Nancy Beck?'

'Go and praise her, if you like!' This was very clever of Mrs Dolphin, but her brother was not so easily caught. He didn't take that view of his duty, and he declined to cross her ladyship's threshold. 'Then she'll come and see you,' said Mrs Dolphin, with decision.

'If she does, I'll tell her Nancy's an angel.'

'If you can say so conscientiously, she'll be delighted to hear it,' Mrs Dolphin replied, as she gathered up her cloak and gloves.

Meeting Rupert Waterville the next day, as he often did, at the St George's Club, which offers a much-appreciated hospitality to secretaries of legation and to the natives of the countries they assist in representing, Littlemore let him know that his prophecy had been fulfilled and that Lady Demesne had been making proposals for an interview. 'My sister read me a most remarkable letter from her,' he said.

'What sort of a letter?'

'The letter of a woman so scared that she will do anything. I may be a great brute, but her fright amuses me.'

'You're in the position of Olivier de Jalin, in the *Demi-Monde*,' Waterville remarked.

'In the *Demi-Monde*?' Littlemore was not quick at catching literary allusions.

'Don't you remember the play we saw in Paris? Or like Don Fabrice in *L'Aventurière*. A bad woman tries to marry an honorable man, who doesn't know how bad she is, and they who do know step in and push her back.'

'Yes, I remember. There was a good deal of lying, all round.'

'They prevented the marriage, however, which is the great thing.'

'The great thing, if you care about it. One of them was the intimate friend of the fellow, the other was his son. Demesne's nothing to me.'

'He's a very good fellow,' said Waterville.

'Go and tell him, then.'

'Play the part of Olivier de Jalin? Oh, I can't; I'm not Olivier. But I wish he would come along. Mrs Headway oughtn't really to be allowed to pass.'

'I wish to heaven they'd let me alone,' Littlemore murmured, ruefully, staring for a while out of the window.

'Do you still hold to that theory you propounded in Paris? Are you willing to commit perjury?' Waterville asked.

'Of course I can refuse to answer questions – even that one.'

'As I told you before, that will amount to a condemnation.'

'It may amount to what it pleases. I think I will go to Paris.'

'That will be the same as not answering. But it's quite the best thing you can do. I have been thinking a great deal about it, and it seems to me, from the social point of view, that, as I say, she really oughtn't to pass.' Waterville had the air of looking at the thing from a great elevation; his tone, the expression of his face, indicated this lofty flight; the effect of which, as he glanced down at his didactic young friend, Littlemore found peculiarly irritating.

'No, after all, hanged if they shall drive me away!' he exclaimed abruptly; and walked off, while his companion looked after him.

10

THE morning after this Littlemore received a note from Mrs Headway – a short and simple note, consisting merely of the words, 'I shall be at home this afternoon; will you come and see me at five? I have something particular to say to you.' He sent no answer to this inquiry, but he went to the little house in Chesterfield Street at the hour that its mistress had designated.

'I don't believe you know what sort of woman I am!' she exclaimed, as soon as he stood before her.

'Oh, Lord!' Littlemore groaned, dropping into a chair. Then he added, 'Don't begin on that sort of thing!'

'I shall begin – that's what I wanted to say. It's very important. You don't know me – you don't understand me. You think you do – but you don't.'

'It isn't for the want of your having told me – many, many times!' And Littlemore smiled, though he was bored at the prospect that opened before him. The last word of all was, decidedly, that Mrs Headway was a nuisance. She didn't deserve to be spared!

She glared at him a little, at this; her face was no longer the face that smiled. She looked sharp and violent, almost old; the change was complete. But she gave a little angry laugh. 'Yes, I know; men are so stupid. They know nothing about women but what women tell them. And women tell them things on purpose, to see how stupid they can be. I've told you things like that, just for amusement, when it was dull. If you believed them, it was your own fault. But now I am serious, I want you really to know.'

'I don't want to know. I know enough.'

'How do you mean, you know enough?' she cried with a flushed face. 'What business have you to know anything?' The poor little woman, in her passionate purpose, was not obliged to be consistent, and the loud laugh with which Littlemore greeted this interrogation must have seemed to her unduly harsh. 'You shall know what I want you to know, however. You think me a bad woman – you don't respect me; I told you that in Paris. I have done things I don't understand, myself, today; that I admit, as fully as you please. But I've completely changed, and I want to change everything. You ought to enter into that; you ought to see what I want. I hate everything that has happened to me before this; I loathe it, I despise it. I went on that way trying – one thing and another. But now I've got what I want. Do you expect me to go down on my knees to you? I believe I will, I'm so anxious. You can help me – no one else can do a thing – no one can do anything – they are only waiting to see if he'll do it. I told you in Paris you could help me, and it's just as true now. Say a good word for me, for God's sake! You haven't lifted your little finger, or I should know it by this time. It will just make the difference. Or if your sister would come and see me, I should be all right.

Women are pitiless, pitiless, and you are pitiless too. It isn't that she's anything so great, most of my friends are better than that! – but she's the one woman who *knows*, and people know that she knows. *He* knows that she knows, and he knows she doesn't come. So she kills me – she kills me! I understand perfectly what he wants – I shall do everything, be anything, I shall be the most perfect wife. The old woman will adore me when she knows me – it's too stupid of her not to see. Everything in the past is over; it has all fallen away from me; it's the life of another woman. This was what I wanted; I knew I should find it some day. What could I do in those horrible places? I had to take what I could. But now I've got a nice country. I want you to do me justice; you have never done me justice; that's what I sent for you for.'

Littlemore suddenly ceased to be bored; but a variety of feelings had taken the place of a single one. It was impossible not to be touched; she really meant what she said. People don't change their nature; but they change their desires, their ideal, their effort. This incoherent and passionate protestation was an assurance that she was literally panting to be respectable. But the poor woman, whatever she did, was condemned, as Littlemore had said of old, in Paris, to Waterville, to be only half-right. The color rose to her visitor's face as he listened to this outpouring of anxiety and egotism; she had not managed her early life very well, but there was no need of her going down on her knees. 'It's very painful to me to hear all this,' he said. 'You are under no obligation to say such things to me. You entirely misconceive my attitude – my influence.'

'Oh yes, you shirk it – you only wish to shirk it!' she cried, flinging away fiercely the sofa-cushion on which she had been resting.

'Marry whom you please!' Littlemore almost shouted, springing to his feet.

He had hardly spoken when the door was thrown open, and the servant announced Sir Arthur Demesne. The baronet entered with a certain briskness, but he stopped short on seeing that Mrs Headway had another visitor. Recognizing Littlemore, however, he gave a slight exclamation, which might have passed for a greeting. Mrs Headway, who had risen as he came in, looked with extraordinary earnestness from one of the men to the other; then, like a person who had a sudden inspiration, she clasped her hands together and cried out, 'I'm so glad you've met; if I had arranged it, it couldn't be better!'

'If you had arranged it?' said Sir Arthur, crinkling a little his high, white forehead, while the conviction rose before Littlemore that she had indeed arranged it.

'I'm going to do something very strange,' she went on, and her eye glittered with a light that confirmed her words.

'You're excited, I'm afraid you're ill.' Sir Arthur stood there with his hat and his stick; he was evidently much annoyed.

'It's an excellent opportunity; you must forgive me if I take advantage.' And she flashed a tender, touching ray at the baronet. 'I have wanted this a long time – perhaps you have seen I wanted it. Mr Littlemore has known me a long, long time; he's an old, old friend. I told you that in Paris, don't you remember? Well, he's my only one, and I want him to speak for me.' Her eyes had turned now to Littlemore; they rested upon him with a sweetness that only made the whole proceeding more audacious. She had begun to smile again, though she was visibly trembling. 'He's my only one,' she continued; 'it's a great pity, you ought to have known others. But I'm very much alone, I must make the best of what I have. I want so much that some one else than myself should speak for me. Women usually can ask that service of a relative, or of another woman. I can't; it's a great pity, but it's not my fault, it's my misfortune. None of my people are here; and I'm terribly alone in the world. But Mr Littlemore will tell you; he will say he has known me for years. He will tell you whether he knows any reason – whether he knows anything against me. He's been wanting the chance; but he thought he couldn't begin himself. You see I treat you as an old friend, dear Mr Littlemore. I will leave you with Sir Arthur. You will both excuse me.' The expression of her face, turned towards Littlemore, as she delivered herself of this singular proposal had the intentness of a magician who wishes to work a spell. She gave Sir Arthur another smile, and then she swept out of the room.

The two men remained in the extraordinary position that she had created for them; neither of them moved even to open the door for her. She closed it behind her, and for a moment there was a deep, portentous silence. Sir Arthur Demesne, who was very pale, stared hard at the carpet.

'I am placed in an impossible situation,' Littlemore said at last, 'and I don't imagine that you accept it any more than I do.'

The baronet kept the same attitude; he neither looked up nor answered. Littlemore felt a sudden gush of pity for him. Of course he couldn't accept the situation; but all the same, he was half sick with anxiety to see how this nondescript American, who was both so valuable and so superfluous, so familiar and so inscrutable, would consider Mrs Headway's challenge.

'Have you any question to ask me?' Littlemore went on.

At this Sir Arthur looked up. Littlemore had seen the look before; he had described it to Waterville after the baronet came to call on him in Paris. There were other things mingled with it now – shame, annoyance, pride; but the great thing, the intense desire to *know*, was paramount.

'Good God, how can I tell him?' Littlemore exclaimed to himself.

Sir Arthur's hesitation was probably extremely brief; but Littlemore heard the ticking of the clock while it lasted. 'Certainly, I have no question to ask,' the young man said in a voice of cool, almost insolent surprise.

'Good-day, then.'

'Good-day.'

And Littlemore left Sir Arthur in possession. He expected to find Mrs Headway at the foot of the staircase; but he quitted the house without interruption.

On the morrow, after lunch, as he was leaving the little mansion at Queen Anne's Gate, the postman handed him a letter. Littlemore opened and read it on the steps of his house, an operation which took but a moment. It ran as follows: –

DEAR MR LITTLEMORE, – It will interest you to know that I am engaged to be married to Sir Arthur Demesne, and that our marriage is to take place as soon as their stupid old Parliament rises. But it's not to come out for some days, and I am sure that I can trust meanwhile to your complete discretion.

Yours very sincerely,
NANCY H.

P.S. – He made me a terrible scene for what I did yesterday, but he came back in the evening and made it up. That's how the thing comes to be settled. He won't tell me what passed between you – he requested me never to allude to the subject. I don't care; I was bound you should speak!

Littlemore thrust this epistle into his pocket and marched away with it. He had come out to do various things, but he forgot his business for the time, and before he knew it had walked into Hyde Park. He left the carriages and riders to one side of him and followed the Serpentine into Kensington Gardens, of which he made the complete circuit. He felt annoyed, and more disappointed than he understood – than he would have understood if he had tried. Now that Nancy Beck had succeeded, her success seemed offensive, and he was almost sorry he had not said to Sir Arthur – 'Oh, well, she was pretty bad, you know.' However, now the thing was settled, at least they would leave him alone. He walked off his irritation, and before he went about the business he had come out for, had ceased to think about Mrs Headway. He went home at six o'clock, and the servant who admitted him informed him in doing so that Mrs Dolphin had requested he should be told on his return that she wished to see him in the drawing-room. 'It's another trap!' he said to himself, instinctively; but, in spite of this reflection, he went upstairs. On entering the apartment in which Mrs Dolphin was accustomed to sit, he found that she had a visitor. This visitor, who was apparently on the point of departing, was a tall, elderly woman, and the two ladies stood together in the middle of the room.

'I'm so glad you've come back,' said Mrs Dolphin, without meeting her brother's eye. 'I want so much to introduce you to Lady Demesne, and I hoped you would come in. Must you really go – won't you stay a little?' she added, turning to her companion; and without waiting for an answer, went on hastily – 'I must leave you a moment – excuse me. I will come back!' Before he knew it, Littlemore found himself alone with Lady Demesne, and he understood that, since he had not been willing to go and see her, she had taken upon herself to make an advance. It had the queerest effect, all the same, to see his sister playing the same tricks as Nancy Beck!

'Ah, she must be in a fidget!' he said to himself as he stood before Lady Demesne. She looked delicate and modest, even timid, as far as a tall, serene woman who carried her head very well could look so; and she was such a different type from Mrs Headway that his present vision of Nancy's triumph gave her by contrast something of the dignity of the vanquished. It made him feel sorry for her. She lost no time; she went straight to the point. She evidently felt that in the situation in which she had placed herself, her only advantage could consist in being simple and business-like.

'I'm so glad to see you for a moment. I wish so much to ask you if you can give me any information about a person you know and about whom I have been in correspondence with Mrs Dolphin. I mean Mrs Headway.'

'Won't you sit down?' asked Littlemore.

'No, I thank you. I have only a moment.'

'May I ask you why you make this inquiry?'

'Of course I must give you my reason. I am afraid my son will marry her.'

Littlemore was puzzled for a moment; then he felt sure that she was not yet aware of the fact imparted to him in Mrs Headway's note. 'You don't like her?' he said, exaggerating in spite of himself the interrogative inflexion.

'Not at all,' said Lady Demesne, smiling and looking at him. Her smile was gentle, without rancor; Littlemore thought it almost beautiful.

'What would you like me to say?' he asked.

'Whether you think her respectable.'

'What good will that do you? How can it possibly affect the event?'

'It will do me no good, of course, if your opinion is favorable. But if you tell me it is not, I shall be able to say to my son that the one person in London who has known her more than six months thinks her a bad woman.'

This epithet, on Lady Demesne's clear lips, evoked no protest from Littlemore. He had suddenly become conscious of the need to utter the simple truth with which he had answered Rupert Waterville's first question at the Théâtre Français. 'I don't think Mrs Headway respectable,' he said.

'I was sure you would say that.' Lady Demesne seemed to pant a little.

'I can say nothing more – not a word. That's my opinion. I don't think it will help you.'

'I think it will. I wished to have it from your own lips. That makes all the difference,' said Lady Demesne. 'I am exceedingly obliged to you.' And she offered him her hand; after which he accompanied her in silence to the door.

He felt no discomfort, no remorse, at what he had said; he only felt relief. Perhaps it was because he believed it would make no difference. It made a difference only in what was at the bottom of all things – his own sense of fitness. He only wished he had remarked to Lady Demesne that Mrs Headway would probably make her son a capital wife. But that, at least, would make no difference. He requested his sister, who had wondered greatly at the brevity of his interview with Lady Demesne, to spare him all questions on this subject; and Mrs Dolphin went about for some days in the happy faith that there were to be no dreadful Americans in English society compromising her native land.

Her faith, however, was short-lived. Nothing had made any difference; it was, perhaps, too late. The London world heard in the first days of July, not that Sir Arthur Demesne was to marry Mrs Headway, but that the pair had been privately, and it was to be hoped, as regards Mrs Headway, on this occasion indissolubly, united. Lady Demesne gave neither sign nor sound; she only retired to the country.

'I think you might have done differently,' said Mrs Dolphin, very pale, to her brother. 'But of course everything will come out now.'

'Yes, and make her more the fashion than ever!' Littlemore answered, with cynical laughter. After his little interview with the elder Lady Demesne, he did not feel himself at liberty to call again upon the younger; and he never learned – he never even wished to know – whether in the pride of her success she forgave him.

Waterville – it was very strange – was positively scandalized at this success. He held that Mrs Headway ought never to have been allowed to marry a confiding gentleman; and he used, in speaking to Littlemore, the same words as Mrs Dolphin. He thought Littlemore might have done differently.

He spoke with such vehemence that Littlemore looked at him hard – hard enough to make him blush.

'Did you want to marry her yourself?' his friend inquired. 'My dear fellow, you're in love with her! That's what's the matter with you.'

This, however, blushing still more, Waterville indignantly denied. A little later he heard from New York that people were beginning to ask who in the world was Mrs Headway.

CRAPY CORNELIA

1

THREE times within a quarter of an hour – shifting the while his posture on his chair of contemplation – had he looked at his watch as for its final sharp hint that he should decide, that he should get up. His seat was one of a group fairly sequestered, unoccupied save for his own presence, and from where he lingered he looked off at a stretch of lawn freshened by recent April showers and on which sundry small children were at play. The trees, the shrubs, the plants, every stem and twig just ruffled as by the first touch of the light finger of the relenting year, struck him as standing still in the blest hope of more of the same caress; the quarter about him held its breath after the fashion of the child who waits with the rigour of an open mouth and shut eyes for the promised sensible effect of his having been good. So, in the windless, sun-warmed air of the beautiful afternoon, the Park of the winter's end had struck White-Mason as waiting; even New York, under such an impression, was 'good', good enough – for *him*: its very sounds were faint, were almost sweet, as they reached him from so seemingly far beyond the wooded horizon that formed the remoter limit of his large shallow glade. The tones of the frolic infants ceased to be nondescript and harsh, were in fact almost as fresh and decent as the frilled and puckered and ribboned garb of the little girls, which had always a way, in those parts, of so portentously flaunting the daughters of the strange native – that is of the overwhelmingly alien – populace at him.

Not that these things in particular were his matter of meditation now; he had wanted, at the end of his walk, to sit apart a little and think – and had been doing that for twenty minutes, even though as yet to no break in the charm of procrastination. But he had looked without seeing and listened without hearing: all that had been positive for him was that he hadn't failed vaguely to feel. He had felt in the first place, and he continued to feel – yes, at forty-eight quite as much as at any point of the supposed reign of younger intensities – the great spirit of the air, the fine sense of the season, the supreme appeal of Nature, he might have said, to his time of life; quite as if she, easy, indulgent, indifferent, cynical Power, were offering him the last chance it would rest with his wit or his blood to embrace. Then with that he had been entertaining, to the point and with the prolonged consequence of accepted immobilization, the certitude that if he did call on Mrs Worthingham and find her at home he couldn't in justice to himself not put to her the question that had lapsed the other time, the last time, through the irritating and persistent, even if accidental, presence of others. What friends she had – the people who so stupidly, so wantonly stuck! If they *should*, he and she, come to an understanding, that would presumably have to include certain members of her singularly ill-composed circle, in whom it was incredible to him that he should ever take an interest. This defeat, to do himself justice – he had bent rather predominantly on *that*, you see; ideal justice to *her*, with her possible conception of what it should consist of being another and quite a different matter – he had had the fact of the Sunday afternoon to thank for; she didn't 'keep' that day for him, since they hadn't, up to now, quite begun to cultivate the appointment or assignation founded on explicit sacrifices. He might at any rate look to find this pleasant practical Wednesday – should he indeed, at his actual rate, stay it before it ebbed – more liberally and intendingly given him.

The sound he at last most wittingly distinguished in his nook was the single deep note of half-past five borne to him from some high-perched public clock. He finally got up with the sense that the time from then on *ought* at least to be felt as sacred to him. At this juncture it was – while he stood there shaking his garments, settling his hat, his necktie, his shirt-cuffs, fixing the high polish of his fine shoes as if for some reflection in it of his straight and spare and grizzled, his refined and trimmed and dressed, his altogether distinguished person, that of a gentleman abundantly settled, but of a bachelor markedly nervous – at this crisis it was, doubtless, that he at once most measured and least resented his predicament. If he should go he would almost to a certainty find her, and if he should find her he would almost to a certainty come to the point. He wouldn't put it off again – there was that high consideration for him of justice at least to himself. He had never yet denied himself anything so apparently fraught with possibilities as the idea of proposing to Mrs Worthingham – never yet, in other words, denied himself anything he had so distinctly wanted to do; and the results of that wisdom had remained for him precisely the precious parts of experience. Counting only the offers of his honourable hand, these had been on three remembered occasions at least the consequence of an impulse as sharp and a self-respect that hadn't in the least suffered, moreover, from the failure of each appeal. He had been met in the three cases – the only ones he at all compared with his present case – by the frank confession that he didn't somehow, charming as he was, cause himself to be superstitiously believed in; and the lapse of life, afterward, had cleared up any doubts.

It *wouldn't* have done, he eventually, he lucidly saw, each time he had been refused; and the candour of his nature was such that he could live to think of these very passages as a proof of how right he had been – right, that is, to have put himself forward always, by the happiest instinct, only in impossible conditions. He had the happy consciousness of having exposed the important question to the crucial test, and of having escaped, by that persistent logic, a grave mistake. What better proof of his escape than the fact that he was now free to renew the all-interesting inquiry, and should be exactly about to do so in different and better conditions? The conditions were better by as much more – as much more of his career and character, of its situation, his reputation he could even have called it, of his knowledge of life, of his somewhat extended means, of his possibly augmented charm, of his certainly improved mind and temper – as was involved in the actual impending settlement. Once he had got into motion, once he had crossed the Park and passed out of it, entering, with very little space to traverse, one of the short new streets that abutted on its east side, his step became that of a man young enough to find confidence, quite to find felicity, in the sense, in almost any sense, of action. He could still enjoy almost anything, absolutely an unpleasant thing, in default of a better, that might still remind him he wasn't so old. The standing newness of everything about him would, it was true, have weakened this cheer by too much presuming on it; Mrs Worthingham's house, before which he stopped, had that gloss of new money, that glare of a piece fresh from the mint and ringing for the first time on any counter, which seems to claim for it, in any transaction, something more than the 'face' value.

This could but be yet more the case for the impression of the observer introduced and committed. On our friend's part I mean, after his admission and while still in the hall, the sense of the general shining immediacy, of the still unhushed clamour of the shock, was perhaps stronger than he had ever known it. That broke out from every corner as the high pitch of interest, and with a candour that – no, certainly – he had never seen equalled; every particular expensive object shrieking at him in its artless pride that it had just 'come home'. He met the whole vision with something of the grimace produced on persons without goggles by the passage from a shelter to a blinding light; and if he had – by a perfectly possible chance – been 'snap-shotted' on the spot, would have struck you as showing for his first tribute to the temple of Mrs Worthingham's charming presence a scowl almost of anguish. He wasn't constitutionally, it may at once be explained for him, a goggled person; and he was condemned in New York to this frequent violence of transition – having to reckon with it whenever he went out, as who should say, from himself. The high pitch of interest, to his taste, was the pitch of history, the pitch of acquired and earned suggestion, the pitch of association, in a word; so that he lived by preference, incontestably, if not in a rich gloom, which would have been beyond his means and spirits, at least amid objects and images that confessed to the tone of time.

He had ever felt that an indispensable presence – with a need of it moreover that interfered at no point with his gentle habit, not to say his subtle art, of drawing out what was left him of his youth, of thinly and thriftily spreading the rest of that choicest jam-pot of the cupboard of consciousness over the remainder of a slice of life still possibly thick enough to bear it; or in other words of moving the melancholy limits, the significant signs, constantly a little further on, very much as property-marks or staked boundaries are sometimes stealthily shifted at night. He positively cherished in fact, as against the too inveterate gesture of distressfully guarding his eyeballs – so many New York aspects seemed to keep him at it – an ideal of adjusted appreciation, of courageous curiosity, of fairly letting the world about him, a world of constant breathless renewals and merciless substitutions, make its flaring assault on its own inordinate terms. Newness *was* value in the piece – for the acquisitor, or at least sometimes might be, even though the act of 'blowing' hard, the act marking a heated freshness of arrival, or other form of irruption, could never minister to the peace of those already and long on the field; and this if only because maturer tone was after all most appreciable and most consoling when one staggered back to it, wounded, bleeding, blinded, from the riot of the raw – or, to put the whole experience more prettily, no doubt, from excesses of light.

2

If he went in, however, with something of his more or less inevitable scowl, there were really, at the moment, two rather valid reasons for screened observation; the first of these being that the whole place seemed to reflect as never before the lustre of Mrs Worthingham's own polished and prosperous little person – to smile, it struck him, with her smile, to twinkle not only with the gleam of her lovely teeth, but with that of all her rings and brooches and bangles and other gewgaws, to curl and spasmodically cluster as in emulation of her charming complicated yellow tresses, to surround the most animated of pink-and-white, of ruffled and ribboned, of frilled and festooned Dresden china shepherdesses with exactly the right system of rococo curves and convolutions and other flourishes, a perfect bower of painted and gilded and moulded conceits. The second ground of this immediate impression of scenic extravagance, almost as if the curtain rose for him to the first act of some small and expensively mounted comic opera, was that she hadn't, after all, awaited him in fond singleness, but had again just a trifle inconsiderately exposed him to the drawback of having to reckon, for whatever design he might amiably entertain, with the presence of a third and quite superfluous person, a small black insignificant but none the less oppressive stranger. It was odd how, on the instant, the little lady engaged with her did affect him as comparatively black – very much as if that had absolutely, in such a medium, to be the graceless appearance of any item not positively of some fresh shade of a light colour or of some pretty pretension to a charming twist. Any witness of their meeting, his hostess should surely have felt, would have been a false note in the whole rosy glow; but what note so false as that of the dingy little presence that she might actually, by a refinement of her perhaps always too visible study of effect, have provided as a positive contrast or foil? whose name and intervention, moreover, she appeared to be no more moved to mention and account for than she might have been to 'present' – whether as stretched at her feet or erect upon disciplined haunches – some shaggy old domesticated terrier or poodle.

Extraordinarily, after he had been in the room five minutes – a space of time during which his fellow-visitor had neither budged nor uttered a sound – he had made Mrs Worthingham out as all at once perfectly pleased to see him, completely aware of what he had most in mind, and singularly serene in face of his sense of their impediment. It was as if for all the world she didn't take it for one, the immobility, to say nothing of the seeming equanimity, of their tactless companion; at whom meanwhile indeed our friend himself, after his first ruffled perception, no more adventured a look than if advised by his constitutional kindness that to notice her in any degree would perforce be ungraciously to glower. He talked after a fashion with the woman as to whose power to please and amuse and serve him, as to whose really quite organized and indicated fitness for lighting up his autumn afternoon of life his conviction had lately strained itself so clear; but he was all the while carrying on an intenser exchange with his own spirit and trying to read into the charming creature's behaviour, as he could only call it, some confirmation of his theory that she also had her inward flutter and anxiously counted on him. He found support, happily for the conviction just named, in the idea, at no moment as yet really repugnant to him, the idea bound up in fact with the finer essence of her appeal, that she had her own vision too of her quality and her price, and that the last appearance she would have liked to bristle with was that of being forewarned and eager.

He had, if he came to think of it, scarce definitely warned her, and he probably wouldn't have taken to her so consciously in the first instance without an appreciative sense that, as she was a little person of twenty superficial graces, so she was also a little person with her secret pride. She might just have planted her mangy lion – not to say her muzzled house-dog – there in his path as a symbol that she wasn't cheap and easy; which would be a thing he couldn't possibly wish his future wife to have shown herself in advance, even if to him alone. That she could make him put himself such questions was precisely part of the attaching play of her iridescent surface, the shimmering interfusion of her various aspects; that of her youth with her independence – her pecuniary perhaps in particular, that of her vivacity with her beauty, that of her facility above all with her odd novelty; the high modernity, as people appeared to have come to call it, that made her so much more 'knowing' in some directions than even he, man of the world as he certainly was, could pretend to be, though all on a basis of the most unconscious and instinctive and luxurious assumption. She was 'up' to everything, aware of everything – if one counted from a short enough time back (from week before last, say, and as if quantities of history had burst upon the world within the fortnight); she was likewise surprised at nothing, and in that direction one might reckon as far ahead as the rest of her lifetime, or at any rate as the rest of his, which was all that would concern him: it was as if the suitability of the future to her personal and rather pampered tastes was what she most took for granted, so that he could see her, for all her Dresden-china shoes and her flutter of wondrous befrilled contemporary skirts, skip by the side of the coming age as over the floor of a ball-room, keeping step with its monstrous stride and prepared for every figure of the dance.

Her outlook took form to him suddenly as a great square sunny window that hung in assured fashion over the immensity of life. There rose toward it as from a vast swarming *plaza* a high tide of motion and sound; yet it was at the same time as if even while he looked her light gemmed hand, flashing on him in addition to those other things the perfect polish of the prettiest pink finger-nails in the world, had touched a spring, the most ingenious of recent devices for instant ease, which dropped half across the scene a soft-coloured mechanical blind, a fluttered fringed awning of charmingly toned silk, such as would make a bath of cool shade for the favoured friend leaning with her there – that is for the happy couple itself – on the balcony. The great view would be the prospect and privilege of the very state he coveted – since didn't he covet it? – the state of being so securely at her side; while the wash of privacy, as one might count it, the broad fine brush dipped into clear umber and passed, full and wet, straight across the strong scheme of colour, would represent the security itself, all the uplifted inner elegance, the condition, so ideal, of being shut out from nothing and yet of having, so gaily and breezily aloft, none of the burden or worry of anything. Thus, as I say, for our friend, the place itself, while his vivid impression lasted, portentously opened and spread, and what was before him took, to his vision, though indeed at so other a crisis, the form of the 'glimmering square' of the poet; yet, for a still more remarkable fact, with an incongruous object usurping at a given instant the privilege of the frame and seeming, even as he looked, to block the view.

The incongruous object was a woman's head, crowned with a little sparsely feathered black hat, an ornament quite unlike those the women mostly noticed by White-Mason were now 'wearing', and that grew and grew, that came nearer and nearer, while it met his eyes, after the manner of images in the cinematograph. It had presently loomed so large that he saw nothing else – not only among the things at a considerable distance, the things Mrs Worthingham would eventually, yet unmistakably, introduce him to, but among those of this lady's various attributes and appurtenances as to which he had been in the very act of cultivating his consciousness. It was in the course of another minute the most extraordinary thing in the world: everything had altered, dropped, darkened, disappeared; his imagination had spread its wings only to feel them flop all grotesquely at its sides as he recognized in his hostess's quiet companion, the oppressive alien who hadn't indeed interfered with his fanciful flight, though she had prevented his immediate declaration and brought about the thud, not to say the felt violent shock, of his fall to earth, the perfectly plain identity of Cornelia Rasch. It was she who had remained there at attention; it was she their companion hadn't introduced; it was she he had forborne to face with his fear of incivility. He stared at her – everything else went.

'Why, it has been *you* all this time?'

Miss Rasch fairly turned pale. 'I was waiting to see if you'd know me.'

'Ah, my dear Cornelia' – he came straight out with it – 'rather!'

'Well, it isn't,' she returned with a quick change to red now, 'from having taken much time to look at me!'

She smiled, she even laughed, but he could see how she had felt his unconsciousness, poor thing; the acquaintance, quite the friend of his youth, as she had been, the associate of his childhood, of his early manhood, of his middle age in fact, up to a few years back, not more than ten at the most; the associate too of so many of his associates and of almost all of his relations, those of the other time, those who had mainly gone for ever; the person in short whose noted disappearance, though it might have seemed final, had been only of recent seasons. She was present again now, all unexpectedly – he had heard of her having at last, left alone after successive deaths and with scant resources, sought economic salvation in Europe, the promised land of American thrift – she was present as this almost ancient and this oddly unassertive little rotund figure whom one seemed no more obliged to address than if she had been a black satin ottoman 'treated' with buttons and gimp; a class of object as to which the policy of blindness was imperative. He felt the need of some explanatory plea, and before he could think had uttered one at Mrs Worthingham's expense. 'Why, you see we weren't introduced!'

'No – but I didn't suppose I should have to be named to you.'

'Well, my dear woman, you haven't – do me that justice!' He could at least make this point. 'I felt all the while –!' However it would have taken him long to say what he had been feeling; and he was aware now of the pretty projected light of Mrs Worthingham's wonder. She looked as if, out for a walk with her, he had put her to the inconvenience of his stopping to speak to a strange woman in the street.

'I never supposed you knew her!' – it was to him his hostess excused herself.

This made Miss Rasch spring up, distinctly flushed, distinctly strange to behold, but not vulgarly nettled – Cornelia was incapable of that; only rather funnily bridling and laughing, only showing that this was all she had waited for, only saying just the right thing, the thing she could make so clearly a jest. 'Of course if you *had* you'd have presented him.'

Mrs Worthingham looked while answering at White-Mason. 'I didn't want you to go – which you see you do as soon as he speaks to you. But I never dreamed –!'

'That there was anything between us? Ah, there are no end of things!' He, on his side, though addressing the younger and prettier woman, looked at his fellow-guest; to whom he even continued: 'When did you get back? May I come and see you the very first thing?'

Cornelia gasped and wriggled – she practically giggled; she had lost every atom of her little old, her little young, though always unaccountable, prettiness, which used to peep so, on the bare chance of a shot, from behind indefensible features, that it almost made watching her a form of sport. He had heard vaguely of her, it came back to him (for there had been no letters; their later acquaintance, thank goodness, hadn't involved that), as experimenting, for economy, and then as settling, to the same rather dismal end, somewhere in England, at one of those intensely English places, St Leonards, Cheltenham, Bognor, Dawlish – which, awfully, *was* it? – and she now affected him for all the world as some small, squirming, exclaiming, genteelly conversing old maid of a type vaguely associated with the three-volume novels he used to feed on (besides his so often encountering it in 'real life') during a faraway stay of his own at Brighton. Odder than any element of his ex-gossip's identity itself, however, was the fact that she somehow, with it all, rejoiced his sight. Indeed the supreme oddity was that the manner of her reply to his request for leave to call should have absolutely charmed his attention. She didn't look at him; she only, from under her frumpy, crapy, curiously exotic hat, and with her good little near-sighted insinuating glare, expressed to Mrs Worthingham, while she answered him, wonderful arch things, the overdone things of a shy woman. 'Yes, you may call – but only when this dear lovely lady has done with you!' The moment after which she had gone.

3

FORTY minutes later he was taking his way back from the queer miscarriage of his adventure; taking it, with no conscious positive felicity, through the very spaces that had witnessed shortly before the considerable serenity of his assurance. He had said to himself then, or had as good as said it, that, since he might do perfectly as he liked, it couldn't fail for him that he must soon retrace those steps, humming, to all intents, the first bars of a wedding march; so beautifully had it cleared up that he was 'going to like' letting Mrs Worthingham accept him. He was to have hummed no wedding-march, as it seemed to be turning out – he had none, up to now, to hum; and yet, extraordinarily, it wasn't in the least because she had refused him. Why then hadn't he liked as much as he had intended to like it putting the pleasant act, the act of not refusing him, in her power? Could it all have come from the awkward minute of his failure to decide sharply, on Cornelia's departure, whether or no he would attend her to the door? He hadn't decided at all – what the deuce had been in him? – but had danced to and fro in the room, thinking better of each impulse and then thinking worse. He had hesitated like an ass erect on absurd hind legs between two bundles of hay; the upshot of which must have been his giving the falsest impression. In what way that was to be for an instant considered had their common past committed him to crazy Cornelia? He repudiated with a whack on the gravel any ghost of an obligation.

What he could get rid of with scanter success, unfortunately, was the peculiar sharpness of his sense that, though mystified by his visible flurry – and yet not mystified enough for a sympathetic question either – his hostess had been, on the whole, even more frankly diverted: which was precisely an example of that newest, freshest, finest freedom in her, the air and the candour of assuming, not 'heartlessly', not viciously, not even very consciously, but with a bright pampered confidence which would probably end by affecting one's nerves as the most impertinent stroke in the world, that every blest thing coming up for her in any connection was somehow matter for her general recreation. There she was again with the innocent egotism, the gilded and overflowing anarchism, really, of her doubtless quite unwitting but none the less rabid modern note. Her grace of ease was perfect, but it was all grace of ease, not a single shred of it grace of uncertainty or of difficulty – which meant, when you came to see, that, for its happy working, not a grain of provision was left by it to mere manners. This was clearly going to be the music of the future – that if people were but rich enough and furnished enough and fed enough, exercised and sanitated and manicured, and generally advised and advertised and made 'knowing' enough, *avertis* enough, as the term appeared to be nowadays in Paris, all they had to do for civility was to take the amused ironic view of those who might be less initiated. In *his* time, when he was young or even when he was only but a little less middle-aged, the best manners had been the best kindness, and the best kindness had mostly been some art of not insisting on one's luxurious differences, of concealing rather, for common humanity, if not for common decency, a part at least of the intensity or the ferocity with which one might be 'in the know'.

Oh, the 'know' – Mrs Worthingham was in it, all instinctively, inevitably and as a matter of course, up to her eyes; which didn't, however, the least little bit prevent her being as ignorant as a fish of everything that really and intimately and fundamentally concerned *him*, poor dear old White-Mason. She didn't, in the first place, so much as know who he was – by which he meant know who and what it was to *be* a White-Mason, even a poor and a dear and old one, 'anyway'. That indeed – he did her perfect justice – was of the very essence of the newness and freshness and beautiful, brave social irresponsibility by which she had originally dazzled him: just exactly that circumstance of her having no instinct for any old quality or quantity or identity, a single historic or social value, as he might say, of the New York of his already almost legendary past; and that additional one of his, on his side, having, so far as this went, cultivated blankness, cultivated positive prudence, as to her own personal background – the vagueness, at the best, with which all honest gentlefolk, the New Yorkers of his approved stock and conservative generation, were content, as for the most part they were indubitably wise, to surround the origins and antecedents and queer unimaginable early influences of persons swimming into their ken from those parts of the country that quite necessarily and naturally figured to their view as 'God-forsaken' and generally impossible.

The few scattered surviving representatives of a society once 'good' – *rari nantes in gurgite vasto* – were liable, at the pass things had come to, to meet, and even amid old shades once sacred, or what was left of such, every form of social impossibility, and, more irresistibly still, to find these apparitions often carry themselves (often at least in the case of the women) with a wondrous wild gallantry, equally imperturbable and inimitable, the sort of thing that reached its maximum in

Mrs Worthingham. Beyond that who ever wanted to look up their annals, to reconstruct their steps and stages, to dot their i's in fine, or to 'go behind' anything that was theirs? One wouldn't do that for the world – a rudimentary discretion forbade it; and yet this check from elementary undiscussable taste quite consorted with a due respect for them, or at any rate with a due respect for oneself in connection with them; as was just exemplified in what would be his own, what would be poor dear old White-Mason's, insurmountable aversion to having, on any pretext, the doubtless very queer spectre of the late Mr Worthingham presented to him. No question had he asked, or would he ever ask, should his life – that is should the success of his courtship – even intimately depend on it, either about that obscure agent of his mistress's actual affluence or about the happy headspring itself, and the apparently copious tributaries, of the golden stream.

From all which marked anomalies, at any rate, what was the moral to draw? He dropped into a Park chair again with that question, he lost himself in the wonder of why he had come away with his homage so very much unpaid. Yet it didn't seem at all, actually, as if he could say or conclude, as if he could do anything but keep on worrying – just in conformity with his being a person who, whether or no familiar with the need to make his conduct square with his conscience and his taste was never wholly exempt from that of making his taste and his conscience square with his conduct. To this latter occupation he further abandoned himself, and it didn't release him from his second brooding session till the sweet spring sunset had begun to gather and he had more or less cleared up, in the deepening dusk, the effective relation between the various parts of his ridiculously agitating experience. There were vital facts he seemed thus to catch, to seize, with a nervous hand, and the twilight helping, by their vaguely-whisked tails; unquiet truths that swarmed out after the fashion of creatures bold only at eventide, creatures that hovered and circled, that verily brushed his nose, in spite of their shyness. Yes, he had practically just sat on with his 'mistress' – heaven save the mark! – as if *not* to come to the point; as if it had absolutely come up that there would be something rather vulgar and awful in doing so. The whole stretch of his stay after Cornelia's withdrawal had been consumed by his almost ostentatiously treating himself to the opportunity of which he was to make nothing. It was as if he had sat and watched himself – that came back to him: Shall I now or shan't I? Will I now or won't I? Say within the next three minutes, say by a quarter past six, or by twenty minutes past, at the furthest – always if nothing more comes up to prevent.

What had already come up to prevent was, in the strangest and drollest, or at least in the most preposterous, way in the world, that not Cornelia's presence, but her very absence, with its distraction of his thoughts, the thoughts that lumbered after her, had made the difference; and without his being the least able to tell why and how. He put it to himself after a fashion by the image that, this distraction once created, his working round to his hostess again, his reverting to the matter of his errand, began suddenly to represent a return from so far. That was simply all – or rather a little less than all; for something else had contributed. 'I never dreamed you knew her,' and 'I never dreamed *you* did,' was inevitably what had been exchanged between them – supplemented by Mrs Worthingham's mere scrap of an explanation: 'Oh, yes – to the small extent you see. Two years ago in Switzerland when I was at a high place for an "aftercure", during twenty days of incessant rain, she was the only person in an hotel of roaring, gorging, smoking Germans with whom I couldn't have a word of talk. She and I were the only speakers of English, and were thrown together like castaways on a desert island and in a raging storm. She was ill besides, and she had no maid, and mine looked after her, and she was very grateful – writing to me later on and saying she should certainly come to see me if she ever returned to New York. She *has* returned, you see – and there she was, poor little creature!' Such was Mrs Worthingham's tribute – to which even his asking her if Miss Rasch had ever happened to speak of him caused her practically to add nothing. Visibly she had never thought again of anyone Miss Rasch had spoken of or anything Miss Rasch had said; right as she was, naturally, about her being a little clever queer creature. This was perfectly true, and yet it was probably – by being *all* she could dream of about her – what had paralysed his proper gallantry. Its effect had been not in what it simply stated, but in what, under his secretly disintegrating criticism, it almost luridly symbolized.

He had quitted his seat in the Louis Quinze drawing-room without having, as he would have described it, done anything but give the lady of the scene a superior chance not to betray a defeated hope – not, that is, to fail of the famous 'pride' mostly supposed to prop even the most infatuated women at such junctures; by which chance, to do her justice, she had thoroughly seemed to profit. But he finally rose from his later station with a feeling of better success. He had by a happy turn of his hand got hold of the most precious, the least obscure of the flitting, circling things that brushed his ears. What he wanted – as justifying for him a little further consideration – was there before him from the moment he could put it that Mrs Worthingham had no data. He almost hugged that word – it suddenly came to mean so much to him. No data, he felt, for a conception of the sort of thing the New York of 'his time' had been in his personal life – the New York so unexpectedly, so vividly, and, as he might say, so perversely called back to all his senses by its identity with that of poor Cornelia's time: since even she had had a time, small show as it was likely to make now, and his time and hers had been the same. Cornelia figured to him while he walked away as by contrast and opposition a massive little bundle of data; his impatience to go to see her sharpened as he thought of this: so certainly should he find out that wherever he might touch her, with a gentle though firm pressure, he would, as the fond visitor of old houses taps and fingers a disfeatured, over-papered wall with the conviction of a wainscot-edge beneath, recognize some small extrusion of history.

4

THERE would have been a wonder for us meanwhile in his continued use, as it were, of his happy formula – brought out to Cornelia Rasch within ten minutes, or perhaps only within twenty, of his having settled into the quite comfortable chair that, two days later, she indicated to him by her fireside. He had arrived at her address through the fortunate chance of his having noticed her card, as he went out, deposited, in the good old New York fashion, on one of the rococo tables of Mrs Worthingham's hall. His eye had been caught by the pencilled indication that was to affect him, the next instant, as fairly placed there for his sake. This had really been his luck, for he shouldn't have liked to write to Mrs Worthingham for guidance – *that* he felt, though too impatient just now to analyse the reluctance. There was nobody else he could have approached for a clue, and with this reflection he was already aware of how it testified to their rare little position, his and Cornelia's – position as conscious, ironic, pathetic survivors together of a dead and buried society – that there would have been, in all the town, under such stress, not a member of their old circle left to turn to. Mrs Worthingham had practically, even if accidentally, helped him to acknowledge; the last nail in the coffin of the poor dear extinct past had been planted for him by his having thus to reach his antique contemporary through perforation of the newest newness. The note of this particular recognition was in fact the more prescribed to him that the ground of Cornelia's return to a scene swept so bare of the associational charm was certainly inconspicuous. What had she then come back for? – he had asked himself that; with the effect of deciding that it probably would have been, a little, to 'look after' her remnant of property. Perhaps she had come to save what little might still remain of that shrivelled interest; perhaps she had been, by those who took care of it for her, further swindled and despoiled, so that she wished to get at the facts. Perhaps on the other hand – it was a more cheerful chance – her investments, decently administered, were making larger returns, so that the rigorous thrift of Bognor could be finally relaxed.

He had little to learn about the attraction of Europe, and rather expected that in the event of his union with Mrs Worthingham he should find himself pleading for it with the competence of one more in the 'know' about Paris and Rome, about Venice and Florence, than even she could be. He could have lived on in *his* New York, that is in the sentimental, the spiritual, the more or less romantic visitation of it; but had it been positive for him that he could live on in hers? – unless indeed the possibility of this had been just (like the famous *vertige de l'abîme*, like the solicitation of danger, or otherwise of the dreadful) the very hinge of his whole dream. However that might be, his curiosity was occupied rather with the conceivable hinge of poor Cornelia's: it was perhaps thinkable that even Mrs Worthingham's New York, once it should have become possible again at all, might have put forth to this lone exile a plea that wouldn't be in the chords of Bognor. For himself, after all, too, the attraction had been much more of the Europe over which one might move at one's ease, and which therefore could but cost, and cost much, right and left, than of the Europe adapted to scrimping. He saw himself on the whole scrimping with more zest even in Mrs Worthingham's New York than under the inspiration of Bognor. Apart from which it was yet again odd, not to say perceptibly pleasing to him, to note where the emphasis of his interest fell in this fumble of fancy over such felt oppositions as the new, the latest, the luridest power of money and the ancient reserves and moderations and mediocrities. These last struck him as showing by contrast the old brown surface and tone as of velvet rubbed and worn, shabby, and even a bit dingy, but all soft and subtle and still velvety – which meant still dignified; whereas the angular facts of current finances were as harsh and metallic and bewildering as some stacked 'exhibit' of ugly patented inventions, things his medieval mind forbade his taking in. He had, for instance, the sense of knowing the pleasant little old Rasch fortune – pleasant as far as it went;

blurred memories and impressions of what it had been and what it hadn't, of how it had grown and how languished and how melted; they came back to him and put on such vividness that he could almost have figured himself testify for them before a bland and encouraging Board. The idea of taking the field in any manner on the subject of Mrs Worthingham's resources would have affected him on the other hand as an odious ordeal, some glare of embarrassment and exposure in a circle of hard unhelpful attention, of converging, derisive, unsuggestive eyes.

In Cornelia's small and quite cynically modern flat – the house had a grotesque name, 'The Gainsborough', but at least wasn't an awful boarding-house, as he had feared, and she could receive him quite honourably, which was so much to the good – he would have been ready to use at once to her the greatest freedom of friendly allusion: 'Have you still your old "family interest" in those two houses in Seventh Avenue? – one of which was next to a corner grocery, don't you know? and was occupied as to its lower part by a candy-shop where the proportion of the stock of suspectedly stale popcorn to that of rarer and stickier joys betrayed perhaps a modest capital on the part of your father's, your grandfather's or whoever's tenant, but out of which I nevertheless remember once to have come as out of a bath of sweets, with my very garments, and even the separate hairs of my head, glued together. The other of the pair, a tobacconist's, further down, had before it a wonderful huge Indian who thrust out wooden cigars at an indifferent world – you could buy candy cigars too at the popcorn shop, and I greatly preferred them to the wooden; I remember well how I used to gape in fascination at the Indian and wonder if the last of the Mohicans was like him; besides admiring so the resources of a family whose "property" was in such forms. I haven't been round there lately – we must go round together; but don't tell me the forms have utterly perished!' It was after *that* fashion he might easily have been moved, and with almost no transition, to break out to Cornelia – quite as if taking up some old talk, some old community of gossip, just where they had left it; even with the consciousness perhaps of overdoing a little, of putting at its maximum, for the present harmony, recovery, recapture (what should he call it?) the pitch and quantity of what the past had held for them.

He didn't in fact, no doubt, dart straight off to Seventh Avenue, there being too many other old things and much nearer and long subsequent; the point was only that for everything they spoke of after he had fairly begun to lean back and stretch his legs, and after she had let him, above all, light the first of a succession of cigarettes – for everything they spoke of he positively cultivated extravagance and excess, piling up the crackling twigs as on the very altar of memory; and that by the end of half an hour she had lent herself, all gallantly, to their game. It was the game of feeding the beautiful iridescent flame, ruddy and green and gold, blue and pink and amber and silver, with anything they could pick up, anything that would burn and flicker. Thick-strown with such gleanings the occasion seemed indeed, in spite of the truth that they perhaps wouldn't have proved, under cross-examination, to have rubbed shoulders in the other life so very hard. Casual contacts, qualified communities enough, there had doubtless been, but not particular 'passages', nothing that counted, as he might think of it, for their 'very own' together, for nobody's else at all. These shades of historic exactitude didn't signify; the more and the less that there had been made perfect terms – and just by his being there and by her rejoicing in it – with their present need to have *had* all their past could be made to appear to have given them. It was to this tune they proceeded, the least little bit as if they knowingly pretended – he giving her the example and setting her the pace of it, and she, poor dear, after a first inevitable shyness, an uncertainty of wonder, a breathlessness of courage, falling into step and going whatever length he would.

She showed herself ready for it, grasping gladly at the perception of what he must mean; and if she didn't immediately and completely fall in – not in the first half-hour, not even in the three or four others that his visit, even whenever he consulted his watch, still made nothing of – she yet understood enough as soon as she understood that, if their finer economy hadn't so beautifully served, he might have been conveying this, that and the other incoherent and easy thing by the comparatively clumsy method of sound and statement. 'No, I never made love to you; it would in fact have been absurd, and I don't care – though I almost know, in the sense of almost remembering! – who did and who didn't; but you were always about, and so was I, and, little as you may yourself care who *I* did it to, I daresay you remember (in the sense of having known of it!) any old appearances that told. But we can't afford at this time of day not to help each other to have had – well, everything there was, since there's no more of it now, nor anyway of coming by it *except so*; and therefore let us *make* together, let us make over and recreate, our lost world; for which we have after all and at the worst such a lot of material. You were in particular my poor dear sisters' friend – they thought you the funniest little brown thing possible; so isn't that again to the good? You were mine only to the extent that you were so much in and out of the house – as how much, if we come to that, wasn't one in and out, south of Thirtieth Street and north of Washington Square, in those days, those spacious, sociable, Arcadian days, that we flattered ourselves we filled with the modern fever, but that were so different from any of *these* arrangements of pretended hourly Time that dash themselves forever to pieces as from the fiftieth floors of sky-scrapers.'

This was the kind of thing that was in the air, whether he said it or not, and that could hang there even with such quite other things as more crudely came out; came in spite of its being perhaps calculated to strike us that these last would have been rather and most the unspoken and the indirect. They were Cornelia's contribution, and as soon as she had begun to talk of Mrs Worthingham – *he* didn't begin it! – they had taken their place bravely in the centre of the circle. There they made, the while, their considerable little figure, but all within the ring formed by fifty other allusions, fitful but really intenser irruptions that hovered and wavered and came and went, joining hands at moments and whirling round as in chorus, only then again to dash at the slightly huddled centre with a free twitch or peck or push or other taken liberty, after the fashion of irregular frolic motions in a country dance or a Christmas game.

'You're so in love with her and want to marry her!' – she said it all sympathetically and yearningly, poor crapy Cornelia; as if it were to be quite taken for granted that she knew all about it. And then when he had asked how she knew – why she took so informed a tone about it; all on the wonder of her seeming so much more 'in' it just at that hour than he himself quite felt he could figure for: 'Ah, how but from the dear lovely thing herself? Don't you suppose *she* knows it?'

'Oh, she absolutely "knows" it, does she?' – he fairly heard himself ask that; and with the oddest sense at once of sharply wanting the certitude and yet of seeing the question, of hearing himself say the words, through several thicknesses of some wrong medium. He came back to it from a distance; as he would have had to come back (this was again vivid to him) should he have got round again to his ripe intention three days before – after his now present but then absent friend, that is, had left him planted before his now absent but then present one for the purpose. 'Do you mean she – at all confidently! – expects?' he went on, not much minding if it couldn't but sound foolish; the time being given it for him meanwhile by the sigh, the wondering gasp, all charged with the unutterable, that the tone of his appeal set in motion. He saw his companion look at him, but it might have been with the eyes of thirty years ago; when – very likely! – he had put her some such question about some girl long since dead. Dimly at first, then more distinctly, didn't it surge back on him for the very strangeness that there had been some such passage as this between them – yes, about Mary Cardew! – in the autumn of '68?

'Why don't you realize your situation?' Miss Rasch struck him as quite beautifully wailing – above all to such an effect of deep interest, that is, on her own part and in him.

'My situation?' – he echoed, he considered; but reminded afresh, by the note of the detached, the far-projected in it, of what he had last remembered of his sentient state on his once taking ether at the dentist's.

'Yours and hers – the situation of her adoring you. I suppose you at least know it,' Cornelia smiled.

Yes, it was like the other time and yet it wasn't. *She* was like – poor Cornelia was – everything that used to be; that somehow was most definite to him. Still he could quite reply, 'Do you call it – her adoring me – *my* situation?'

'Well, it's a part of yours, surely – if you're in love with her.'

'Am I, ridiculous old person! in love with her?' White-Mason asked.

'I may be a ridiculous old person,' Cornelia returned – 'and, for that matter, of course I *am*! But she's young and lovely and rich and clever: so what could be more natural?'

'Oh, I was applying that opprobrious epithet –!' He didn't finish, though he meant he had applied it to himself. He had got up from his seat; he turned about and, taking in, as his eyes also roamed, several objects in the room, serene and sturdy, not a bit cheap-looking, little old New York objects of '68, he made, with an inner art, as if to recognize them – made so, that is, for himself; had quite the sense for the moment of asking them, of imploring them, to recognize *him*, to be for him things of his own past. Which they truly were, he could have the next instant cried out; for it meant that if three or four of them, small sallow carte-de-visite photographs, faithfully framed but spectrally faded, hadn't in every particular, frames and balloon skirts and false 'property' balustrades of unimaginable terraces and all, the tone of time, the secret for warding and easing off the perpetual imminent ache of one's protective scowl, one would verily but have to let the scowl stiffen or to take up seriously the question of blue goggles, during what might remain of life.

5

WHAT he actually took up from a little old Twelfth-Street table that piously preserved the plain mahogany circle, with never a curl nor a crook nor a hint of a brazen flourish, what he paused there a moment for commerce with, his back presented to crapy Cornelia, who sat taking that view of him, during this opportunity, very protrusively and frankly and fondly, was one of the wasted mementoes just mentioned, over which he both uttered and suppressed a small comprehensive cry. He stood there another minute to look at it, and when he turned about still kept it in his hand, only holding it now a little behind him. 'You *must* have come back to stay – with all your beautiful things. What else does it mean?'

'"Beautiful"?' his old friend commented with her brow all wrinkled and her lips thrust out in expressive dispraise. They might at that rate have been scarce more beautiful than she herself. 'Oh, don't talk so – after Mrs Worthingham's! *They're* wonderful, if you will: such things, such things! But one's own poor relics and odds and ends are one's own at least; and one *has* – yes – come back to them. They're all I have in the world to come back to. They were restored, and what I was paying—!' Miss Rasch woefully added.

He had possesion of the small old picture; he hovered there; he put his eyes again to it intently; then again held it a little behind him as if it might have been snatched away or the very feel of it, pressed against him, was good to his palm. 'Mrs Worthingham's things? You think them beautiful?'

Cornelia did now, if ever, show an odd face. 'Why, certainly, prodigious, or whatever. Isn't that conceded?'

'No doubt every horror, at the pass we've come to, is conceded. That's just what I complain of.'

'Do you *complain*?' – she drew it out as for surprise: she couldn't have imagined such a thing.

'To me her things are awful. They're the newest of the new.'

'Ah, but the old forms!'

'Those are the most blatant. I mean the swaggering reproductions.'

'Oh, but,' she pleaded, 'we can't all be *really* old.'

'No, we can't, Cornelia. But *you* can—!' said White-Mason with the frankest appreciation.

She looked up at him from where she sat as he could imagine her looking up at the curate at Bognor. 'Thank you, sir! If that's all you want—!'

'It *is*,' he said, 'all I want – or almost.'

'Then no wonder such a creature as that,' she lightly moralized, 'won't suit you!'

He bent upon her, for all the weight of his question, his smoothest stare. 'You hold she certainly won't suit me?'

'Why, what can I tell about it? Haven't you by this time found out?'

'No, but I think I'm finding.' With which he began again to explore.

Miss Rasch immensely wondered. 'You mean you don't expect to come to an understanding with her?' And then, as even to this straight challenge he made at first no answer: 'Do you mean you give it up?'

He waited some instants more, but not meeting her eyes – only looking again about the room. 'What do you think of my chance?'

'Oh,' his companion cried, 'what has what I think to do with it? How can I think anything but that she must like you?'

'Yes – of course. But how much?'

'Then don't you really know?' Cornelia asked.

He kept up his walk, oddly preoccupied and still not looking at her. 'Do you, my dear?'

She waited a little. 'If you haven't really put it to her I don't suppose she knows.'

This at last arrested him again. 'My dear Cornelia, she doesn't know—!'

He had paused as for the desperate tone, or at least the large emphasis of it, so that she took him up. 'The more reason then to help her to find it out.'

'I mean,' he explained, 'that she doesn't know anything.'

'Anything?'

'Anything else, I mean – even if she does know *that.*'

Cornelia considered of it. 'But what else need she – in particular – know? Isn't that the principal thing?'

'Well' – and he resumed his circuit – 'she doesn't know anything that *we* know. But nothing,' he re-emphasized – 'nothing whatever!'

'Well, can't she do without that?'

'Evidently she can – and evidently she does, beautifully. But the question is whether *I* can!'

He had paused once more with his point – but she glared, poor Cornelia, with her wonder. 'Surely if you know for yourself—!'

'Ah, it doesn't seem enough for me to know for myself! One wants a woman,' he argued – but still, in his prolonged tour, quite without his scowl – 'to know *for* one, to know *with* one. That's what you do now,' he candidly put to her.

It made her again gape. 'Do you mean you want to marry *me*?'

He was so full of what he did mean, however, that he failed even to notice it. 'She doesn't in the least know, for instance, how old I am.'

'That's because you're so young!'

'Ah, there you are!' – and he turned off afresh and as if almost in disgust. It left her visibly perplexed – though even the perplexed Cornelia was still the exceedingly pointed; but he had come to her aid after another turn. 'Remember, please, that I'm pretty well as old as you.'

She had all her point at least, while she bridled and blinked, for this. 'You're exactly a year and ten months older.'

It checked him there for delight. 'You remember my birthday?'

She twinkled indeed like some far-off light of home. 'I remember everyone's. It's a little way I've always had – and that I've never lost.'

He looked at her accomplishment, across the room, as at

some striking, some charming phenomenon. 'Well, *that's* the sort of thing I want!' All the ripe candour of his eyes confirmed it.

What could she do therefore, she seemed to ask him, but repeat her question of a moment before? – which indeed, presently she made up her mind to. 'Do you want to marry *me*?'

It had this time better success – if the term may be felt in any degree to apply. All this candour, or more of it at least, was in his slow, mild, kind, considering head-shake. 'No, Cornelia – not to *marry* you.'

His discrimination was a wonder; but since she was clearly treating him now as if everything about him was, so she could as exquisitely meet it. 'Not at least,' she conclusively smiled, 'until you've honourably tried Mrs Worthingham. Don't you really *mean* to?' she gallantly insisted.

He waited again a little; then he brought out: 'I'll tell you presently.' He came back, and as by still another mere glance over the room, to what seemed to him so much nearer. 'That table *was* old Twelfth-Street?'

'Everything here was.'

'Oh, the pure blessings! With you, ah, with you, I haven't to wear a green shade.' And he had retained meanwhile his small photograph, which he again showed himself. 'Didn't we talk of Mary Cardew?'

'Why, do you remember it?' – she marvelled to extravagance.

'You make me. You connect me with it. You connect it with *me*.' He liked to display to her this excellent use she thus had, the service she rendered. 'There are so many connections – there will *be* so many. I feel how, with you, they must all come up again for me: in fact you're bringing them out already, just while I look at you, as fast as ever you can. The fact that you knew every one –!' he went on; yet as if there were more in that too than he could quite trust himself about.

'Yes, I knew every one,' said Cornelia Rasch; but this time with perfect simplicity. 'I knew, I imagine, more than you do – or more than you did.'

It kept him there, it made him wonder with his eyes on her. 'Things about *them* – our people?'

'Our people. Ours only now.'

Ah, such an interest as he felt in this – taking from her while, so far from scowling, he almost gaped, all it might mean! 'Ours indeed – and it's awfully good they are; or that we're still here for them! Nobody else is – nobody but you: not a cat!'

'Well, I *am* a cat!' Cornelia grinned.

'Do you mean you can tell me things –?' It was too beautiful to believe.

'About what really *was*?' She artfully considered, holding him immensely now. 'Well, unless they've come to you with time; unless you've learned – or found out.'

'Oh,' he reassuringly cried – reassuringly, it most seemed, for himself – 'nothing has come to me with time, everything has gone from me. How I find out now! What creature has an idea –?'

She threw up her hands with the shrug of old days – the sharp little shrug his sisters used to imitate and that she hadn't had to go to Europe for. The only thing was that he blessed her for bringing it back. 'Ah, the ideas of people now –!'

'Yes, their ideas are certainly not about *us*.' But he ruefully faced it. 'We've none the less, however, to live with them.'

'With their ideas –?' Cornelia questioned.

'With *them* – these modern wonders; such as they are!' Then he went on: 'It must have been to help me you've come back.'

She said nothing for an instant about that, only nodding instead at his photograph. 'What has become of yours? I mean of *her*.'

This time it made him turn pale. 'You remember I *have* one?'

She kept her eyes on him. 'In a "pork-pie" hat, with her hair in a long net. That was so "smart" then; especially with one's skirt looped up, over one's hooped magenta petticoat, in little festoons, and a row of very big onyx beads over one's braided velveteen sack – braided quite plain and very broad, don't you know?'

He smiled for her extraordinary possession of these things – she was as prompt as if she had had them before her. 'Oh, rather – "don't I know?" You wore brown velveteen, and, on those remarkably small hands, funny gauntlets – like mine.'

'Oh, do *you* remember? But like yours?' she wondered.

'I mean like hers in my photograph.' But he came back to the present picture. 'This is better, however, for really showing her lovely head.'

'Mary's head was a perfection!' Cornelia testified.

'Yes – it was better than her heart.'

'Ah, don't say that!' she pleaded. 'You weren't fair.'

'Don't you think I was fair?' It interested him immensely – and the more that he indeed mightn't have been; which he seemed somehow almost to hope.

'She didn't think so – to the very end.'

'She didn't?' – ah, the right things Cornelia said to him! But before she could answer he was studying again closely the small faded face. 'No, she doesn't, she doesn't. Oh, her charming sad eyes and the way they *say* that, across the years, straight into mine! But I don't know, I don't know!' White-Mason quite comfortably sighed.

His companion appeared to appreciate this effect. 'That's just the way you used to flirt with her, poor thing. Wouldn't you like to have it?' she asked.

'This – for my very own?' He looked up delighted. 'I really may?'

'Well, if you'll give me yours. We'll exchange.'

'That's a charming idea. We'll exchange. But you must come and get it at my rooms – where you'll see my things.'

For a little she made no answer – as if for some feeling. Then she said: 'You asked me just now why I've come back.'

He stared as for the connection; after which with a smile: 'Not to do *that* –?'

She waited briefly again, but with a queer little look. 'I can do those things now; and – yes! – that's in a manner why. I came,' she then said, 'because I knew of a sudden one day – knew as never before – that I was old.'

'I see. I see.' He quite understood – she had notes that so struck him. 'And how did you like it?'

She hesitated – she decided. 'Well, if I liked it, it was on the principle perhaps on which some people like high game!'

'High game – that's good!' he laughed. 'Ah, my dear, we're "high"!'

She shook her head. 'No – not you – yet. I at any rate didn't want any more adventures,' Cornelia said.

He showed their small relic again with assurance. 'You wanted *us*. Then here we are. Oh, how we can talk! – with all those things you know! You *are* an invention. And you'll see there are things *I* know. I shall turn up here – well, daily.'

She took it in, but after a moment only answered. 'There was something you said just now you'd tell me. Don't you mean to try –?'

'Mrs Worthingham?' He drew from within his coat his pocket-book and carefully found a place in it for Mary Cardew's carte-de-visite, folding it together with deliberation over which he put it back. Finally he spoke. 'No – I've decided. I can't – I don't want to.'

Cornelia marvelled – or looked as if she did. 'Not for all she has?'

'Yes – I know all she has. But I also know all she hasn't. And, as I told you, she herself doesn't – hasn't a glimmer of a suspicion of it; and never will have.'

Cornelia magnanimously thought. 'No – but she knows other things.'

He shook his head as at the portentous heap of them. 'Too many – too many. And other indeed – *so* other. Do you know,' he went on, 'that it's as if *you* – by turning up for me – had brought that home to me?'

'For you,' she candidly considered. 'But what – since you can't marry me! – can you do with me?'

Well, he seemed to have it all. 'Everything. I can live with you – just this way.' To illustrate which he dropped into the other chair by her fire; where, leaning back, he gazed at the flame. 'I can't give you up. It's very curious. It has come over me as it did over you when you renounced Bognor. That's it – I know it at last, and I see one can like it. I'm "high". You needn't deny it. That's my taste. I'm old.' And in spite of the considerable glow there of her little household altar he said it without the scowl.

MORE ABOUT PENGUINS AND PELICANS

For further information about books available from Penguins please write to Dept EP, Penguin Books Ltd, Harmondsworth, Middlesex UB7 0DA.

In the U.S.A.: For a complete list of books available from Penguins in the United States write to Dept CS, Penguin Books, 625 Madison Avenue, New York, New York 10022.

In Canada: For a complete list of books available from Penguins in Canada write to Penguin Books Canada Ltd, 2801 John Street, Markham, Ontario L3R 1B4.

In Australia: For a complete list of books available from Penguins in Australia write to the Marketing Department, Penguin Books Australia Ltd, P.O. Box 257, Ringwood, Victoria 3134.

In New Zealand: For a complete list of books available from Penguins in New Zealand write to the Marketing Department, Penguin Books (N.Z.) Ltd, P.O. Box 4019, Auckland 10.

HENRY JAMES

'He is as solitary in the history of the novel as Shakespeare in the history of poetry' – Graham Greene in *The Lost Childhood*

THE PORTRAIT OF A LADY

The poignant story of an American princess in Europe and her involvement in the toils of European guile.

THE BOSTONIANS

Intending to write 'a very American tale', Henry James drew attention, in *The Bostonians*, to 'the situation of women, the decline of the sentiment of sex, the agitation in their behalf'.

THE EUROPEANS

'This small book, written so early in James's career, is a masterpiece of major quality' – F. R. Leavis in *The Great Tradition*

Also published

WASHINGTON SQUARE
RODERICK HUDSON
THE WINGS OF THE DOVE
WHAT MAISIE KNEW
THE AWKWARD AGE
THE GOLDEN BOWL
THE SPOILS OF POYNTON
THE AMBASSADORS
SELECTED SHORT STORIES
THE TURN OF THE SCREW AND OTHER STORIES
THE ASPERN PAPERS AND OTHER STORIES
THE PRINCESS CASAMASSIMA
THE TRAGIC MUSE